A Song in the Dark
High Fantasy Novel (Book 1)
C. Graves

CONTENTS

Chapter One

Streamwatch

S moke crawls along a serpentine path as it winds into an azure sky; beneath it, golden fields stretch towards the horizon in every direction. A great hill punctuates the landscape as it rises in the distance.

It is a beautiful day.

A young woman in her early twenties dashes toward the hill. Her hair swirls around her like a living flame, echoing the inferno that awaits ahead. Her emerald eyes shimmer, on the brink of emptying the radiant well of tears she struggles to contain.

As she runs, she calls to the man who trails behind her, "Hurry, Baldwin!"

Baldwin wears heavy armor. A blue and white tabard flutters behind him as he manages to keep pace despite the labored breaths that huff and puff their way out of his helm.

Reaching the summit of the hill, they pause, gasping for air.

Before them, Streamwatch Village lies engulfed in flames, its buildings reduced to smoldering ruins. Skeletal remains line the streets here and there, victims of whatever horrific event wrought such ruin to the once-thriving community.

The scale of destruction wrought by the infamous Gregorious Vile is staggering.

Aileen and Baldwin stand in silence for a moment, the flickering light of the flames dancing on their skin as they take in the devastation of what once was their home.

How could this happen? Why?

"It's too late..." Aileen whispers in despair.

"Streamwatch Village... lost. So many innocent lives," Baldwin laments.

"Perhaps... but we can make sure this never happens again," Aileen says. Her determination ignites as she charges down the hill toward the burning village.

Baldwin calls after her, "Aileen!"

He follows without hesitation.

———

The central courtyard of Streamwatch Village greets them, consumed by an unnatural green fire that crackles menacingly.

Unholy flames hiss at the heroes as they position themselves in the square, enveloped by the relentless gloom that harbors a dark and oppressive presence.

A dark figure, hidden in the shadows of a watch tower, observes Aileen and Baldwin's approach. He sees mere bodies, potential soldiers for his growing horde.

As the Greater Light retreats beneath the cluttered buildings of Streamwatch, a sinister figure emerges from the shadows, enveloped in a shimmering green aura, glaring down at the square.

The figure laughs. The laughter is a deep, terrible sound that resounds through the empty cobblestone streets.

"You dare challenge me here?" The air around him crackles with dangerous energy, and noxious fumes swirl, emanating darkness and despair.

Baldwin stands resolute, "You will pay for what you have done to these people, Gregor!"

Gregorious Vile, undeterred, sneers, "These *people* will be your undoing! I am afraid you find yourself outnumbered. Servants, arise!"

With that, green energy spirals down and pours into the ground at the base of the tower. After a tense moment, a spectral, virescent mist rises from the ground like spores and covers the bones of the fallen.

They rise in unison and threaten the pair of heroes.

Meanwhile, Aileen has found a vantage point from which she can support her staunch ally. She gracefully ascends the ruins, steps as sure as a gazelle; Aileen races for higher ground.

Aileen reaches for an arrow and readies for action as she perches among the burned-out ruins.

Surrounded by skeletal forms, Baldwin laughs, "Always loved a challenge." A masterful swing of his weapon strikes the skeletons with force; the air crackles in response.

Bone shards scatter in all directions as three skeletons collapse to the ground, their bony limbs clattering. Baldwin stands tall. Courage radiates from his victorious stance.

An arrow, perfectly aimed, strikes a skeleton's skull. With a sickening thud, the skull detaches from the frame, rolls across the ground, and comes to rest under a nearby cart, out of view.

The undead creature's body begins to run in frantic circles. Its arms and legs flail about akimbo as it desperately searches for its misplaced cranium. The creature grabs a nearby lantern, tests it for size, but discards it. The creature resumes a futile search for the missing skull.

The quiet of the burning ruins breaks into a thunderous clash of steel against rattling bones. More fiends enter the fray as Baldwin fights toward the tower entrance.

The first of a series of skeletal warriors threatens to clamber up to Aileen's defensive position. She bolts toward the far edge of the second floor, racing for the remains of an exterior wooden wall. She leaps to the nearest building as she reaches the ledge, but her adversaries remain close behind.

Aileen gracefully leaps from building to building as she ascends higher. Her agility carries her steadily toward Gregorious Vile, the epicenter of this fierce battle.

With heroic resolve, Baldwin makes a final push toward the tower. A skeletal warrior emerges from the entrance; Baldwin crushes it and dashes inside, out of the necromancer's sight.

Aileen leaps towards a tower window on the third floor, narrowly escaping a trio of skeletons. She falters, clinging to the ledge by a thread.

Below, skeletal archers aim at her vulnerable frame.

Teetering from the ledge, Aileen begins to slip into the abyss below, but a steel gauntlet reaches out, grabs her by the arm, and pulls her to safety inside.

Arrows and crossbow bolts pepper the wall where she had moments before dangled, bouncing harmlessly off the stone.

A headless skeleton stumbles past the entrance of the tower. It picks up a large stone and tries to replace its missing head. In frustration, it casts the stone away.

Aileen and Baldwin reunite, racing up the spiral staircase before bursting through a wooden door to face Gregorious Vile. His eyes and mouth emit a vibrant harlequin color as he sneers from the shadows. "At last, you have arrived! Prepare for your doom!"

Baldwin unsheathes his sword, ready for battle, "Not this time, Gregor!"

As Baldwin leaps towards Gregor, Aileen draws her weapon.

Thick fumes envelop the tower as Gregorious Vile chants. The smell is acrid and painful. It sears the sinuses and leaves a lingering feeling of overbearing spicy mustard or horseradish.

"Nothorel, arise!"

The cloud forms an impenetrable barrier through which it is impossible to see. Vapor and tears block out the faintest shadow or silhouette. Suddenly, the upper floor explodes with some unknown force.

As the smoke slowly dissipates, the imposing figure of Gregorious Vile comes into view, dreadfully perched atop Nothorel, an ancient, skeletal dragon. Nothorel's eyes are deep, abyssal wells, possessing an otherworldly malice capable of driving lesser men screaming into the depths of insanity.

Within those black sockets, unholy malachite flames flicker and dance, casting an eerie glow that illuminates the surrounding area. The dragon's bones, bleached white from ages long past, glint under the flames' light, giving Nothorel a spectral appearance that is both awe-inspiring and terrifying.

A sprawling pumpkin field thrives at the base of the ancient tower; living vines of rich color contrast against the stark, lifeless creatures surrounding the heroes.

The vibrant green of the vines weaves through the rich, earthy tones of the pumpkin patch, offering a glimpse of nature's beauty in the face of death and despair.

Aileen throws her head back, huffing, "Oh, come on!"

Baldwin points his sword at Gregorious Vile, "That's cheating!"

Their nemesis replies slowly, "No... it's not!"

Nothorel casts his deadly, confused gaze between the trio, appearing increasingly perplexed by their argument. The ancient destroyer seems enthralled in the banter.

Baldwin shouts, "We said no dragons!"

Gregorious Vile raises a hand, summoning dark flame, "This is a skeleton!"

Baldwin insists, "Of a dragon!"

Gregorious Vile, now defeated, laments, "It's not fair. You always make me play the bad guy! I don't want to be Gregorious Vile. I wanted to be Gregor the Gray! Or maybe Gregor the White!"

Aileen and Baldwin appear dejected.

Meanwhile, a headless skeleton wanders the pumpkin field below, frantically searching for a suitable head. It grabs a pumpkin and tests it for fit.

The macabre form bursts into a spontaneous and joyful jig.

CHAPTER TWO

THE TALE BEGINS

Aileen gazes intently across the table. Her eyes hold you in place. The lines on her face tell a story of laughter. Deep crow's feet frame her eyelids. Once likened to a magnificent blaze, her red hair now bears streaks of muted grey. Yet, her age adds a timeless beauty under the candlelight's soft glow.

Her look penetrates as if she's peering into your spirit and soul. Weighing your worth on unseen scales. Taking a deep breath, Aileen's eyes glaze with a faraway look, transporting her to another time and place. She resumes her story in a voice tinged with nostalgia. "I was only a child when this story began. It was autumn. We were traveling to the King's Harvest Festival. Wind and wave danced playfully atop the surface of Blackwater River as we made our way..."

CHAPTER THREE

BLACKWATER

Autumn rains engorge the Blackwater River, which sings a vibrant melody as it flows downstream, flanked by the Old Gloamwood forest. The waters snake their way toward the tranquil Stillwater Lake.

Along its verdant banks unfolds a scene with three young figures: Aileen, a girl with her arms defiantly crossed, stands beside Baldwin and Gregor, two adolescent boys. The wind whips Aileen's white dress violently and tugs at her fiery red locks of hair.

Baldwin is tall, his broad shoulders outlined against the backdrop of his attire. He has dark brown hair and eyes. Draped in a faded blue vest, he sports a ragged white shirt tucked into his tattered brown pants, which bear the marks of caked mud and dirt from recent adventures.

His feet are encased in oversized boots, adding to his rugged appearance. For a fleeting moment, a wooden bucket crowns his head, serving as an impromptu helmet, before he nonchalantly discards his makeshift headgear.

Gregor is a slender young man. His strawberry-red hair is complemented by piercing grey eyes. He holds a lengthy wooden branch, a relic once belonging to the nefarious Gregorious Vile, repurposed now as a makeshift walking stick. A tan tabard covers his frame, which falls over a green shirt and trousers.

Aileen impatiently taps her dainty foot against the lush grass, looking at her older brother sternly. "Gregor, you're a cheater and a liar!" she accuses. The sole of her boot smacks against the soft soil of the bank menacingly.

Gregor blushes, steps back, and defensively raises his arms. "I am not! I was just..."

Baldwin interjects, shock widening his eyes as he raises his hands in disbelief. "But you promised no dragons, giants, or ghosts, Gregor!"

Gregor halts his retreat, glaring at Baldwin. He re-enters the fray and threatens Baldwin with a sharp index finger. "Oh really? You said you'd be the bad guy, Balds!"

Baldwin, now on the defensive, steps back, his hands morph from a gesture of alarm to one of surrender. "Well, yeah, but that's scary," he murmurs sheepishly.

Gregor rolls his eyes at Baldwin's reply. Amidst their argument, Aileen struggles to hold back her laughter, though her amused eyes give her away. Finally, she can no longer contain herself; the dam bursts, and Aileen's laughter pours alongside the flowing waters.

Seeing Aileen's laughter, Baldwin frowns, "Let's just go. We're going to be late for the festival," he suggests, seeking an escape from the dispute.

Gregor tries to let the argument go but gets a final quick jab, "Fine, but I know why you're changing the subject, Balds. We're going to talk about this later!"

At the mention of the festival, Aileen breaks into prancing steps and advances along the riverbank. Blackwater's rolling waves become Aileen's constant companion.

Baldwin and Gregor amuse themselves by skimming stones across the river's glistening surface. Their laughter mingles with the gentle sounds of water lapping over stone.

A mischievous stone thrown by Gregor skims perilously close to Aileen. Its spray narrowly misses her. She whirls around and fixes Gregor with a stern glare. "Gregor! You almost splashed water on me! Do that again, and I'm telling Mom!" she warns. Her severe facade crumbles into giggles.

Gregor shakes his head dismissively.

Aileen resumes her walk and steps onto a mossy, slippery stone at the water's edge. "Careful, Aileen!" Gregor shouts, concern in his voice as he dashes toward her.

Her footing falters, but Gregor is swift to act and reaches her in time to pull Aileen back to the safety of the solid ground, away from the river's swell.

Gregor breathes a sigh of relief before he continues, "Stay away from the water, Aileen. You know mom doesn't want us playing too close!"

Gregor's eyes flash anger for a moment, but he sighs, and they suddenly yield to a look of loving concern, "If you fall into the river, we're all going to be in more trouble than if I just splash you."

Aileen isn't discouraged for a moment.

She quips, "You always think you're right, Gregor. Does your brother always have to be right, too, Baldwin?"

Baldwin pauses to think, then confesses, "Arek enlisted. I don't think he's been right since."

Gregor, intrigued, raises his eyebrows. "Is that what he told you?"

Shaking his head, Baldwin replies, "No, that's what his arms master tells him."

As the trio continues their walk, the warm smell of confections intermingled with smoked meats assails their senses. Soon after, the muffled sound of voices filters through the trees of Old Gloamwood. At last, the festival comes into view. It is a breathtaking sight as pennants and banners flutter in the breeze. Smoke rises from various points around the grounds. Kites taken upon the wind soar to dizzying heights, slowly moving back and forth in a beautiful waltz among the clouds.

Many guests line the festival's impromptu streets and narrow alleys. Makeshift stalls and carts line the fields as hawkers cry out for attention. Each makes impossible promises about their one-of-a-kind, fantastic thingamajig.

Aileen, Baldwin, and Gregor approach the entrance gate with boundless wonder. A great banner stretched between two towering wooden poles proudly proclaims, "King Beaumont's Harvest Festival."

A regal welcome for the young children.

CHAPTER FOUR

The Harvest Festival

The festival bursts into life. Vibrant banners flutter in the breeze, filling the sky with a kaleidoscope of colors and shapes. The air hums with the melodies of strings, drums, and woodwinds, mingling with the joyous sounds of laughter and conversation that fill the atmosphere.

The tantalizing aromas of freshly baked goods, succulent roast meats, and spicy mulled wines drift through the air, drawing festival-goers towards them with an irresistible barrage of scents.

The spectacle immediately captivates Aileen, Baldwin, and Gregor. Aileen's delight is palpable as she spots puppeteers captivating a group of children with their performance.

Baldwin notices a commotion in the wrestling ring. He glances over to see an armored man throw his arms into the air to celebrate victory as the crowd's cheers echo in his ears.

Gregor is fascinated by a cart that opens into a makeshift stage where tales of strange creatures from the Beaumont region are shared.

Aileen's eyes sparkle with excitement. She pleads, "Can we please watch the puppet show?"

Meanwhile, a trio of battle-hardened men enters the festival, their presence starkly contrasting with its vivacity. They survey the crowd with keen eyes, searching before disappearing into the throng.

Amidst a friendly debate over which attraction to visit first, the children are momentarily distracted by the festival's lively hustle and bustle, losing sight of the mysterious men.

Aileen, Gregor, and Baldwin embrace the festival's spirited ambiance and agree to experience everything the festival offers together.

CHAPTER FIVE

PUPPET SHOW

Wind lifts vibrant banners and pennants playfully as they hang from the puppet show's stage. The effect is a dazzling array of colors set against the azure backdrop of a cloudless autumn sky. Each decorative flag bears a distinct coat of arms. Together, this all creates a magnificent scene.

Several rows of benches are arranged in a welcoming semicircle around the stage. They await the attendees as they file in. Children eagerly take their seats. Aileen, Baldwin, and Gregor find a spot in the central row of benches. One of the dangerous-looking men observes from afar among the audience. His attention seldom strays from the trio.

The stage itself is a picturesque depiction of a farm, complete with a wooden silo and a bright red farmhouse. A cornfield stretches across the stage's foreground, adding to the rustic charm. Three animals graze nearby —a sheep with wool as white as snow on the left, a mottled cow in the center, and a black rooster on the right. The rooster diligently pecks at the ground for delicious grubs to win his darling hens' affection.

A dragon emerges from the left. Its sinister presence shatters the peaceful farm scene as it stalks back and forth.

After several menacing passes, the dragon rears its head and releases a thunderous "Rooooaaaar!"

It pounces on the unsuspecting sheep. The sheep's desperate bleats, "Baaahaaahaahaaa..." fill the air, but to no avail; it disappears beneath the stage. The dragon's head pursues it below the stage, accompanied by gobbling from below.

Aileen gasps in shock from the sudden turn of events. Baldwin and Gregor observe her reaction, smile, and continue watching.

The terrible beast once more crosses the stage in its quest for food. Its malevolent gaze fixates on the unfortunate cow that stands lost in the cornfield.

"Raawwweeeerrrr... *ahouhou**houph**!*" A cough disrupts the creature's roar and slightly shatters the puppet show's illusion, but the children watching remain unfazed.

The dragon charges at the cow, which emits a confused and despairing "Mooooooo?!?" before appearing to succumb, dipping below the stage in defeat.

The dragon poses triumphantly above its prey before it drives its head down. From beneath, the sound of exaggeratedly loud chewing fills the air.

Aileen watches with her eyes wide and hands covering her mouth in shock.

Baldwin and Gregor are barely able to contain their laughter. They beam at Aileen with broad smiles.

In a defiant display, the dragon lifts its head toward the heavens and rages, "Raaaawrr!" Its voice pierces the sky. The menacing beast then pivots towards the black rooster and performs a taunting dance that signals its readiness for another onslaught.

Amidst this spectacle, Aileen stands with her hands over her eyes. She dares only to peek through her fingers.

The rooster, previously occupied with finding morsels for his hens, turns his gaze upon the dragon. He faces the great adversary that threatens his flock. The air is tense as the last two contenders stare each other down among the standing rows of corn. This tension of the showdown is drawn out for several seconds while someone blows dust across the stage with a fan.

The dragon targets the rooster and charges forward. The rooster takes flight in a display of agility. Flapping his wings vigorously, the rooster lands atop the dragon and forces it to retreat beneath the stage. Victoriously, the rooster dances proudly for his beloved hens.

Taking his place as the sole ruler of the roost, he calls forth his hens, "Cock-a-doodle-rooooooaaaar!!!" These rush in and begin to peck at the ground, their actions punctuated by exaggerated eating sounds.

This elicits laughter and cheers from all who witness the affectionate display.

Aileen's concerns melt amidst the laughter, and she joins in the crowd's merriment.

Chapter Six

Wrestling Ring

A field is encircled by wooden posts. It is muddy and worn, as though an army trampled it. A heavily armored soldier stands at each post, seemingly remnants of an ancient battle.

One of the dangerous men watches from the sidelines. Nothing on the festival grounds escapes his wandering gaze. He has light blue eyes that possess lethal brilliance. His head is shaven, but he sports a mustache and a long beard that comes to a sharp point below his chin.

Amidst the growing crowd that gathers at the fringes of this makeshift arena, a figure who seems to be a referee calls out, signaling the commencement of the match.

"Leorick Eversham of Beaumont, present yourself for the match!" the referee cries.

Leorick, one of the armored figures, strides into the center. His boots slog through the mire. He is the smaller of the two contenders but carries himself with confidence. Each step is deliberate and calculated as he crosses the field and approaches the referee.

He wears a familiar white tabard adorned with a blue field, a rampant lion, and a gold crown. These are the arms of Beaumont, the same arms Baldwin imagined himself wearing when he played the hero earlier in the day.

Leorick arrives at the center of the field and nods to the judge. At last, he turns to face the spectators and salutes.

The man's gaze lingers on Baldwin, who smiles briefly.

The referee then summons the second contender. "Brom Hawthorne of Holmsfield, present yourself for the match!"

Brom enters the arena. His heavy steps leave deep impressions on the soft earth as he approaches and nods to the referee. He strikes an imposing figure, almost a full head taller than Leorick. His tabard bears a green field with three standing sheaves of grain arranged around a chevron.

The men's heavy armor occasionally catches the sunlight, casting dazzling bolts of light into the crowd. With a grin of anticipation, the official lays out the simple rules: "Longswords only. No deathblows."

Preparations are complete, and the referee sets the stage for the duel. "Mud backs and Filthy paws are disqualifications. Are the contenders ready?"

Both nod.

The referee signals, "Return to your fields."

Extracting themselves from the clingy mud, the fighters return to their posts, and the referee exits the arena.

With a final cry of "Honor for thy king!" the match begins.

The fighters surge towards one another and clash in a tumultuous symphony of metal. They are tidal waves of steel cast about in the field of mire. The sudden trampling of steel boots and crashing human frames make it clear why the whole area is little more than sludge.

They wield swords more as staves than blades in a frenetic search for dominance. The pommels strike each other's helms, the blades sneaking between limbs and offering leverage for grapples and counters.

As the duel unfolds, Brom slips a leg beneath Leorick and throws him over his hips. Leorick crashes into the muddy soil, eliciting a collective gasp from the local crowd, who have rallied behind their hometown hero.

He catches himself on a hand and a knee.

Somehow, Leorick avoids going down on all fours, a disqualification termed filthy paws. Resilient, Leorick quickly regains his footing, narrowly avoiding defeat.

The crowd, including Aileen and Gregor, erupts in excitement, though Baldwin's reaction shifts from shock to deep sorrow.

Meanwhile, in the arena, the fighters' movements grow increasingly sluggish.

Their armor is now caked in mud.

Brom has started to move about wildly—a series of chaotic maneuvers that force Leorick to adjust his stance repeatedly. Brom makes a desperate lunge at Leorick. He attempts to grapple and throw his adversary once again.

This time, Leorick is ready.

Leorick locks the arm.

Brom spirals to the ground and takes a seat.

Leorick pounces.

Mud. Brom.

It's over.

The referee pulls a bone whistle to his lips and signals the end.

"Mudback! That's the match! Congratulations, Leorick of Beaumont!"

The announcement unleashes a wild roar of cheers throughout the crowd.

Leorick extends a hand to help his opponent stand and then celebrates a hard-won victory.

Balwin wears a frown.

CHAPTER SEVEN

FERGUS THE FABLER

A wooden carriage adorned with images of fantastical beasts has been transformed into an impromptu stage. Bold letters engraved in the carriage announce, "Fergus the Fabler." On the stage, a tall, slender man in eccentric attire stalks back and forth. He dramatically mimics some fearsome creature. He appears to be either a man lost to raving madness or something infinitely more sinister.

His face contorts as it stretches into wild, bestial shapes. His tale goes on, "...with a maw as large as the waterwheel we passed on the way through Riverview!"

Despite the rabid tone, an ever-growing crowd of captivated listeners hangs on every word, gasping at the tales spun before them. The stranger holds all eyes locked. He entrances his prey as he weaves a yarn as a serpent might hypnotically enthrall a flock of doves before it strikes.

Amidst this entranced assembly, Aileen, Baldwin, and Gregor look for a place to rest and enjoy the show.

The mad talebearer goes on.

"Behold the tyrannical, the terrifying, the fearsome Groasque!"

At the end of his tale, the crowd breaks from their stupefaction and bursts into applause and cheers.

Finally securing a spot on a long wooden bench, the ninth in a series of twelve arrayed before the booth, Aileen, Baldwin, and Gregor settle in.

A new tale unfolds before the audience can contain their enthusiastic cheers.

"Now, travel with me far to the north. See a land covered in perpetuity by frost and snow! Harsh winds, ever blowing, ever blowing..."

The speaker scans the crowd with wild eyes.

Perhaps Fergus resembles a crafty mad scientist more than a mere lunatic. Coat tails flash to and fro across the stage. Striped red and black, they only deepen the fascinating nature of his wondrous show.

"Haunted by small devilish creatures that look like dog men, with sharp fangs and deadly spears, there live children of Adam the likes of which you have never seen!"

As he speaks, his skinny fingers reach towards the heavens, desperately trying to mimic the towering stature of the legendary Byneørsk. His gaunt form briefly assumes a posture that hints at the massive bulk and intimidating presence of the mighty Byneørsk warriors, formidable beings hailing from the frozen, barren wastes of Njoldr. His gestures, though feeble, evoke images of these fierce fighters, wrapped in furs against the biting cold, their eyes alight with the fire of battle as they stand resolute against any threat that might dare challenge them.

"Great and mighty, spanning three or sometimes even four span in height! And yet their noble blood and mighty stature..."

The storyteller collapses into a low bow, "Has not exempted them from hardship. Alas, they cruelly face a foe most heinous..."

Fergus begins to rise as he lifts his arms a bit. "Most hideous..." The phenomenal storyteller's arms spread higher. "Most horrific!"

His arms again stretch upwards, hands morphing into fearsome claws, "The Vaelskar, giant embodiments of cruel frost, death, and despair! These monstrous and tortuous beings tower above the mighty Byneorsk. Rising to the astonishing height of seven to eight span!"

Exhausted, the storyteller exhales, "No, no dear friends. You must not take this deadly trek northward with me. The peril is far too great. Stay here. Stay here."

The crowd's response is a thunderous cheer filled with swirling emotions.

Recognition of his unrivaled genius.

Reverence for his narrative artistry.

Relief that Njoldr is a world away.

Meanwhile, a third sinister figure lurks behind a stall; his sharp gaze traces everyone and everything in the crowd. He occasionally halts passersby, questioning them thoroughly before resuming his silent vigil.

CHAPTER EIGHT
HEADING HOME

The Greater Light wanes across the celestial sea and casts a soft glow as the children weave through the bustling crowd. Their faces are lit with joyous smiles as they flail their arms about in an excited conversation.

Aileen's eyes beam with excitement, "That was great! Those giants sound scary!"

Baldwin replies with a smile, "Yes! I liked the puppet show! I think you were more afraid of that cow-eating dragon than the stories of the giants."

Their laughter melds with the surrounding chatter.

Gregor adds, "Yeah! I loved the puppet show, too! Hey, Baldwin?"

"Yeah, Greg?" Baldwin turns to him.

Gregor hesitates before asking, "Uhm, about the wrestling... You seemed upset. What happened?"

Baldwin's smile falters, "It was... never mind. Nothing. Hey, look! Smoked meat! Let's grab a bite."

They halt at a stall, where a middle-aged man greets them warmly. "Hey, kids, do you want ribs or a leg?"

Rows of roasted turkey legs alternate with beef ribs cut into portions of three rib bones. Each hangs behind him over a crackling fire. Directly above the fire, sizzling meats are developing a nice sear before they, too, will be hung up in a path of smoke to stay warm.

Each child chooses a turkey leg, which a teenage boy retrieves with a long hook. The children exchange a few coppers and walk toward the festival's exit as people pour in and out through the gate leading back toward Riverview.

On the outskirts of the festival grounds, the three hardened men continue their investigation.

Once again, the gentle gurgling of the Blackwater River accompanies the children south toward Riverview. It's early evening, and the Greater Light still casts a soft, warm glow as it begins to set. Aileen, Baldwin, and Gregor meander down the path, their day at the festival still fresh in their minds.

Aileen's voice brims with excitement as she breaks the serene silence. "Today was incredible. I loved the festival."

Baldwin responds with a mix of enthusiasm and curiosity. "It was exciting, but I can't get those giant stories out of my head. I wonder if they're true."

Gregor chimes in, attempting to push away Baldwin's apprehension. "I don't know, but I don't think we should dwell on it too much. We have enough danger around here without worrying about giants."

Intrigued, Aileen probes further. "Oh? Do you think so, Gregor? What kind of danger?"

Ahead, a bridge spans a narrow stretch of the Blackwater River.

Gregor gestures towards the bridge with a mischievous smile and teases, "Well, you never know. There could be a great, big Uerg living under that bridge, ready to get you when we cross over!"

"Stop it!" Baldwin interjects, though his protest soon dissolves into laughter along with Gregor and Aileen. Caught up in the moment's laughter, Baldwin offers, "Oh yeah. Those stories were probably made up as well. I bet we could even make up our own!"

Inspired by Baldwin's suggestion, Gregor exclaims, "Brilliant, Baldwin! Let's stop and make it a game. Who can think of the scariest, real monster!"

Baldwin and Gregor gather stones from the ground excitedly while Aileen dashes towards the bridge. Standing back up, the conversation takes a playful turn.

"Real?" Baldwin questions.

"Fine, make-believe..." Gregor concedes, only to shoot Baldwin an evil grin, "...but yeah, the realest!"

Chapter Nine

Bed Hair Nightmare

The trio steps onto the bridge and leans over to toss stones into the river below. Some stones skim gracefully across the water, while others plunge in with a splash and vanish.

Aileen exclaims, "I want to go first!"

Gregor responds, "Okay, Aileen. Remember, it has to be a scary monster!"

Aileen's lips curl into a mischievous grin, "Oh, it is. It's really scary, Gregor!"

"Have you ever heard of the Naoishlatt?" Aileen asks.

Baldwin interjects with a hint of fear, "Nope, stop!"

Gregor's voice is filled with anticipation, "Yes!"

Aileen begins, "Once upon a time, she was a breathtakingly beautiful woman..."

As Aileen narrates, the children envision a stunning young woman gazing at her reflection in a mirror. The woman admires herself, entranced by her beauty. She tosses her hair back over her shoulder, turns her head to one side, and cuts her eyes toward the image of herself.

She is exquisitely tainted. Her smile is a vibrant crimson cherry that has gone off. Sickly sweet lips reek of foulness and poison. Beautiful eyes are radiant pools of acid. They lure any who might test their waters to enter suffering and death.

Aileen continues to spin her yarn, "...but vanity was her downfall. She only ever cared about herself. She only ever cared about her looks. Upon her death..."

The envisioned woman suddenly drops the mirror and grasps her throat. She dramatically chokes and coughs, overly theatrical in her demise.

Just before she dies, she throws her head back, raises a dainty hand to her forehead, and collapses, "Uuuungh..."

At last, she collapses to the floor of the imaginary stage and rests beside the shattered remnants of the mirror that she once used to admire herself.

Aileen adds, "She discovered that she was unable to rest."

The image of the beautiful woman fades from their minds, replaced by a man sleeping peacefully in his bed amidst a shadowy void. The sleeping man stirs and turns over in his bed. He smiles slightly and smacks his lips as he dreams.

Aileen narrates, "On the darkest nights, while men slumber peacefully, she roams the woods and remote villages..."

A window materializes behind the sleeping man. Moonlight streams in through the darkness.

Something moves through the trees in the darkness outside and draws closer to the window. Their branches stir as whatever it is seems to bring a powerful gust of wind.

Baldwin, increasingly uneasy, says, "I don't like this, Greg!"

Gregor dismisses him, "Stop being a baby!"

Aileen goes on, "...searching for open windows..."

The window snaps open with a crack!

Baldwin whispers in alarm to Gregor, "Oh no!"

Aileen elaborates, "...or doors left unlocked..."

Baldwin's fear escalates, and he gasps loudly, "Oh no!"

"And if she gets inside..."

A ghostly Naoischlatt crawls through the window and stands over the sleeping man.

Aileen concludes, "Her hair, stretching nine spans long, comes to life. It slithers down, creeping inside to steal his very breath."

CHAPTER TEN

LAKESHORE LOBSTER

Gregor exclaims, "That was scary. Great story, Aileen! I could barely hear it over someone crying..."

Baldwin retorts with a vengeful, mischievous grin, "Hey! Okay, well... let me tell you a story then!"

Gregor challenges mockingly, "Go ahead *hero*..."

Baldwin, slightly disheartened, begins his narrative.

"Nearby, in the depths of Stillwater Lake..."

The children's imaginations paint a serene lakeshore scene. Waters lap gently against the shore. Gregor tosses stones into the lake.

"...is a massive, deadly creature with claws as big as Gregor!"

A massive, reddish claw pierces the water's surface.

"Monstrous, boasting eight legs along a segmented body."

The lake's surface churns violently as more of the crimson claw emerges.

"The creature's head protrudes sharply from its body. It hosts a deadly beak akin to an eagle's!"

A creature crawls forth from the boiling waters of the lake as Baldwin continues.

"Even Gregor would cry like a baby at the sight of the Ceanidh!"

The vision of Gregor runs in a circle, cries, and then sprints away from the imaginary scene.

"Hey!" protests Gregor.

Baldwin chuckles, "Well, you would!"

Gregor seeks to move on. "Are you done?"

Baldwin pauses and thinks before he concedes, "Hmm, yeah. Your turn, I guess."

CHAPTER ELEVEN

MAGICKS IN THE AIR

Baldwin queries, "How are we going to judge, though?" Gregor smirks, "Oh, don't worry, you'll know. In Old Gloamwood, just across this bridge, there live a group of creatures known as Boglins..."

Baldwin interrupts skeptically, "Boglins??? Is that your scary monster? Laaaame..."

A Boglin materializes in the imaginative grey expanse before the children. It sports a bizarre trumpet in place of its nose. The odd entity engages in a clumsy yet humorous dance.

Gregor insists, "Yes, Boglins!"

Aileen remarks, "Gregor, Boglins aren't that scary."

The amusing Boglin frowns and then vanishes with an audible poof.

Gregor teases, "Just wait! Because you've never heard of... Boglin hedge wizards!"

The comical Boglin reappears, still dancing absurdly, now donned in a wizard's robe and a pointed hat. An audible and exaggerated yawn from Baldwin breaks the silence.

Gregor continues, "All Boglins look different. Some have horns..."

The Boglin's color shifts. It gestures to the musical instrument in place of its nose.

"...some have tails..."

A massive tail, reminiscent of a dragon's, sprouts from the Boglin, causing it to express surprised joy. The tail then shrinks to a size more befitting the creature, prompting it to sigh, snap its fingers in disappointment, and sulkily kick a stone.

"...but none compare to the monstrous hedge wizards!"

The Boglin disappears, replaced by a taller, more menacing hedge wizard. It extends a gnarled hand, conjuring a flickering purple orb of flame between its twisted, malevolent claws.

Now laughing with a hint of madness, Gregor declares, "If Boglins are wild and chaotic creatures, their hedge wizards are living nightmares made of terror and madness!"

The hedge wizard throws its head back in a sinister laugh. Gregor's laughter fills the air as he begins to cackle gleefully, "They don't even need to walk! They can float across the ground, levitating!" The hedge wizard hovers back and forth within the imaginary arena.

Baldwin concedes, "That's enough! You win, you win!"

Aileen agrees, "Yeah! I still have to sleep tonight! I think we're done here."

Gregor exclaims triumphantly, "Yes! I won!"

As Aileen and Baldwin roll their eyes, the trio cross the bridge.

Gregor struts ahead, a picture of victory, while Aileen and Baldwin share a look of amusement, shaking their heads at Gregor's antics.

CHAPTER TWELVE

SPLASH

Baldwin asks with a hint of skepticism, "So, Gregor, you think those Boglins are real? I've heard that sometimes strange lights can be seen from Old Gloamwood at night."

He gestures toward the ominous forest. The darkness beyond Old Gloamwood's boughs is pierced with thousands of tiny points of light. Each pair represents the possibility of a sinister creature, ready to pounce from the young boy's imagination and into reality at any moment.

Gregor responds with conviction, "Oh yeah, they're real!"

Baldwin winces.

Gregor adds, "But I doubt they're near here. We would've seen one by now, don't you think?"

Baldwin concedes, "I guess so. I don't think I want to."

As they resume picking up stones to throw into the lake, Aileen runs out of sight again. Gregor smiles at his sister as she joyfully bounds toward their home, a small farm on the outskirts of Riverview.

Once Aileen is out of earshot, Baldwin says, "I don't think it's fair, Greg. You know I'm afraid of things. Why did we play a scary game?"

Gregor tries to reassure him, "It's just a game. What are you scared of?"

Baldwin wrestles with his fears before he confesses, "I don't want to be. I just..."

Their conversation is abruptly interrupted by a loud splash from the lake. They look up in alarm to find Aileen missing.

In the river.

"Aileen!!!"

CHAPTER THIRTEEN
GREGOR DESPAIRS

Aileen is ensnared. She flounders about in the water as she struggles to free herself from the tangled mesh of a net. Her curious bobbing motions are melancholic reminders of the prancing steps of joy she traced on her way to the festival.

She is being swept downstream at a bewildering pace. A shadowy figure snakes through the water ahead of her, but it's impossible to tell what the form might be.

Far ahead, a part of Blackwater River washes into a narrow branch that flows into a small cave. The water thunders at the juncture as it rages against the stone and soil that rise from its surface and force it to split. The spray catches on the wind and flies into the fading light of dusk. White, bubbling foam swirls against the firmament's radiant red, violet, and blue as the Greater Light wanes.

It is a beautiful day.

Onshore, Baldwin and Gregor sprint down the shoreline in a vain effort to catch up to Aileen. Their labored breathing is a testament to their fatigue.

She slips further away.

For a moment, Aileen rises upon an eddy formed by the currents, which crash against the stone outcropping before the rapids whisk her away. She disappears into the cave's shadowy embrace.

A single word echoes in Gregor's mind.

Hopeless.

Ignited by a fierce resolve, Baldwin and Gregor push themselves to their limits. They finally reach the sinister cave into which Aileen passed not long ago. Inside, they find a spacious cavern, its center dominated by a deep pool. Nearby, the outline of a rectangular object and fresh scrapes on the stone floor suggest something of significant weight was pushed over the side and into the depths. Baldwin and Gregor fixate on the ominous pool.

Their hope fades.

Gregor's cries pierce the silence, "Aileen! No! No! Help!"

Panic etched across his face, he scans desperately for any sign of another way out.

Baldwin, struck by the grim reality, acknowledges, "She's... She's gone? She's gone!"

Baldwin notices Gregor's terror and his resolve crumbles. Tears mar the wanna-be hero's face.

Gregor, overwhelmed by despair, pleads, "No! No, she can't be. Help me, Baldwin!" Gregor pleads but has no idea what they should do. Gregor's question hangs in the air, more a prayer to his Creator than a request to Baldwin.

Baldwin is paralyzed by fear. Finally, he admits, "Gregor! What do we do? I want to help, but I can't! I'm sorry!"

"Help!" Gregor's plea echoes in the cavern as he collapses. The weight of their predicament renders him helpless.

Gregor cries.

Chapter Fourteen

Sinking

A foreboding darkness engulfs the cave and clings to every crevice like a vile miasma. The ground forms a stone semicircle, and at its heart is a deep pool fed by the rushing waters of the Blackwater River.

An ancient stone sarcophagus rests nearby, its lid ajar and propped against its side. An ominous, sticky, oily residue smears the sarcophagus' rim.

Near the water's edge, two Mehr—slimy, fish-like humanoids with scales ranging from indigo to deep purple—stand guard. Their large, white eyes are devoid of emotion. Their mouths are full of sharp teeth stained green and brown from algae and blood. Gills flutter along their necks. Striking fins arc from their heads down their backs.

The cave is momentarily still, the Mehr poised in anticipation. Suddenly, the sound of splashing draws their attention. A third Mehr emerges, swimming to the pool's edge, followed by Aileen, who struggles within a net. Her screams are broken only by moments of panicked gurgling as she dips below the surface.

The two Mehr on the bank swiftly pull her from the water. As she is dragged towards the sarcophagus, the net drops away. Aileen's wild scrambling hands catch one of the creatures by surprise, slipping into its gills and causing it to release her momentarily. "Gregor! Help!" Aileen cries out in desperation. She takes a fleeting step toward the cave, but the other Mehr grasps her. It drags her backward, leaving deep claw marks in the flesh of her left arm.

She screams, kicks, bites. Aileen refuses to surrender to her wicked captors.

The third Mehr, climbing from the pool, utters an arcane phrase, its voice echoing like water in a chasm, "Oopw'p fdna pw'pu."

They thrust Aileen into the sarcophagus with indifference. She falls clumsily backward and lands in a heap.

She raises a hand in a vain effort to resist, but the two Mehr force the lid shut. Aileen is sealed in a hopeless fate. Darkness envelops her. She cries in despair. She apologizes to Gregor. Her mournful wails fill the void as the sarcophagus is pushed into the pool, sinking with a haunting splash.

Inside, Aileen fights against her confinement. Her efforts weaken until only her breathing and the eerie sound of underwater echoes remain.

Pitch-black despair.

Aileen begins to hum—the melody transforms the oppressive darkness. She cuts her tune short, leaving the claustrophobic chamber again dark and hopeless.

She takes a deep breath.

A radiant song floods the dark chamber, filling it with her native tongue, Saeldring. Aileen sings of hope and deliverance, her voice a beacon in the darkness.

Screaming in fear, terror flees from Aileen.

A Loresinger is born.

Sinking down, into the pool,

into the depths of the world.

She carries hope

to the darkness below

until her brother comes

and carries them all

out of this place

back to the land of the son.

As she sings, orbs of light materialize, each revealing scenes of Gregor and Baldwin and their struggles and triumphs.

In the dim light of a secluded cave, Gregor kneels beside a pool, tears streaming down his face without restraint.

In the next orb, he dashes into the melancholy clutches of Old Gloamwood, whose shadowy boughs envelop him completely. Baldwin follows Gregor, unaware that a mysterious, shadowy figure is pursuing them.

Meanwhile, orbs of light flit by, casting a warm illumination over Aileen in the dark confines of her tomb.

These visions culminate in a final scene of liberation. Aileen and Gregor escape into the daylight from the depths of their captivity.

The orbs vanish, leaving Aileen alone once more in the darkness.

Yet, a sense of peace envelops her.

"It's going to be okay, Gregor. Be careful. I love you," she whispers. She resigns to live out the tale she's just seen unfold.

With a deafening thump, the sarcophagus' descent comes to an end.

Aileen speaks and sings in Saeldring—a language of the Sonebraén people dwelling in the southern kingdoms of Chancelmir.

In Saeldring, her song reads as follows:

Aef a dohl fodha linne

   Steach do'n tua de doimhne

Tha giùlan dòchas

   d'on dorchadas shìos

gus an tànaig a brathàir

   Agus a 'giùlan iad uile

eos às an toll sios

   agus air ais gu tìr de àthair

CHAPTER FIFTEEN

RISING

G regor kneels beside the pool. Tears stream down his face as he gazes into its depths. He cautiously tests the water with his hands before submerging his head. His eyes scan for signs of a floor, but his gaze finds only darkness. The pool is fathomless.

Gregor raises his head and vigorously shakes the water from his hair. He appears lost in thought for a brief moment before he dismisses an idea with a shake of his head. "I'd never make it down to the bottom," he murmurs.

Drying his tears, Gregor rises, a newfound determination in his eyes.

Baldwin starts, "Greg, you don't think she's dr..." Gregor interrupts him firmly, "No! I don't know what happened, but I'm sure she's alright. We have to find her, somehow."

"Someone in Riverview could help!" Baldwin suggests.

Turning towards Baldwin with a hopeful smile, Gregor agrees, "Yeah, let's go!"

Baldwin and Gregor burst from the cave and race southward along the path adjacent to the Blackwater River. Crashing falls roar in camaraderie beside them. The sun offers a fleeting glimmer on the horizon before it succumbs to darkness.

It is night.

As the path veers left, they leave the roaring Blackwater River behind. Finally, fatigue sets in. Their pace falters to a jog. Heavy breaths fill the silence between them until Baldwin can no longer bear it. "Hey Gregor, what are we going to say?" Baldwin's voice is burdened with concern for Aileen.

"I don't know. I'll tell them what we saw and ask for help." Gregor responds, his gaze distant.

"Do you think they will blame us?" Baldwin presses.

Gregor doesn't answer. He quickens his steps. Urgency drives him on. They approach a wider road, Old Gloamwood Trail, and turn right. As Riverview comes into sight, Gregor pulls ahead of Baldwin. The tiny hamlet appears desolate. Her inhabitants are likely still at the festival.

They cross a small stone bridge over the Blackwater River. Moss thrives in the crevices between stones, a testament to the ancient bridge's endurance over time.

The boys rush over the bridge and into the tiny hamlet.

Riverview.

Chapter Sixteen

Weary Traveler

The Weary Traveler has been a beacon for travelers for over a century. With its haggard bones, this ancient roadhouse is responsible for the tiny hamlet's existence. It is nestled on the left as one approaches Riverview from Old Gloamwood.

A lone mare is tied to a post near the entrance. As Baldwin and Gregor draw near, the mare quenches her thirst from a trough. Unfazed by the boys' hurried pace, the horse continues to drink.

The boys sprint past the horse, bound up the steps, and burst through the door where they search for assistance.

Inside, The Weary Traveler wears its emptiness like a cloak. Tonight, its only guests are Welt and Curn, an odd pair united by their day's toils and tales. With his thinning hair and grey beard, Welt carries an air of authority. Curn, of middle age, boasts a head of red hair.

Baldwin and Gregor struggle to articulate their plea for help while gasping for air.

Orsen Griegs, the robust man behind the bar and the proprietor of The Weary Traveler, calls out to them with concern and curiosity.

"Gregor! Baldwin! What's got you boys in such a rush? Were you being chased? Should the fellars and I be preparin' for something?" Orsen inquires, his voice echoing around the sparse room.

A brief chuckle shared between Orsen, Welt, and Curn fills the room as the boys attempt to regain their breath.

"No! It's Aileen..." Gregor manages to say, eliciting raised eyebrows from the three men. "... she's fallen into the river!" he continues, prompting a quick, concerned response from Orsen, "Aye, the poor lass. Ya just left her then?"

Gregor, desperate, clarifies, "No! She went into a cave and something... I think something took her!"

Orsen, skeptical yet concerned, suggests, "Ach, lads. Was it one of those Boglin ya always tell us about? Ye canna keeps makin' up these wild tales, Greg."

But Gregor insists, "No! This isn't just a story! She's in trouble! Can you help us?" Baldwin echoes the urgency, "It's true, Mr. Griegs! It's true!"

Torn between his duties and the boys' plea, Orsen responds, "Aye Greg, best not be a game. I ha'e a business to run 'ere."

Welt and Curn stand up. They glance toward Gregor with a mix of disappointment and resolve.

"We'll check 'er out, Orsen. Ya stay put and 'ave our meat ready when we get back," Welt declares, showing a glimmer of hope amidst the concern.

Curn, with a stern look, adds, "And if 'is ain't trouble, son, it will be. We know yer pa."

With that, the boys hasten back into the night. The men follow more slowly, their steps heavy with the weight of the unfolding situation.

Halfway between the Weary Traveler and the bridge over the Blackwater River, the flickering light of a torch moves along the trail toward Riverview. "It's our lucky day. Look! 'ere comes Justin. He can babysit for us." Welt exclaims.

Welt and Curn descend the steps, eagerly waving at the approaching young guard. "'ey! Justin, we got something fer ya!" Welt shouts.

Justin is a young guard distinguished by his short, jet-black hair. He is clad in a sturdy chainmail hauberk. A sheathed arming sword hangs gracefully from his belt. He holds a flickering torch that illuminates his determined path forward. A tabard emblazoned with the Beaumont family's coat of arms is draped over his armor. It is a symbol of his loyalty and service. The fabric of the tabard rustles softly with each deliberate step he takes.

They rush to meet him.

"Well? What's the trouble?" Justin inquires.

"It's about Ail…" starts Gregor.

"No trouble, Justin, just thissun says his sis is lost. Curn an I's goin' to fetch 'er, but meats 'bout done. Can ye take the lads fer us?" Welt interjects. Justin nods in agreement and gestures for Gregor and Baldwin to accompany him.

Chapter Seventeen

Something Fishy

J ustin calls out, "Come on, boys. What's happened?" The boys catch up with Justin and head back towards the bridge together. Meanwhile, Welt and Curn make their way back to the roadhouse.

With a hint of panic, Gregor says, "Aileen fell in the river, but I think something took her." Justin picks up the pace. Upon hearing something might have taken Aileen, he glances at Gregor.

Gregor continues, "We chased her downstream, but she went into a cave. It took us a while to catch up, and when we did, she was gone!"

Justin responds, "Well, let's go see this cave. This isn't one of your stories, is it?" Gregor seems on the verge of tears.

Noticing Gregor's distress, Justin softens, sighing deeply, "It's okay, Greg. We'll figure it out, but let's hurry. I'm still on duty and shouldn't be away too long."

As the Lesser Light rises, full and magnificent, bats occasionally fly past, hunting for insects against the backdrop of the vibrant celestial body. The sound of crickets fills the air, and the familiar babble of the Blackwater River draws closer as they approach the ancient bridge.

Justin suddenly stops and signals Baldwin and Gregor to halt. "Hold, did you hear that?" he whispers.

The boys exchange nervous glances.

Gregor asks, "Hear what?"

Justin replies, "Something moved near the bridge. Stay here."

Justin draws his blade and approaches the old bridge. He vanishes down the embankment.

Baldwin is uneasy. He looks nervously around the darkness and says, "Greg?"

"Yeah, Bald?" replies Gregor.

"He looks serious. I... I think he believes us now," Baldwin observes.

After a moment, Gregor moves towards the slope Justin had investigated, followed by a hesitant Baldwin.

Justin examines what appears to be a net. He calls out, "Someone was fishing. I have no idea why they'd run, but I never saw them."

Rejoining the boys, Justin says, "They must have been up to something; they left their net down there."

As the group regathers near the bridge, a bat swoops at Justin's flickering torch. The dark form causes a moment of panic and startles them all.

Nervous and hoping to put this whole ordeal behind him, Justin leads the boys across the bridge, his voice firm, "Let's go find your sis."

The boys follow, with Justin appearing slightly unnerved. His sword remains drawn and ready.

Grateful, Gregor says, "Hey, Justin? Thank you for helping us."

CHAPTER EIGHTEEN
FIND THE GIRL

The cave, shrouded in darkness, gradually brightens as the flicker of approaching torchlight pierces the gloom.

Footsteps echo.

Justin queries, "Is this the right place?"

Gregor confirms, "Yeah, she went right in. She was in the water."

The sound of footsteps intensifies, and the cave is bathed in the wavering light. The trio navigates the cavern, their search intent yet unclear. Justin seeks guidance, "Help me out, boys. What am I supposed to be looking for?"

Gregor gestures towards the dark, enigmatic waters of the pool, "She went down there!"

Justin appears shaken, "There? In that pool? You saw her in the pool? Mercy!"

Gregor clarifies, "No! I didn't see her!"

Justin is puzzled. "Wait, so you're not sure she's down there? She could have just left the cave and headed home, right?"

Gregor, visibly distressed, asserts, "She'd never do that! You know she'd have come to find me. I heard her call for help!"

Empathetic yet realistic, Justin says, "Oh Greg, I'm sorry, but if she went down in there..."

Baldwin interjects, "Gregor says he knows she's okay!"

Justin replies, "I'm sorry, Gregor. There's nowhere else from here. She either left the cave or..." His tone is skeptical yet sorrowful.

"She's down there! Something had her!" Gregor insists.

Justin proposes, "Let's go check if she went home. If she's not there..." Justin's demeanor shows his heartache as he exits the cave. "Come on, boys."

Gregor and Baldwin walk outside with Justin. They all turn back toward Riverview. Baldwin and Gregor trail behind.

Gregor offers, "Thanks again for helping Justin." A farewell cloaked in sincere gratitude.

"I wish we had found her, Greg," Justin answers with a disheartened voice.

Gregor begins to plot a conspiracy with his friend Baldwin. He silently tugs Baldwin's sleeve to get his attention. Baldwin's eyes are wide. The boys deliberately slow their pace, allowing Justin some distance, then stealthily detour back the way they came.

Moments later, Justin senses his solitude. "Aww, come on..."

He calls into the void, "Baldwin! Gregor! Come back here, boys!"

But it's futile; the boys have vanished into the still night air.

CHAPTER NINETEEN
No Help in Sight

Under cover of darkness, illuminated solely by the soft luminescence of the Lesser Light above, Gregor and Baldwin find a shadowy nook to hide in. They do their best to blend into the night.

Baldwin's whisper cuts through the silence, "Gregor, what are we doing?"

Gregor's response is a hushed, determined whisper, "We're going to find help."

"We tried that," Baldwin points out.

Gregor pleads, "Let's try one more place, please, Balds."

Baldwin lets out a frustrated sigh.

"Where now, Greg?" he asks.

Gregor suggests, "Some people are probably still at the festival."

Baldwin loses hope. His head droops, and he shakes it in resignation. He finally gives a reluctant nod. "Alright, let's go."

With that decision made, the boys slowly rise to their feet. They carefully begin their journey back to the familiar path, navigating through the darkness with only the soft, ethereal glow of the Lesser Light to guide their steps.

Gregor adds, "If you hear anyone or see any lights, we'll have to hide."

Baldwin nods in agreement wordlessly.

By the time they arrive, the festival is over. The Lesser Light casts its glow upon the grounds from overhead. A bonfire burns near the entrance, and another illuminates the back of the area. These fires provide light and warmth to a small group of men tasked with cleaning up after the day's celebrations. Only three workers remain, focused on their tasks. The men attempt to ignore the boys.

A shadowy figure lurks on the periphery. One of the threatening-looking men appears weary and frustrated. He scans his surroundings.

Gregor urgently approaches the first worker. Meanwhile, the foreboding figure finds a concealed spot to observe as Gregor and Baldwin enter the area.

Gregor pleads, "Sir, I need help! My sister fell into the river."

The worker, preoccupied with moving and neatly stacking wooden crates, barely acknowledges him.

The sinister onlooker edges closer, intrigued by the conversation.

Gregor persists, "Please! I need someone to help me!"

The worker responds tersely, "We have a business to attend to, boy. We got no time for your nonsense. I have a family to see, and it's not getting any earlier."

Gregor insists, "It's serious!"

The worker interrupts, "Listen, kid. If I don't get these boxes loaded, my family won't eat tomorrow. That is serious. Sorry, can't help right now."

Gregor attempts to speak again, but the worker cuts him off, "No kid! I have to get this done! If it can wait, I'll try to help when I finish!"

Gregor looks dejected. He turns and retreats from the festival grounds, leaving the comforting light of the fires behind.

Baldwin, torn between the worker and his friend, finally dashes after Gregor.

Unnoticed, the menacing figure silently follows them into the night.

Chapter Twenty

Run to Her

Outside the festival grounds, a menacing figure steps off the beaten path and disappears into the underbrush. The dangerous-looking man's hair is shiny and black, hanging just to his shoulders, and his beard is meticulously groomed.

Cloaked in dark leather armor and draped with tan furs over his shoulders, he cuts a formidable figure. A katzbalger sword, sheathed and silent, hangs at his side. Suddenly, he emits a loud call, mimicking a wolf's howl with uncanny precision. Moments later, two other men join him.

The man commands the group with his dangerous aura, "Something's happening. Two boys ran up. One said that his sister fell into the river."

"You think it's related?" inquires a second man, distinguishable by his bald head and long beard.

"Could be. They were frantic. I'll try and catch up. You pups get things ready," commands the leader, exuding authority. The two men hasten back towards the festival, while the first sets off down the trail towards Riverview, moving with a silence that belies his urgency.

He makes swift progress through shadows as the night resonates with the song of crickets. The Lesser Light bathes the landscape in a light that appears all the more luminous, positioned directly overhead.

Gregor sprints as fast as he can.

His breaths come in heavy gasps. He's no longer guided by a plan but driven by a primal urge towards the woods.

Baldwin struggles to keep pace. He knows he must catch up. Only the radiant glow from the heavens above keeps Gregor in his sight.

Unbeknownst to both, a shadowy figure is effortlessly tailing them, keeping up with a relaxed jog.

"Gregor! Wait up!" Baldwin calls out, but his plea goes unanswered. Gregor's relentless pace towards the foreboding Old Gloamwood remains unchecked.

As they approach, the dark forest looms ominously under the Lesser Light's glow, and the world beyond is swallowed in pitch darkness.

"Please, Greg!" Baldwin's calls are desperate now, but exhaustion takes its toll, reducing his pace to a weary walk. "Gregor, I can't keep up!" he exclaims, resigning himself to his slower speed.

Gregor vanishes into the shadowy undergrowth as he crosses into the woods.

Baldwin halts, overwhelmed by despair, "No... Gregor, no."

He tries once more to muster the strength to run, managing only a feeble jog.

The lurking figure slows, observing Baldwin from afar as he approaches the wood's edge, but dares not enter.

"Gregor?" Baldwin's voice is hopeful yet tentative.

Silence follows until Baldwin's shout, "Gregor!" pierces the quiet.

After a tense pause, Gregor responds, "Come on Balds!"

"I'm scared, Gregor. Where are you?" Baldwin's voice trembles.

Movement stirs near the wood's edge, and Gregor emerges, visibly agitated, "COME. ON. NOW!"

He grabs Baldwin, dragging him into the brush. Baldwin yelps as thorns scrape his face.

Chapter Twenty-One

Brave, but...

Gregor and Baldwin emerge from a thicket and find themselves on a trail. Sharp thorns along the wood's edge reveal why Gregor is so frustrated about returning. Gregor exhales a heavy sigh. Thorn stings visibly mark his face and arms in the dim forest. "I have an idea, Balds. You have to trust me."

Baldwin, filled with uncertainty, asks, "Uh, Gregor? What are we doing? Why are we here?"

Gregor bites his lip and pauses for a moment. He confides. "I know a way down there, Baldwin."

Baldwin, puzzled, queries, "What?"

Gregor looks determined, "I know how we can get to Aileen. It's supposed to be just a story, but I think maybe..."

Baldwin looks shocked, "No. No, Gregor!"

Gregor shakes his head. "Listen! Howling Grotto. They say it goes deep."

Baldwin protests, "Gregor! We can't! They also say it's one way. If we go in there..."

"We have to Baldwin!" Gregor pauses and takes a deep breath. "I have to."

Baldwin, attempting bravery, voices his fears, "I can't, Greg. You know, I'm afraid."

"What are you afraid of, Balds?" Gregor inquires gently.

"Everything! But right now, mostly that place! This is nuts!" Baldwin exclaims and takes a deep breath.

After a moment of reflection, Baldwin confides, "Remember back at the festival? You asked why I looked upset while we watched the wrestling?"

Gregor responds, "Yeah?"

Baldwin answers, and his voice sounds weary. He suddenly seems to have aged many times his years: "I was upset because... I want to be like them. Strong. Brave. I can't. Gregor. I want to be, but I am always so scared."

Giving a comforting gesture, Gregor assures, "It's okay, Baldwin. It's okay. I'm sorry for dragging you out here."

Baldwin appears more hopeful and asks, "So we can go now?"

Gregor somberly says, "You can go, Baldwin."

Baldwin, shocked, insists, "You're coming too, right? What if she's home and Justin and your parents are waiting for you there!"

Gregor responds with a voice of resolution. His mind is set. "Balds, you know that's not true. I have to do this. I can't just abandon Aileen."

As Baldwin walks away, tears streaming down his face, Gregor calls, "Hey Balds?"

Through his sobs, Baldwin replies, "Yeah, Greg?"

Gregor expresses his gratitude, "Thanks for trying, Balds. See ya when Aileen and I get back."

Gregor strides into the woods while Baldwin, motionless, silently prays. His lifelong friend grows more distant with each step.

Turning back with determination, Baldwin brandishes his wooden sword and follows, loudly declaring, "I'm coming, Greg!"

As they navigate the uncertain path, a clamor of movement echoes through the forest behind them, causing them to halt. The darkness conceals the source of the noise.

Gregor whispers, "Baldwin? I think maybe you were right."

With a quiver in his voice, Baldwin agrees.

"I'm afraid maybe I was."

CHAPTER TWENTY-TWO

The Wolf Who Cried Boy

A sinister figure lingers at the forest's edge, ears tuned to the wilderness. Shortly, distant, muffled voices pierce the silence.

"Foolish boys," he mutters, unsheathing a short sword and venturing deeper into the woods.

Tracing the path the boys took, he pauses to listen once more. Baldwin's voice echoes in the distance, "I'm coming, Greg!"

The man scowls, cursing softly, "Shut up..." Stealthily, sword in hand, he advances down the trail, his steps silent as shadows.

Nearby movement rustles; the man's anger flares. Exasperated, he sighs, "Kids."

A sudden crash resonates behind him. Quickly, he conceals himself, retrieving a thick rope from his pack.

He secures the ends so the rope hangs across the worn trail through the woods, ready for the unsuspecting.

Meanwhile, Gregor and Baldwin stiffen in fear as the noise grows closer. A heavyweight of the forest fast approaches. They strain to see down the path for a moment.

"What is it?" Baldwin asks.

"I don't know," Gregor responds.

A chilling scream — part squeal, part roar — sends the boys fleeing in terror.

"WHAT IS IT?" Baldwin yells.

"I DON'T KNOW!" Gregor panics.

As the boys blindly run along the path, Gregor slips and skids along the dirt and leaf-covered floor. The woods suddenly fall silent again, except for the chirping of crickets and some curious owl's occasional inquiry of "Who?".

Baldwin keeps running momentarily, then turns and stops to check on his friend.

Baldwin, "Hey Gregor?"

Gregor spits dirt and leaves from his mouth. In frustration, he takes a deep breath and asks, "What?"

Baldwin, "What was it?"

Gregor's voice is at the edge of anger, "*I. Don't. Know.* Why don't you come help me up?"

Baldwin walks back to Gregor and helps him up. The two walk further along the path.

"I don't like it here," Baldwin admits.

The trail opens onto a clearing with two exits opposite the side from which they came.

A large tree dominates the center of the clearing. The boys don't realize it, but the other side of the tree is the form of a woman.

Baldwin looks nervously around the clearing, lit only by the Lesser Light's glowing rays. "So, what exactly is the plan, Gregor?"

Gregor struggles to come up with a solution. All he says is, "We go in."

Baldwin is nonplussed. "That doesn't sound like a plan."

Gregor throws his hands into the air in surrender and loudly shouts at his friend. "It's not a plan, Balds. We just look for her, I don't know."

A sinister figure steps into the clearing behind the two boys, covered in sweat, disheveled, and angry.

Baldwin's eyes are wide in terror. He points behind Gregor, who looks over his shoulder at the threatening figure before him and gasps.

He stands over the boys menacingly. A short sword is still drawn and now stained with blood. Everything about this man looks threatening now. When he speaks, it's in a deep, measured voice that borders on aggression.

"Looking for someone?"

Chapter Twenty-Three

Unclearing

Baldwin and Gregor stand together in a clearing. They have stumbled into the heart of the forest, commanded by a majestic tree - the tree is Her.

Three paths diverge from this clearing. A menacing figure approaches from the glade's edge by one of the trails. Baldwin and Gregor cower before his presence. The dangerous man looms over the boys, causing them to step back instinctively in caution. Baldwin and Gregor move in unison, speechless and taken aback.

Observing them, the intimidating figure glances at his blade with a sigh and shakes his head in disappointment.

With a quick motion, he cleans the blade on his pants, sheathes it, and attempts to tidy himself up by brushing leaves from his hair. The effort does little to enhance his appearance. He takes a deep breath for another attempt.

A voice, softer and full of concern, crosses the clearing. "I am trying to help."

Baldwin and Gregor share a brief, silent glance before responding.

Baldwin's voice is firm, "We just want to go home."

Gregor interjects sharply, "Baldwin!" His stern gaze falls on his friend before he adds, "I'm looking for my sister! If you can help, I need it."

Baldwin sighs heavily, his frustration palpable, and murmurs to Gregor, "We don't know this guy."

Gregor replies, "We need... I need help, Baldwin."

The stranger interjects, "Your friend is right. You don't know me. You don't have any reasons why you should trust me." He rests his hand on his sword's hilt, "I show up here, in the middle of the woods, with a sword drawn, and ask if you're looking for someone. You have every reason to distrust me."

Baldwin glances at Gregor and shrugs in the man's direction as if to say, "Listen to him!"

The stranger leans in, "On the other hand, I can't figure out if you are a couple of brilliant and brave kids with the potential to be something..." The boys brighten at the praise momentarily. He continues, "...or the two dumbest kids I have ever seen. Did I overhear you say that your plan is not to have a plan? Just march down into the depths." He uses his fingers to pantomime an imaginary person as they walk downstairs.

"Go find your sister," he says, his tone mocking as he mimics searching, "and then just stroll back out?" His fingers puppet a gesture of walking back up and out of someplace dark and lost beneath the surface of the world.

He emphasizes his point by making a downward gesture as if throwing something away. "I know that plan. That plan gets people very, very dead. Or possibly worse."

Gregor looks emotionally drained.

He has nothing left.

It has been Gregor's worst day, and the truth hits home.

Gregor sighs, his shoulders slump, and he begins to sob quietly.

The man sighs, places a firm hand on Gregor's shoulder, and concludes, "You may not trust me, but I doubt you'll find anyone else willing to believe you, let alone help. I have a couple of friends. We'll find your sister."

Gregor straightens, a spark of resolve in his eyes, "We're going with you!"

Baldwin, taken aback, interjects, "We?"

Baldwin exhales sharply but realizes that if Gregor is determined to go, he has no choice but to follow.

"I mean, yeah... We are going with you," Baldwin concedes.

The man reacts with alarm, "No. No! You two almost got yourselves killed. Almost got me killed! Do you know what you spooked into charging down that trail?"

Gregor implores, "We'll do whatever you say! We... I need help finding Aileen!"

The man insists, "I told you I'll go find her."

Gregor is quick-witted and takes this opportunity to go on the offense: "Okay, what does she look like?"

Caught off guard, the man replies, "What?"

Gregor presses, "My sister. What does she look like?"

The man sighs, rolling his eyes in exasperation. "I don't know. She's a girl. Uhm, red hair?"

Gregor rolls his eyes in return, "Yes, my sister's a girl. Brilliant deduction, inspector!"

Stamping his foot, Gregor challenges, "You don't know my sister, so how are you going to find her?"

The man, weary of the argument, answers, "I assumed she'd be the one underground?"

Gregor counters, "What if there are others? She didn't just fall in. I think something took her! What if they took others."

Here, the dangerous man winces. He knows something, and Gregor's words have him trapped.

He resigns, "I'll consider it. Don't do anything rash without me. Go home, see your family, and get some rest."

Hope lights up Gregor's face for the first time in a long while.

The man looks relieved as he sets a condition, "There's going to be some rules if I decide you two can tag along."

Gregor and Baldwin simultaneously roll their eyes.

The man continues, "First rule: keep your mouths shut about this whole thing, especially about me."

The boys respond with laughter and affirmative nods.

Gregor starts, "Who are we gonna..."

But the man interrupts before Gregor can finish: "Second rule: Pack and prepare for the worst. Include extra shoes, clothing, and a rope. Bring a knife if you have one."

Gregor inquires, "Anything else?"

With a determined look, the man says, "You're lost, alone, starving, and out of water. You're in the wastelands of Njoldr... no, Uru'Kaz. It's freezing at night. It's pouring rain. Someone is trying to kill you both. What do you wish you had with you? Bring that. Understood?"

The boy's eyes are vast, but they nod.

"Good. The third rule: stay close. If I say something, you obey. No questions. No hesitation. Hesitation kills. Do you understand?" He fixes a stern gaze on the two.

Baldwin swallows hard.

Both boys nod, their eyes trapped in those of the mysterious stranger.

The man adds, "Fourth rule: Tell your family you love them, especially your moms. They're going to need that. We don't know when we'll be back, and..."

He pauses, locking eyes with Gregor with piercing intensity,"...your parents just lost their daughter. Tell them you love them before you go."

Gregor's voice is full of hope as he asks, "If we agree, can we come?"

The man hesitates, "I don't know. We'll see. I still think it's a terrible idea. Listen, whether or not I allow you to go with me..." He pauses, taking a deep breath, "Your parents are in pain. Will it hurt you to tell them you love them?"

Gregor and Baldwin both shake their heads in agreement with his sentiment.

The man continues, "If I decide to let you two tag along, we won't know how long we will be gone. Just do it, boys."

They nod in understanding.

A somber silence envelops them for a few moments.

Gregor finally breaks the silence, "We'll head back and rest like you said. Will you be here tomorrow?"

"I have things I must attend to, but don't worry. I'll find you. I promise I will at least let you know my decision," the man replies with a sense of finality.

With that, he steps forward, grasps the boys, and guides them out of the clearing, back onto the trail leading away from Old Gloamwood.

On the far side of the clearing, a pair of eyes open, emitting an eerie green glow in the dimming light.

Chapter Twenty-Four
A Brief Reunion

Baldwin and Gregor tread a narrow path toward the fields adjacent to the Killough family farm. Their footsteps disrupt the tranquility of the evening. In the distance, torch in hand, a solitary figure moves purposefully through the fields toward a gathering in front of the Killough homestead.

James Killough, Gregor's father, gestures authoritatively to the individual holding the flaming torch aloft. James has a distinguished, greying beard. He wears the unadorned yet sturdy tunic and trousers that are the hallmark of a dedicated farm owner.

James queries, "Anything, Justin?"

Justin responds with a hint of agonized guilt, "Sorry, sir. There has been no sign of them since we headed back. The rest are still searching by the festival grounds."

The torchbearer, Justin, approaches the assembly near the farm, his light casting long shadows on the ground.

By now, Gregor and Baldwin have halved the distance to the farmhouse.

Abruptly, a figure within the group spots the boys, barely visible in the fringe of Justin's torchlight.

James's voice, laden with concern, cuts through the night, "Boys! Is that you?"

Without hesitation, the group runs towards the two boys. Justin, realizing who's been spotted, redirects his steps towards them.

Gregor calls out, "Dad! Has anyone found Aileen?"

James's response is thick with emotion: "Oh, son. My son. Your mother's worried sick!" Tears trace lines in the poor farmer's cheeks as the man avoids giving his son an answer.

Racing ahead of the others, James enfolds Gregor in his muscular embrace. The young boy disappears into his father's arms, pulling him tightly, as protective and mighty as a mother bear.

He then yells back towards the farm, commanding, "Someone fetch Loren and Millie. And find Bertram! Quickly!"

After a moment, James releases Gregor, only to embrace him again, his concern evident.

James inquires, ensuring their safety, "Are you boys alright? Baldwin, you okay, son?"

Baldwin answers with a trace of worry, "I'm fine, Mr. Killough. Is my dad upset?"

James soothes, "Oh, he's just worried. Out looking for you near the festival."

Standing, James places his strong hands on both boys, guiding them toward the farmhouse with a reassuring presence.

With a note of warmth in his voice, James encourages, "Come on, boys. Let's go see your moms."

Chapter Twenty-Five
Prepare for the Worst

In the quaint corner of the family's home lies Gregor's modest room, furnished with a chest, a dresser, and a standing closet. The centerpiece, Gregor's bed, cradles him in slumber. Warped with age, an open door reveals the room's humble character through its weathered boards.

Darkness envelops the space, yet warmth and coziness pervade. A solitary window punctures an exterior wall, its aged shutters betraying the room's exterior face. Slivers of the Greater Light pierce through shutter cracks, casting fragmented beams across the room. These rays, though faint, mask the unknown lurking within Gregor's sanctuary.

Sounds of subtle movement break the silence; a latch clicks. A burst of light floods the room as Loren Killough swings open the shutters. The light looks like flames as it dances upon her striking, long, red hair. As Gregor's mother, her presence is commanding yet tender.

Loren's voice cuts through the morning haze, "Time to rise, Gregor. We will look for Aileen, and I thought you would join us. Everyone has been worried sick."

Blinded momentarily by the light, Gregor stirs, his voice groggy. "Ugh, morning mom. I'm so tired."

Loren responds with a mix of understanding and resolve: "It's no wonder. You were awake all night. Now, let's get up, son."

Gregor, hesitant, pleads for a moment longer, "Okay, Mom. You guys go ahead. I need to look for a few things first."

Gregor starts to lie back down as Loren walks to the door and closes his eyes for a moment. He sits back up in bed with a start as he remembers the last rule the dangerous man gave him.

"Mom!" Gregor calls out, halting Loren in her tracks.

Startled, Loren turns, "Gregor! What is it, son? You gave me a fright!"

"I love you, Mom. Can I get a hug? I missed you." Moved, Loren reassures, "Oh, sweetie, of course. You know we love you, sweet boy." Returning to his side, they share a heartfelt embrace. Loren's kiss on his forehead is the silent promise of a mother's unconditional love.

"We're going to go look for your sister now."

"Okay, Mom. I'm going to get ready, and then I'll look for her, too," Gregor commits as Loren exits, closing the door behind her.

Gregor surveys his room, his determination renewed. He retrieves an empty backpack beneath his bed and prepares for the journey ahead.

Gregor stands and begins walking through his room as we hear people start to meet somewhere outside.

"Extra Shoes," Gregor grabs a pair of shoes from a pile near the head of his bed. He returns to the pack and puts them in the bottom. "clothing," Gregor grabs two tunics from a dresser, then opens another drawer and retrieves a pair of trousers.

He rolls them up and packs them tightly into the bottom of the backpack as he methodically prepares for this journey.

James Killough appears at the window and greets his son, "Morning Gregor. We're off to find your sister. See you in a bit?"

Heartened by his father's appearance, Gregor responds affectionately, "Hey Dad! Love you!"

Gregor reaches through the window and hugs his father.

James beams through the window and, touched by his son's words, reciprocates, "Well, what's gotten into you, boy? I love you, too. We'll see you in a bit." The old farmer walks back out of view, and we hear the search party leave the farm.

With his father's departure, Gregor shoulders his backpack, his resolve firm. "Just need some rope, a knife, and things for a dangerous adventure." He muses, seizing a tall walking stick from the main room.

He tests the long stick as a weapon and smiles.

"Things for a dangerous adventure."

Chapter Twenty-Six

Gathering of Wolves

A long the trail stand three menacing figures engaged in some conspiracy. One of the three is Cunung, who confronted Baldwin and Gregor the night before. Judging from the soft gurgling sound, an unseen river is near.

The youngest of the trio, Yasodir Drovic, is known as Jas. His golden blonde hair sets him apart from the others. Clad in dark leather armor, his vibrant locks give him a striking appearance. He carries a hand axe at his waist, a departure from the other men's preference for short swords. "Yeah. But now kids are involved," he comments, his voice tinged with concern.

Cunung, the group leader, inquires with a hint of urgency, "How many people are down there?"

Jas replies uncertainly, "I don't know, Cunung."

Cunung retorts, "That's the point. I have yet to decide if they're going, but he's right. He might be able to help."

Jas, in frustration, mutters under his breath, "This idea is a nightmare."

Cunung nods with a frown. "Yeah."

The look of despair doesn't leave Jas' face as he says, "They're just kids."

Cunung still frowns. He sighs and looks away. "I know. We'll do our best to avoid violence, but their safety has to come first."

The older man, Niko, joins the conversation. "This plan is going rabid."

Cunung nods.

CHAPTER TWENTY-SEVEN

DEPTHS OF THE WORLD

As the sun sets, the clearing is enveloped in darkness, punctuated only by the occasional flicker of fireflies. The air is heavy with anticipation. It is as if the forest holds her breath.

Gregor and Baldwin are conversing near a large tree, unaware they are in Her clearing. The ancient tree sleeps unseen by the two boys. Her eyes remain closed on the other side of the tree.

Excitedly, Gregor voices his appreciation, "Thanks for coming, Baldwin. It's heroic." Baldwin responds, visibly buoyed by the praise, "You know I love your sister too, right? I can't just leave her down there." Gregor probes further, "So you think she is down there now?" Baldwin admits his uncertainty, "Well, I don't know if she's down there for sure. You have a feeling, and I trust you. So I guess... I guess I do."

Cunung steps into the clearing. He approaches unheard despite the dry leaves that cover the forest floor.

With a subdued laugh, he announces his presence, "You didn't make yourselves too difficult to find. I see you're both prepared. Well done."

Baldwin quickly responds with a determined voice, "We did just like you said! Can we go? Please? I, I want to help Aileen."

Cunung sighs. "Yeah, boys, you can come." His eyes are marked by years of experience. They seem full of anguish as the man surrenders. "Did you tell your..."

Gregor interjects, "We told them. You're right. They needed to hear it."

Cunung replies with a somber nod. "They always do, son. Let's go."

As the group sets off along a path to their right, none notice Her eyes opening to watch their departure from the clearing.

A solitary firefly blinks into existence in the wake of the group. It trails behind them.

Chapter Twenty-Eight
Howling Grotto

Howling Grotto is cut into a hill deep within Old Gloamwood. Its appearance is unassuming, little more than a stony crevice. A strong wind flows across the entrance. As the wind rises, a haunting scream shrieks forth from within. It's likely nothing more than the wind.

Gregor, Baldwin, and Cunung approach the entrance to Howling Grotto, which descends into the Dark Below. The glow of a lone firefly unwittingly accompanies the trio.

"I'm Gregor." the young boy says to break the nervous tension as they approach the dark hole in the world. "I'm Baldwin. Gregor calls me Bald sometimes. Or Balds. Please don't," Baldwin responds with a hint of humor.

"Cunung," the man answers a bit awkwardly. "Sorry, just not used to introductions. The circles I keep rarely share names."

"You mentioned friends were helping last night. Did they change their minds?" Gregor inquires, his voice tinged with anticipation.

"Never. I don't expect you'll see them, maybe their handiwork," Cunung explains, his words shrouded in mystery. "They went ahead to make sure things... go well. Stay close."

Chapter Twenty-Nine

A Deadly Trade

Beneath the world's surface lies a vast chamber through which a sprawling network of tunnels snakes in from every direction across multiple levels. Spiraled ramps ascend the chamber walls, granting access to higher-level tunnels, while a stone-carved stage commands attention on one side of the room. Behind it, a pair of passageways are hidden—one around five span high on the right, a smaller one around two span high on the left. The larger appears designed for large carts or crowds. The smaller passage would be well suited for individual traffic.

Rows of primitive stone benches sit before the stage formed from sheer stone blocks. The present furnishings are designed for function over comfort. Beneath the facade of decay are furnishings that suggest this chamber was once fit for a nobler purpose.

Despite the chamber's potential grandeur, its opulence, is marred by pervasive filth—litter, unidentified liquids, waste, and possibly feces—taint everything with a layer of grime. The contamination dulls the radiance of the once-rich tapestries in shades of crimson, purple, and blue, edged in silver and gold.

Ssthraza, serpent-like beings, meander through the chamber, entering and exiting the myriad tunnels. Various creatures converge towards the chamber's heart. Most of these beings are humanoid but many are not.

A group of Duerrodar, with their cold blue skin and large white eyes, emerges from a lower ramp. They gravitate toward the stone benches and stand stoically; their powerful, short legs need never rest.

As the crowd settles, a Ssthraza auctioneer makes a slow and deliberate entrance from the left passageway. His green-scaled body is adorned with rising sails from head to tail. He holds a gold-trimmed black book in his gnarled, wicked claws. His demeanor exudes a mix of disdain and wariness. He periodically tastes the air with his flicking tongue, his large eyes scanning the assembly. A cacophony of horns pierces the chamber. The event will soon begin.

Clad in fine purple robes edged in gold—stained with a gradient of brown at every hem—the auctioneer approaches a marble pedestal at the stage's forefront. He makes his grandiose entrance, followed by two Ssthraza guards in heavy, purplish armor. The presence of his entourage is authoritative. Their fangs drip with venom, and their serpentine tails, ending in rattles, move restlessly, signaling their vigilance.

With a hiss, the auctioneer announces in Jathiss, "Tiissss ssha hesss!" calling the halls to silence. His demeanor suggests satisfaction, almost as if he were smiling, as anticipation builds with the sound of something rolling down the passage toward the stage.

The auctioneer turns back to the crowd. He scans their faces and releases a sigh of disappointment.

He begins to speak in Kruumsh in a voice that carries a begrudging tone, "Gom chok bus Kruumsh. Watu bok me mo Jathiss." This roughly translates to, "I forgot we agreed to use Kruumsh. You idiots don't understand Jathiss." With a shudder of disgust, the auctioneer's disdain for the language is palpable. It smacks its jaws as if it struggles to refrain from vomiting.

"Chok bur do tur daba gak. Me mo kuda. Chok kun." This means, "Today, we will conduct only three auctions. No complaints. We are aware." The auctioneer pauses again. It smacks its jaws but manages to suppress the shudder. The distaste remains, yet it is adapting to the unwelcome language.

Behind the auctioneer, a cart rolls in from the broader passage. It carries a sizeable cage housing a single male Sonebraèn in his sixties.

A murmur of disappointment ripples through the crowd. Suddenly, from the crowd emerges a challenge, "Choda gaku!" - "What is this?"

Chaos ensues. The chamber becomes a tumult of shouting. Attendees stand, many shaking their fists in protest. Ssthraza guards position themselves by the auctioneer's side as reinforcements stream into the chamber from an adjoining tunnel.

A Bardelang rises and advances toward the stage. It is a brutish humanoid creature with a fierce visage. He stands a towering two-and-a-half span tall and is covered in thick fur. Large horns curl back from his ears; these are chipped in places, a testament to the many times they have been used to ram and crush his enemies. His breath stinks of decaying flesh as he huffs in rage and stomps toward the auctioneer.

A pair of guards confront the beast and urge it back toward his seat. The Bardelang lashes out in rage. An enormous fist sweeps toward the guard's face. The guard dodges with uncanny speed, biting the Bardelang's arm long enough to inject venom.

Stunned, the Bardelang recoils. It takes a few steps back before collapsing onto a stone bench.

The guards quickly drag the subdued Bardelang away through a nearby tunnel, clearing the chamber.

The crowd gradually calms down, and the remaining guards resume their posts at the doorways, restoring order.

The auctioneer commands in Kruumsh, "Mok udo! Mok udo! Du watu mo kuda. Uk udu ut ubu." Meaning, "Calm down! Calm down!

Told you no complaining. Few slaves to sell." He swiftly flips through the book, searching for the correct page.

With a deliberate motion, his wicked claw slides down a page and stops. "Ubo guk adam da. Bir tuu turmu safo." the auctioneer announces, "Old, weak man here. Bids start 30 silver."

The crowd murmurs in discontent, yet no one steps forward to bid. Seconds pass until a figure in the back tentatively raises a hand. The auctioneer calls out in Kruumsh, "Turmu safo! Uduu mafo." - "Thirty silver! Any higher?"

Chapter Thirty
A Hold for Goods

In the depths, a vast chamber holds merchandise that is being prepared before its auction debut. On one side, the space is dominated by large crates and barrels, while the other is cluttered with bags and piles of various products.

Mushrooms, herbs, and some peculiar-looking weapons lie among these items. A bubbling liquid within a barrel emits an eerie glow, adding a mysterious air to the room. Like the auction hall, this chamber is besieged by filth, suggesting efforts to maintain cleanliness have long been abandoned.

In the chamber's center are two carts. Each features a large cage.

The first cage appears empty. The second confines seven beings: a family of Sonebraèn, consisting of a man, a boy, and two girls, alongside a Taumkin man and two boys. Among the girls is Aileen, and beside her is Seònid, a 14-year-old with blond hair and blue eyes. The empty cart is being prepped for transport through a large tunnel carved into the wall.

A frail Ssthraza worker attempts to remove the chocks from the cart. It is startled when a creature resembling a tiger materializes within the cage and pounces. The cat-like form strikes the cage bars with a resounding crash. The force threatens to topple the cart. The bars hold, but the worker recoils in fear before regaining composure. The snake-like humanoid rises and angrily taunts the beast with a stick.

Within the occupied cart, a poignant scene unfolds as the Taumkin father tries to reassure his sons, "It'll be okay, boys. We'll be okay." They embrace. It is a small comfort in this dark place.

Aileen watches the father and children with a hopeful smile while the caged creature piques Seònid's curiosity. "What is that thing?" Seònid inquires. Aileen recalls her brother's fanciful tales and responds, "No idea. I didn't think things like this were real! My brother would be so excited if he knew."

Confused, Seònid quips, "Is your head okay?"

Aileen tries not to laugh, but smiling, she replies, "Sorry, I just... He likes to tell wild stories. I was thinking of him."

All of the Sonebraèn stare at Aileen now.

Aileen notices the attention. She boldly exclaims, "He's coming to help us." All the other Sonebraèn dismisses the notion with a shake of their heads. One Sonebraèn man scoffs, "Unless your brother is some kind of hero, he's not making it down here."

He lowers his head, gazing at the cage floor, "So, your brother's a soldier, is he?"

Aileen's response is tinged with a hint of disappointment at their skepticism. "He's a boy," Aileen clarifies.

The man chuckles softly, "Of course he is. Why don't we wait for him to show up here."

The sound of footsteps signals the workers' return, who begin to remove the blocks from the cart holding the slaves. The Sonebraèn man muses, "Or perhaps we're moving on. I can't wait to see where we end up next."

Chapter Thirty-One

Sold

Goblins erupt into enthusiastic cheers inside the auction hall as a cart bearing a mighty beast is gradually wheeled back into the larger passageway. The auctioneer announces in Kruumsh, "Uud daba. Sebo udu gu." - "Final auction. Seven slaves up for bid."

The auctioneer glances backward, prompting a tense pause as everyone waits expectantly. Impatient murmurs ripple through the crowd until, finally, the heavy, grinding sound of wheels signals the arrival of the next lot.

After tense moments, the cart carrying Aileen emerges onto the stage.

As they appear, several attendees stand and exit the hall, their disappointment in the day's offerings evident. The auctioneer declares, "Bir tuu omu kafo." - "Bidding starts at ten gold."

The crowd's discontent is palpable, and many more leave, frustrated by the starting price. Now, only about a quarter of the original audience remains.

Then, a hand is raised near the center of the remaining crowd.

The auctioneer calls out, "Omu kafo! Omu tu kafo. Uduu watume?" - "Ten gold! Twelve gold. Any more bids?" Shortly after, another hand signals a bid from the back of the hall. The auctioneer continues, "Omu tu kafo! Omu gu kafo?" - "Twelve gold! Fifteen gold?"

Another bidder from the front counters, prompting the auctioneer to raise the stakes, said, "Omu gu kafo! Tumu?" - "Fifteen gold! Twenty?" After a pause, the Duerrodar confidently raises his great war hammer, bidding twenty gold.

The auctioneer pushes for higher bids, "Tumu kafu! Turmu kafu?" - "Twenty gold! Thirty gold?" Silence hangs heavy in the hall for several seconds until the auctioneer makes one final call, "Turmu kafu? Uduu watume?" - "Thirty gold? Any takers?" Met with silence, he declares, "Turmu kafu. Gu cho!" - "Thirty gold. Last call!"

As the silence persists, he signals with his hand, and Ssthraza workers move the cart back into the large tunnel. Most of the few remaining attendees head towards the exit.

A Duerrodar, speaking the dark language Zuuk, comments, "Zobh guru. Thox ghu." - "Much gold. Little might."

He looks to his companion, who laughs before replying in Zuuk, "Zobh xuu. Zobh vu... Kxo thoguth." - "Great effort. Great might... or a pathetic end."

Ominous laughter fills the increasingly empty hall as the last attendees depart toward the tunnels.

CHAPTER THIRTY-TWO

INSIDE THE GROTTO

Baldwin, Gregor, and Cunung stand poised at Howling Grotto's entrance, an insignificant cleft in the hillside. Cunung vanishes into the shadowy depths. His voice echoes, "Stay close. It's best not to get separated in here."

Baldwin moves to follow. An abrupt gust of wind surges, causing the cave's stones to hum. An eerie melody fills the air. A low moan permeates the atmosphere. This hum escalates into a chilling scream. Baldwin recoils with a start from the entrance and voices his concern, "Gregor, are we sure about this?" Undeterred, Gregor reassures him, "Let's go, Baldwin. We should stick with Cunung; he seems to know more than he's telling us." Gregor steps into the darkness with Baldwin close behind.

Cunung leads them inside with a lantern which casts a soft glow, illuminating their path through the twisting tunnels. Gregor follows eagerly. Baldwin takes his place in the back of the group as he struggles between fascination and apprehension. The cavern's howl, now distant, still sends shivers down his spine as they delve deeper into the earth beneath Aoden, moving towards the ominous Dark Below.

Gregor is awe-struck. His wide eyes scan the passageways as they make their descent. Streaks of reddish clay sporadically mar the white and gray stone patchwork walls. Overhead, diminutive stalactites hang like accusatory fingers, while the path underfoot is dark gray stone veiled in a slick of reddish mud. Stalagmites peek through the mire along the edges, silent witnesses to the trio's descent into the unknown.

Numerous side paths branch off from the main route as they proceed. Cunung ignores these, and the group presses forward at each intersection.

Gregor inquires, "How long has this place been here?"

Baldwin asks, "How deep does it go?"

Cunung responds, "I don't know for certain. This place is ancient, possibly as old as The Wakening."

Descending further, they are enveloped by a repugnant stench. Cunung swiftly produces a white cloth from his pouch to shield his nose. Gregor coughs and follows suit, covering his nose. Baldwin, attempting to dissipate the smell with a wave of his hand, also covers his nose. He gags, his face contorting in revulsion.

"Blech... What is that smell?" Baldwin exclaims, filled with disgust.

Cunung offers, "Don't worry, Baldwin. Just stay near me."

"Why?" Baldwin queries.

"Because I told you yesterday that if I let you come, you would listen and act... Without hesitation." Cunung reminds, shooting Baldwin a stern look before softening slightly. "This cloth reacts to cruel air," he adds.

At the mention of "cruel air," Gregor's interest is piqued. "Cruel air?" he echoes with a hint of excitement. Cunung chuckles momentarily, and then his expression turns grave again. "Down in this place, the air sometimes turns evil. It can even kill a man," he states solemnly.

"What?!" Baldwin blurts out a protest in a mix of nervousness and skepticism.

"Don't worry, Baldwin. We're prepared for it," Cunung reassures. Like I said, stay close."

They descend deeper into the grotto, where the walls are festooned with moss-draped stones and luminous fungi. Ghostly-appearing mushrooms emerge from the stone base, their edges curving back gracefully. These fungi radiate a vibrant blue, accented with yellow concentric rings underneath.

Cunung issues a caution, "And don't touch anything. Unless I tell you that it's safe." He adds, ominously, "Air isn't the only thing that can leave one dead down here," casting a wary eye towards the luminous fungi.

Gregor inquires, "What are those?"

Cunung responds, "I'm not sure. They look like wraith shrooms, beautiful but deadly to the touch. They could also be an edible variety, known as haunting delight."

"Wow," Gregor is impressed. "Can you tell the difference?"

Cunung muses, "Maybe. If I had to. We'd have to turn out the lantern to find out."

Baldwin diligently stays in the middle of the path. Alarmed by Cunung's warning, he insists, "We don't have to!"

Cunung's laughter echoes softly in the dim passage, "Wise choice."

Continuing their descent, they navigate a lengthier path where their light fades before reaching the end. Ahead, the mushrooms cast a soft blue glow, illuminating their way.

Cunung confirms, "Yeah, those are wraith shrooms. It's a good thing we didn't stop for treats."

Moments later, the passage widens, concluding abruptly at a solid wall. To the right, a spherical recess, the size of a fist, is flanked by two cylindrical protrusions.

Gregor sees the end of the passageway and asks, "A dead end?"

"Why would you say that?" Baldwin nervously interjects.

Cunung turns to face them and smiles reassuringly, "No. This is the entrance."

He retrieves an object crafted as a skull from his belt pouch.

Cunung offers a simple question, "Ready?"

CHAPTER THIRTY-THREE

WELCOME TO THE DARK BELOW

G regor and Baldwin exchange puzzled looks.

Gregor asks, "Ready for what?"

Cunung approaches the niche and positions the skull so its eye sockets align with its protrusions. He presses the skull in and rotates it clockwise. A click sounds, and he retrieves the skull. Anticipation hangs heavily in the air as he tucks it back into his pouch and responds, "To go in."

A tense silence ensues. The air is heavy with anticipation. A deep rumble breaks the stillness, and the wall retracts. This unveils a vast abyss. The boys exchange a glance, their eyes wide with wonder and a hint of fear. Cunung strides into the newly opened passage with the boys in tow. They find themselves on a broad ledge at the top of an immense, enigmatic chamber, its depths shrouded in darkness. The path spirals downward, but Cunung's lantern light fails to illuminate the area's floor.

Cunung declares, "Welcome to The Dark Below."

Baldwin's heart pounds in his chest. He keeps a cautious distance from the precipice. His eyes scan the area with awe as he admits, "I don't feel particularly welcome."

Gregor is awestruck, beaming with excitement from the opposite side of Cunung. "Wow! It's real? I didn't think this place was real. Even when..." Gregor's amazement quickly turns to determination as he asks, "Can we go find Aileen?" His voice is filled with hope and a touch of urgency.

Cunung smiles widely and nods.

Tension mounts with each step down the spiraling path. The air is thick with anticipation. The rumble of stone as it grinds against stone again fills the chamber. The door closes, sealing the entrance behind them. The boys exchange a nervous glance as they realize there's no turning back.

CHAPTER THIRTY-FOUR

DXUGOR'S MINING CAMP

The walls of this vast, cylindrical underground chamber are adorned with luminescent mushrooms that cast an ethereal bluish-green light. The air is heavy with the scent of damp earth. The distant echo of pickaxes chipping away at stone fills the chamber. The sound originates from a passageway hewn into the rock wall opposite the entrance.

The floor is punctuated by small holes, each roughly a finger's width. They sporadically release bursts of steam, momentarily revealing their reddish glow beneath. The air is thick with the steam's metallic scent, and the heat from the holes warms the chamber.

This mysterious locale, known as Dxugor's Mining Camp, is guarded by two Duerrodar sentinels at its entrance: Khuz, whose dark blue skin is partially covered by a chainmail breastplate, and Gom, adorned in lighter blue skin and chainmail armor.

Echoes of pickaxes chipping away at stone fill the chamber, a sound originating from a passageway hewn into the rock wall opposite the entrance.

A large black iron brazier with a secure lock dominates the center of the chamber. Next to it stands a stone table.

Several crates and barrels are haphazardly arranged near the table's far end, distanced from the brazier. A closer examination of these crates reveals an eclectic mix of fungi, root vegetables, and fish, seemingly preserved in salt.

While the food might be barely edible, it's not fresh.

Aileen, Seònid, and Leona, a middle-aged Sonebraèn woman, occupy the space.

Gom strides toward the room's center, pulling a keyring from his belt.

With a practiced motion, he inserts a key into the brazier's lock, unlocks it, and tucks it into a pouch at his hip.

With a loud clang, he flings open the brazier's lid and gestures inside.

In Zuuk, Gom announces, "Kuuthu agna." - "Cooking fire." He motions from the food to the brazier. Gom declares, "Agnabaru." - "Flamestone." Upon exposure to the air, a black stone inside the brazier starts to crackle and pop before a soft flame springs to life.

Leona announces, "Looks like it's time to cook. Let's get to it, girls."

She picks a large fish from a crate and places it on the stone table, sliding it toward the brazier's end. Then, she motions for the girls to bring more fish.

Aileen and Seònid collect fish, mushrooms, onions, potatoes, and other supplies from the crates, offering them to Leona for preparation.

Aileen whispers to Seònid, "Everything's going to be alright."

Weariness shadows Seònid's features as she tries to dismiss Aileen's comforting words. "My brother is coming," Aileen persists.

Seònid places an unidentifiable piece of meat, which eerily resembles a tentacle, and pulses once on the table near Aileen. "Look, do you even know where we are?" Seònid questions.

"No," Aileen admits.

After placing a few mushrooms on the table, Aileen returns to the crates alongside Seònid.

"Let's pretend your brother isn't ten years old. He's leading an army of King Richard's finest men. Does he know where we are?" Seònid asks.

"No, I don't think he does," Aileen replies, her voice tinged with uncertainty.

Seònid's face is a canvas of despair and frustration, her eyes glistening with unshed tears. Her voice cracks as she asks, "Then why? Why do you keep saying this, Aileen? Why?"

As they pick vegetables from a crate, Seònid's voice cracks, "Then why? Why do you keep saying this, Aileen? Why?"

"Because I saw it. Gregor was here, and we were rescued. Please, don't cry. I promise it's going to be okay," Aileen reassures, her voice filled with hope.

Seònid's soft sobs break the silence as she places her vegetables on the table and wipes her eyes with dirty hands.

Aileen moves closer, wrapping her arms around Seònid in a gentle embrace.

Seeing Seònid's distress, Leona hurries and envelops them in a comforting hug. "Oh love, it'll be okay. It'll be okay. Don't cry. Shhh...." Leona whispers, offering solace.

Aileen whispers to Seònid, "It's all going to be okay."

CHAPTER THIRTY-FIVE

STEPPING INTO THE UNKNOWN

A vast chamber at the ramp's base unfolds into the distance, shrouded in mystery. Fog obscures the ceiling, with only the soft blue luminescence of lichen and fungi betraying its presence. This entire underground realm casts a spell of surreal beauty. What seemed like a chasm from above is revealed as the majestic sprawl of this grand cavern. Tiny vents dotting the walls emit a subtle orange glow and a whispering hiss of steam. The faint clash of swords and a guttural grunt resound in the far reaches, followed by a heavy thud.

Amidst the sibilant steam, Cunung alone seems alert, his attention fixed on a branching path. Gregor and Baldwin, meanwhile, survey the immense chamber before them.

In a hushed tone, Gregor marvels, "There's a whole world down here." Cunung nods and acknowledges the truth behind Gregor's words. He returns his gaze to the shadowed passage as if expecting someone.

"Cunung, is it like this everywhere?" Baldwin inquires in a whisper.

Shifting his attention, Cunung replies softly, "It may be. No one knows."

Captivated, the boys' gazes linger on their otherworldly surroundings, their minds filled with wonder.

Baldwin, forgetting to lower his voice, exclaims, "Wow."

Cunung lets out a chuckle, shaking his head in amusement. "Come on, boys. We must reach Aileen," Cunung urges, leading the way to a passageway as the boys trail behind him.

"Friends are clearing things ahead of us, but this is a gravely dangerous place. Stay alert," Cunung warns as they enter the tunnel.

This tunnel is similar to the ones in the grotto above, except it has significantly less mud covering its floor. Baldwin spots a black stain on the wall a few feet in, its surface glistening under the dim light. His gaze fixates on the viscous substance, causing him to trip over an iron mace in their path, a clear indicator of a recent skirmish.

Steel clashes against a hard surface somewhere nearby. The sound echoes through the corridor, alarmingly close. A voice cries out in Choduk, "Sothuuuuugggh..." but the sentence is abruptly cut off, and the final words hang suspended in the air. Cunung glances back at the boys, attempting a reassuring smile, but the oppressive atmosphere overshadows the gesture.

Drawing a katzbalger from its sheath, the reflection of his lantern flickers ominously along the blade. "Just in case," Cunung announces.

"Just in case... what?" Gregor inquires.

With the sword in hand, Cunung's smile becomes more authentic, and he seems at ease. "In case our friends up ahead need help. It seems things are getting a little messy. Let's go," he says. A hint of excitement in his voice betrays his confidence as he quickens his pace. Baldwin shakes his head, following closely. Approaching a junction about fifty spans ahead, Cunung raises his hand to stop the boys, signaling them to wait as he stealthily moves towards another intersecting tunnel, with the sound of nearing footsteps growing louder.

Two Goblins emerge from the adjacent tunnel near Cunung, their outlines flickering in the unsteady light of Cunung's lantern.

Garbed in tattered brown, one of them brandishes a spiked black mace. His similarly dressed companion has a short sword sheathed at his belt.

Suddenly, a mace hurtles in a deadly arc toward Cunung's head.

Cunung ducks.

 Skewers the Goblin.

  Drives it towards its ally.

-

A second Goblin

 attempts to flee

  caught - entangled

 hurtling body

falls

 in a heap

-

A flash of motion.

 Cunung is on his foe.

It makes a final cry. Did Cunung's hands move?

Baldwin and Gregor, wide-eyed, watch in awe.

It's over.

Baldwin involuntarily sighs, "Whoa..."

Cunung whispers, "I hope our friends will learn to be quieter here."

Cunung wipes his blade and beckons the boys closer. He puts a finger over his lips and prompts them to proceed cautiously. "Let's go. Be careful."

They continue their journey through the shadowy tunnels leading deeper into the Dark Below, carefully stepping over the Goblin corpses that now obstruct their path.

"Keep an ear out behind us. There may be more on the way," Cunung advises vigilance, a caution that prompts Baldwin to lag behind briefly.

Seizing the opportunity, he sneaks back to the fallen Goblins and searches one of the Goblin's bodies.

Baldwin retrieves the short sword from the creature's belt and conceals it. He hastily rushes to catch up with Cunung and Gregor.

CHAPTER THIRTY-SIX
GETTING TO KNOW YOU

Gregor and Cunung are lost in talk and oblivious to Baldwin's absence. Despite the recent turmoil, the atmosphere is noticeably less tense.

"Hey, Cunung, are you from Beaumont?" Gregor inquires.

"No, I hail from further north," Cunung replies.

"Oh?"

"Yes. My birthplace is Gottleibt."

"That is... quite far north," Gregor remarks, impressed.

Cunung laughs as they continue walking. "Yeah, kissed by the breath of Njoldr."

Cunung glances back at the group. He catches Baldwin's eye briefly and acknowledges him with a nod.

"I guess my home now is in Ulfreich, although I seldom see it," Cunung mentions, his voice hinting melancholy.

Both Gregor and Baldwin can't help but marvel at the mention of Ulfreich.

"The Wolf Kingdom? Really?" Baldwin asks, his interest piqued.

Cunung chuckles at their fascination. "It's just a different location. Maybe a bit colder than here, but it's nothing special."

"It's just... the stories of that place!" Gregor exclaims.

Cunung reassures, "It's beautiful but not that different from here. Who knows, maybe you'll see for yourself someday."

"Oh, I hope!" Gregor's eyes shine with anticipation.

Baldwin chimes in, "Is that where you learned to fight? Are you with the Oberwehren? Do you know my brother, Arek Aoghnes?"

Cunung's smile momentarily fades. "I'm a soldier in my own right, contributing to the empire's cause without officially joining the military." He takes a deep breath and continues, "A friend taught me to fight. Enough to survive anyway."

With a forlorn smile, he adds, "After that, it was the life. People needed help, and helping them sometimes made enemies."

Baldwin nods.

"So, to survive the enemies, I had to fight. That made me better at fighting," Cunung states matter-of-factly, "I had a choice: get better or die."

A heavy silence follows his words. "I am sorry. Let's continue."

CHAPTER THIRTY-SEVEN
DOMRI'S ALCOVE

A t the end of the passageway, the group discovers an entrance leading to a small chamber, revealed as they round a bend in the tunnel. The chamber, illuminated from within, extends a welcoming glow.

The trio steps into the space, finding themselves in a cozy room, approximately five cubic spans in size, with a ceiling that arches into a dome at its center.

An eternal torch, mounted on a stone column at the room's heart, offers a steady flame. A chimney carved into the dome draws smoke upwards and out of the depths.

In each corner of the alcove lies a statuette of a Dar. These figures stand in silent vigil. They each stand a span tall and face the eternal torch in the center of the room. Adorned in splendid armor and wielding rune-inscribed weapons, they command attention.

The chamber walls are etched with petroglyphs, narrating tales of Dar engaged in subterranean battles, hinting at ancient wars between Goblins and other Dar factions. These intricate carvings promise to captivate the boys for hours.

Cunung realizes he may have an opportunity to scout ahead. He warns the young boys, "You two stay here. Touch nothing in this room. I'm just going to make sure this is the way." With that, he exits through a doorway opposite their point of entry.

Baldwin and Gregor begin to explore the chamber. Their eyes scan the walls and ceiling as they absorb Dar history etched in stone.

Baldwin murmurs to Gregor in awe, "Can you believe this place, Greg?"

Gregor replies in a hushed voice, "No, not really. Do you think he's from Ulfreich?"

Baldwin, "Did you see how he handled those Goblins? I thought they were just stories. He moved so fast..."

Baldwin examines a carving that depicts an epic battle between Dar and the Goblins. His hand almost touches the ancient stonework before he abruptly stops himself.

Oblivious to Baldwin's reaction, Gregor comments, "Yeah, I didn't even see what he did."

Baldwin nods thoughtfully. "I think I believe him, Gregor. Why would he be here, though?"

Gregor shrugs, "I don't know, but he knows something, Balds. I hope he's good. I wouldn't be down here if I had any choice."

Their attention is drawn to a carving of Dar warriors repelling a monstrous entity deep underground.

Gregor's gaze shifts as he studies the interplay of shadows on the carved scene.

"Yeah, me either. This place is creepy," Baldwin admits. "If he weren't good, he'd have done something by now. We couldn't stop him."

"Yeah, I think you're right," agrees Gregor. He stops and turns to his friend. A great smile flashes on his face. "Hey Balds. You came with me! You are with me in The Dark Below. It's wild! That's really brave."

Gregor laughs softly, then whispers, "Maybe a little stupid. Why? Why'd you change your mind, Balds?"

Both boys are looking around the room now, careful not to touch anything.

Baldwin contemplates his answer carefully, then finally responds, "I didn't have a choice."

Gregor responds with a whispered laugh, "Don't blame me!"

"No," Baldwin pauses to gaze at a distant wall and says softly, "It was scary to come, but... Thinking that something would happen to you and I'd never see you again, that was worse. You're my best friend, Gregor."

Gregor cocks his head and smiles proudly at his friend. With a wistful sigh, he turns and resumes his exploration of the room. Gregor hovers near one of the passages between their entry point and the exit Cunung took. The passage beyond descends into near-complete darkness, its floor invisible from the chamber. Gregor leans forward to peer into the abyss with a cautious hand on the doorway.

"Well, thanks Baldwin. I can't imagine being down here alone," Gregor steps forward, but his foot finds no solid ground. He tumbles into the darkness of a concealed slide. "WHOAH!!!!" Gregor's scream echoes through the chamber.

"Gregor!" Baldwin cries out, turning just in time to see his friend vanish.

He rushes to the passage's brink and pauses at its edge. The darkness is daunting. Instead of following Gregor, Baldwin urgently races to find Cunung.

Cunung moves cautiously through the serpentine passageway, alert for any trace of his companions. Pausing, he listens intently—the sound of heavy footsteps approaches from behind. Cunung readies his katzbalger and adopts a defensive stance to confront the unseen threat.

Baldwin's voice breaks the tension, "Cunung!"

Relief washes over Cunung as he lowers his weapon. He murmurs in frustration, "Come on..."

Cunung sheaths his sword as Baldwin appears, breathless and eager to reach him. Cunung's concern is immediate, "What is it? Where's Gregor? Why aren't you together?"

Baldwin's reply is tinged with panic: "I don't know! He disappeared in that room! I heard him cry from one of the other tunnels! Help!"

Cunung charges into action without hesitation, "Let's go!"

They retrace their steps through the labyrinthine corridors to the previously visited chamber, their pace swift.

Cunung is unable to suppress a hint of exasperation. "You two are a constant source of trouble, aren't you?"

Baldwin acknowledges their predicament and responds, "Yes! That's what I keep telling Gregor! And you can yell at us for it later!"

A chuckle escapes Cunung, though he attempts to conceal it from Baldwin. "Just... Just keep up, boy," As he runs, he casts a stern look over his shoulder that softens into a smile despite his efforts.

Baldwin's mood shifts to joy upon catching Cunung's smile, which he mirrors with his own.

Despite his frustration and worry for Gregor, Cunung feels a youthful vigor stirred by their adventure.

"I'm not sure if you boys are giving me grey hairs or keeping me young," Cunung muses as they enter the small room.

"Where did you last see him?" he asks.

Baldwin points towards the spot where Gregor was last seen. Cunung's lantern illuminates a hidden trapdoor that opens into a dark chute below. Cunung seizes Baldwin's arm and points into the abyss.

Baldwin gasps.

Cunung hastily retrieves a rope from his pack and prepares for their descent.

Chapter Thirty-Eight

Falling for it

The sound of air rushes past Gregor as his skin scrapes against smooth stones. Gregor tumbles into the abyss. Occasionally, the sharp clatter of wood against stone punctuates the darkness as his staff collides with the chute's floor.

"Baldwin! Help!" cries Gregor. Seconds later, he's flung into a shadowy chamber in a wild spin. Dim light seeps through an entrance on one side and casts ghostly shadows. Gregor attempts to steady his breathing and remain as silent as possible. He stands with a firm grip on his walking staff. The silence is palpable. Gregor tries to calm his racing heart when movement stirs at the entrance.

An unknown voice cuts through the shadow, speaking in Chuduk, "Chu huruchu?" - "Did you hear that?" Gregor's heart sinks.

Gregor presses himself into a corner in an attempt to become invisible. The deliberate sound of footsteps approaches, signaling danger. Gregor's fear is palpable. A shadow darkens the faint light as the footsteps draw closer. Suddenly, a Goblin emerges. It's adorned with mismatched furs and a crude leather breastplate that gives it a bizarre, menacing appearance.

Upon spotting Gregor, it sneers, "Soruusoth..." - "I see a boy." The Goblin's laugh chills Gregor to the bone.

As it steps forward, another set of footsteps can be heard.

Gregor offers a feeble wave, "Uhm, Hi."

The Goblin responds with a deep, sinister laugh devoid of warmth. "Hoooii..." it scoffs, the mockery evident in its voice. A second Goblin appears, and the first repeats the greeting mockingly. They join in laughter that fills the chamber. A sounds as sinister as it is unrelenting.

The second Goblin raises a clawed hand, "Huuuuoooey..." Their laughter intensifies.

Gregor, overwhelmed with fear, clutches his walking staff. He cries to himself.

"I'm so sorry, Aileen. I failed you."

"Hoooeeeeyauuu!" The Goblins continue to mock, and their laughter echoes grotesquely around the chamber.

Finally, the two Goblins produce wicked, serrated blades.

CHAPTER THIRTY-NINE

Heeoouuuyyy!

Cunung and Baldwin focus on reaching Gregor in the small chamber. Baldwin grips a lengthy rope, and Cunung hurries to secure one end to the pedestal bearing the eternal torch. Their efforts intensify when an eerie noise reverberates up from the chute below.

"Hoooii."

Baldwin is perplexed, "What? What was that?"

Cunung is equally bewildered, "Did something just say... there's no way."

Despite their confusion, they struggle to maintain composure, barely stifling their laughter at the bizarre sound. Cunung quickly ties off the rope and signals to Baldwin, who has already fashioned the other end around his wrist. Baldwin plunges into the chute.

The mysterious voice calls again, "Heeoouuuyyy," causing Cunung to chuckle.

Shaking his head in amusement, Cunung mutters, "Who are these kids? What have I gotten myself into?"

Still smiling, he grips the rope firmly and jumps after Baldwin into the void, the strange voice trailing off, "Heeeoooooiii..."

Gregor stands cornered by a pair of Goblins. Their short, rust-coated blades flash in the scant light.

In an attempt to intimidate Gregor, one of the Goblins leaps forward with a shout, "Hoooeey!" Both Goblins burst into laughter as Gregor recoils further into his shrinking space. The other seizes the moment and lunges at Gregor, "Huueii!" Gregor flinches, not just from fright but also from the Goblin's foul breath.

A clattering noise announces another arrival through the chute. "I'm coming, Gregor!!!" Baldwin's voice foreshadows his entrance. He drops into the room with a crash. The Goblins turn, their attention snapped towards the new threat. Rising, Baldwin stares into the eyes of one of the menacing Goblins, "Oh..."

Baldwin steps back toward the corner opposite Gregor.

"Huuuoiii!!!" The Goblins, amused, advance on Baldwin, only to be interrupted by more clattering from the chute.

The Goblins again look at each other and sigh in frustration. They grow tired of this game and turn to face the opening as Cunung slides into the room. This time, the Goblins leap backward and cower before attacking their new, more dangerous foe.

Chaos erupts.

Cunung strikes.

Goblin writhes, its eyes wide.

Its knees hit the ground.

Metal rings against stone.

Goblin clutches its chest.

Claws feebly caress Cunung's blade.

Light fades from its eyes.

Cunung retrieves his side arm.

The Goblins' dark swords still resonate against the cold stone floor.

Turning to Gregor, Cunung wears an impish grin, greeting him with a simple, "Hi?"

A moment of nervous laughter breaks out among them.

Gregor still struggles to process what has just occurred. He can only reply, "I didn't know what to say."

"Hi?" Cunung repeats and motions to the rope touching the chamber floor. Cunung nods, "After you."

Baldwin wipes away tears of laughter as Gregor begins his ascent.

Cunung shakes his head in disbelief. He looks at Baldwin and utters once more, "Hi."

In the dimly lit chamber, Baldwin and Gregor stand close. Gregor's cheeks blush, and his lips bear just a hint of a frown.

Baldwin wears an unwavering grin. "You alright, Gregor?" Baldwin asks with amusement in his voice.

"Yeah, just a little embarrassed," Gregor admits.

Suddenly, a hand emerges, gripping the rope from the chute. Cunung appears. He crawls back into the chamber with a broad grin mirroring Baldwin's. "Don't worry too much, Gregor. It happens to the best of us," Cunung reassures as he steps into the room. "And that's the closest I have ever seen a Goblin come to speaking Saeldring," he smiles.

The warmth in Cunung's voice softens the mood, drawing Baldwin and Gregor into a moment of shared laughter.

Gentle tugs test the rope's strength, but these go unnoticed. A strong pull snaps the rope taut with a crack. The loud noise abruptly interrupts their merriment and demands their attention. The trio rushes to the entrance and peers into the darkness below.

A voice from the depths, speaking in Chuduk, commands, "Krof qof" - "Go up." Claws rake against the walls of the chute.

"Get the rope!" Cunung orders. They hastily grip the taut rope and attempt to pull it up, but this effort is wasted.

"Something's big down there. Pull together!" Cunung's voice commands urgency. Their combined effort dislodges the rope, moving it a quarter span before whatever is below yanks back fiercely, regaining control.

A brief struggle ensues, characterized by desperate cries as the rope briefly breaks free. Something crashes down the chute. A loud caterwaul mixed with a scraping and scratching sound echoes up from below.

"Quickly, again!" Cunung urges. The trio grasp the rope and pull it with all their might. They secure a span of rope before the line goes taut once more, suggesting the presence of a significant weight.

A crowd of Goblins grow in the dimly lit chamber at the base of the chute. Three Goblins participate in the perilous tug of war. Two Goblins lay strewn across the room's center as they recuperate from their fall down the shaft.

Another Goblin prepares to grasp the rope and climb.

Cunung inquires, "Got anything heavy here?"

Gregor's eyes dart to one of the Dar statuettes positioned at each corner of the room.

Cunung nods, "That'll work. Can you drag one over here?"

Gregor drops the rope and hurries to the nearest corner. He attempts to pull the statuette, but it hardly moves.

Muttering under his breath, Gregor urges, "Come on, come on..."

He changes his tactic and pushes from the opposite side. The statuette moves slightly.

Gregor exerts more force with a determined huff and shoves hard against the statuette's weight. It moves a significant half-span.

Cunung encourages, "Great! Keep coming!"

The rope jerks Cunung forward. Cunung and Baldwin both grunt as they struggle against the force.

Baldwin exclaims, "I think we're losing this!"

Cunung takes a deep breath and commands, "Just pull!"

Baldwin and Cunung exert themselves again. The sound of clawed feet scraping the chute walls fills the air.

Gregor pushes with renewed effort. The statuette slides another half-span closer to the chute.

"A span and a half to go," Gregor notes, encouraged by his progress.

Cunung calls, "Great! Faster if you can!" Cunung and Baldwin wrestle with the rope.

Gregor heaves with everything he has. He shoulders into the stone image and advances the statuette further.

The strain shows on everyone's faces. The room's previously vibrant atmosphere now feels heavy and oppressive.

They move in sync, driven by a shared goal.

"Pull!" Cunung shouts. Gregor pushes the statuette, closing another half span.

Only a half-span left.

"Almost there!" Gregor gasps.

Baldwin visibly struggles for breath.

"PULL!" Cunung's shout echoes as he and Baldwin manage a final pull. The rope pulls up from the chute a quarter-span.

Gregor moves the statuette into position before the chute.

A Goblin claws at the opening as it appears at the top of the rope.

Cunung looks toward Gregor, his eyes full of mischief. "It's for you!"

The Goblin reaches out, menacing.

Cunung makes a swift decision, "Let go!"

Baldwin and Cunung they release the rope in unison. The Goblin plummets down the chute. Its cries mingle with those of its allies as it crashes through their massing ranks. Angry screams reverberate up the shaft. They quickly pull up the rope.

Cunung orders, "Drop it!"

The three push the Dar statuette together. It topples over the edge and rattles down the chute. The heavy stone makes a skittering sound in the chute before it crashes into the room full of Goblins. Chaos erupts from below.

"They let go. Does that mean we win?" Cunung says with a wink.

Gregor replies, "Seems like it."

Gregor tries to apologize. He feels ashamed and responsible for the encounter. Cunung cuts him off and praises Gregor for his role in their victory: "Great work figuring that out. We'd have been in trouble without you there. Ready to go?"

Baldwin and Gregor bask for just a moment in the praise. "Yeah, let's go find Aileen," Gregor says.

Baldwin whispers to his friend, "Can't believe we're on an adventure, Greg!"

The worry lifts from Baldwin, and he is full of joy for the moment.

They leave the chamber behind and take the passage Cunung scouted earlier.

CHAPTER FORTY
A Humble Meal

A rugged chamber houses a pair of unadorned stone benches that flank a robust table carved from the surrounding rock.

Time has weathered these benches. The room offers a simple gathering space for Sonebraèn and Taumkin as they await their modest meal without the vigilant Duerrodar guards. Their absence should reassure the huddled mass, but it only fills the room with uncertainty.

A network of tunnels, their mouths hewn into the stone walls, whisper of the mine's labyrinthine depths. Gathered around the table are ten Sonebraèn men. Their faces are etched with the soot and wear of hard labor.

Beside them sit four Sonebraèn boys. The light of youth has dimmed under the heavy shadow of their toil. They seek a flicker of hope in the men's eyes. Three Taumkin men sit nearby, but their usual joy is muted. Three Taumkin boys gaze at the tunnels across the barren chamber.

All males from Aileen's contingent of slaves are among the group of men. They have gathered together in heavy anticipation as they await their meager meal.

Leona, Seònaid, and Aileen enter. They bring food and break the looming silence. Aileen serves each attendee from a platter of bread trenchers. Leona follows with a bounty of steaming vegetables.

Seònaid spoons servings from a bowl of richly sauced meat, setting a place for themselves last.

As Aileen distributes the bread trenchers, snippets of hushed conversation between Sonebraèn and Taumkin men reach her ears.

Edoric whispers, "We have no idea where it leads, but there's a hollow space on the other side."

William cautions of dire consequences, "We have to plan this out. We can't rush it. If we get caught, they won't hesitate to kill us."

Khuz, a formidable Duerrodar guard, interrupts the conversation with his heavy tread. He enters the chamber, and his sharp gaze scrutinizes the gathering. Aileen silently notes the exchange between the two men but continues her duties. Khuz loses interest in the meal preparation and surveys the room. His attention wanders from the slaves.

Edoric asserts, "We have to take our chance. We may not get another." He reclines with his eyes on Khuz and tries to gauge whether the guard suspects anything.

Khuz's eyes methodically sweep the room. He inspects each prisoner for a moment. Edoric advises, "For now, we should avoid that branch. Focus our work on the upper tunnels."

Leona walks around the table and adds hot vegetables to the trenchers next to the meat. When she reaches William, he softly catches her sleeve. He draws her close and whispers something in her ear. She nearly gasps but restrains herself and covers her mouth with a hand. Her eyes are wide with surprise. After a moment, Leona nods in understanding.

She then leans in to whisper a reply to William, their exchange unheard by others. Seònaid and Aileen share a look of curiosity.

Aileen sits at the corner of the table with Seònaid. Leona sits opposite Aileen.

William asks, "So, we continue our work as usual for now?"

"Yes, for the time being. Let's eat." Edoric responds as he tears off a piece of bread. He folds it to scoop up meat and gravy. He follows the spicy beef with a mushroom. Everyone starts to eat, and the buzz of conversation blends with the sounds of their humble yet significant meal.

Seònaid whispers, "Wow, did you hear that? I think you were right, Aileen. We might get out of here."

Aileen responds in a hushed tone, "Something's wrong. This isn't the escape."

Seònaid asks in a soft voice, "What do you mean?" She casts a nervous glance at Aileen.

Aileen whispers, "My brother is going to rescue us."

"Maybe we meet them outside; this has to be related, right?" Seònaid suggests, still whispering.

"It isn't. I saw Gregor in the tunnels with us. Something is wrong," Aileen whispers back.

Seònaid gives Aileen a disapproving look, her eyes narrowing until Aileen notices her stare. Stopping her meal, Aileen looks towards Seònaid and responds with a perplexed shrug, echoing Seònaid's expression. "I just know what I saw, and Gregor came here."

Seònaid rests her elbow on the table and covers her face with her hand. She lets out a long, pained sigh. "I don't understand you, Aileen. You said we'd be rescued."

Aileen accidentally raises her voice in frustration and exclaims, "This isn't it. This feels..." She quickly lowers her voice to a whisper again, "This feels wrong. Like we're being tricked. This isn't what I saw."

Seònaid's eyes focus in the distance. She looks into another, brighter place.

"Seònaid, there's something else," Aileen looks stricken, "something evil wants us to go that way. Something hungry. Something dark and terrible."

"I want to go home, Aileen. I want to see my mom and my dad." Seònaid whispers.

"I know. I'm sorry," Aileen whispers back, her expression filled with pain. Aileen is alone and feels the pain she inflicts upon her only friend in this dark place.

Seònaid whispers, "I want my daddy to hold me high and hug me. I don't want to be here."

"I know, I'm sorry. I want you to be back home, Seònaid. This isn't the way," Aileen whispers reassuringly.

More heavy footsteps approach from the chamber's entrance.

"I want to feel the sun again," Seònaid whispers wistfully.

"Please, Seònaid, this isn't the way. Please trust me," Aileen implores softly.

As Gom enters the room and joins Khuz, Seònaid whispers with resentment, "I hate you, Aileen."

Aileen winces, hurt by her friend's words. After a pause, she asks gently, "Do you believe me?"

Aileen attempts to reach out. Seònaid recoils from her touch. "I don't want to..." Seònaid starts, her eyes pleading.

"But do you?" Aileen insists gently.

"Leave me alone!" Seònaid bursts out, her patience worn thin. Tears well in her eyes as she pushes her trencher aside, crosses her arms, and collapses into them, sobbing. "Yes! Yes... and I hate you even more because I believe you!" Seònaid whispers through her tears.

Leona overhears them and chimes in, "It'll be okay, girls. They've found a way out."

Aileen looks at her mournfully, saying, "Please don't go that way."

Leona laughs off the warning, "Oh, I'm going! You can stay here in this pit if you want! Now eat your meal. If you're coming with us, you'll need your strength. You certainly won't be slowing us down!"

She returns to her meal, dismissing Aileen's concern.

Aileen whispers to herself, "She wasn't with us."

The men finish their meals and rise to approach Khuz. They form a line, and some yawn while they wait.

Khuz retrieves a long chain with shackles and begins to bind each prisoner. He leads the men off through the exit into another part of the mining camp.

The sounds of the rattling chains fade. The women clear the tables and dispose of the trash. They roll the barrel into the kitchen and end another grueling day.

CHAPTER FORTY-ONE

CLAUSTROPHOBIA

C unung leads the boys into the depths of a serpentine passage. They pause at the spot where he had previously assisted Baldwin. "Here we are again," Cunung announces, his voice bears caution.

"Sorry," says Baldwin in a sheepish tone.

Cunung responds with a chuckle, "It's okay. Let's aim for less excitement, though. At least for the time being."

The passage weaves past several intersecting tunnels. It eventually tapers to a narrow section that forces them to sidle through sideways. They must compress their bodies to fit through, so Cunung entrusts the lantern to Baldwin. Before Cunung enters the tight aperture, he threads a length of rope through the lantern's loop.

He instructs Baldwin, "Take the end of this. Once I'm through, pull the rope up to bring the lantern across."

Cunung disappears into the fissure. His progress is audible in the confined space.

"Do you think we're going to find her, Greg?" Baldwin asks. His voice is full of hope and uncertainty.

Gregor asserts, "We're close."

Baldwin asks again, "You believe that?"

"I can't explain it, but I know we're close," Gregor confides. This prompts a nod from Baldwin.

After a moment of silence, Cunung's voice calls from beyond, "Okay, send the lantern over." The voice is muffled as it echoes through the narrow crevice. Baldwin lifts his end of the rope. The lantern slips through the narrow gap as the light dims. Its absence leaves only the faint glow of blue fungi dotting the ceiling.

"See you on the other side, Greg," Baldwin says before he squeezes through the opening. His progress is marked by the sound of his body scraping against the narrow passageway until it fades away. A series of breaths break the silence—not Gregor's, but someone or something else.

Gregor asks, "Hello? Who's there?" His voice is a whisper barely louder than a breath.

No answer comes. The sound of breathing intensifies. Gregor scans the gloomy expanse but sees no one.

As the sound grows louder, a sense of urgency propels him to follow his friends. Gregor scrambles into the crack to elude the unsettling presence that lurks just beyond the edge of his vision.

Cunung and Baldwin patiently await Gregor on the opposite end of the narrow passage, which opens into a broader corridor.

The floor is blanketed with thick mud. The luminous fungi that once lit the way are nowhere to be found, leaving only Cunung's lantern to cast a flickering orange glow over the area. In the distance, a slow, soft, pinging noise can be heard. Gradually, the sound of Gregor forcing his way through the cramped passage that leads to this tunnel becomes audible.

At last, Gregor steps into the room.

"I heard something back there when I was alone," Gregor announces.

Cunung meets Gregor's gaze and nods in acknowledgment.

"You probably did," he confirms.

"What was it?" Gregor inquires, curiosity laced in his voice.

"Let's go," Cunung declares.

"But..." Gregor starts to object.

Cunung interrupts Gregor with a stern look and a decisive shake of his head, "Not here. Let's go."

Chapter Forty-Two
Meeting the Pack

The trio advance through the tunnel. A peculiar pinging sound intensifies as Cunung leads Baldwin and Gregor deeper into the passage. They navigate several twists and turns. Finally, they emerge into a vast underground hollow. The glow of Cunung's lantern illuminates the area, but in the distance, there is another flickering light source.

Two men stand in the heart of the chamber, bordered by columns of porous rock. Niko, the oldest of the three, is clad in black leather armor similar to Cunung's. A wolf emblem marks his shoulder, and he holds a lantern aloft. Beside him, Jas also wears dark leather armor. It bears the same wolf emblem on his knee guards. In his grip, he holds a device, the source of the pinging noise that continues to resonate through the tunnels.

Cunung greets them with a smile, "We caught up. I told these boys we'd probably not see you two."

The men return the gesture with grim smiles. Jas quietly laughs before speaking. "We stopped because we thought you'd want to see this. We could have just saved everyone without you. I figured you'd be jealous."

Niko shakes his head with a grin.

Cunung retorts, "Probably get yourselves caught, and these boys would have to rescue you."

He gently nudges Baldwin and Gregor forward. "This is Baldwin and Gregor. Boys, Jas is the annoying one with the noisemaker. Niko is the annoying one with the lamp."

Baldwin offers a simple, "Hey, I'm Baldwin."

Gregor adds, "Hi."

Cunung laughs under his breath before he asks, "So, what is *that*?" His voice is marked with curiosity.

Jas explains, "One of those little guys sold it to me. The Tinkernel? Supposed to be a tracker. We're picking up someone. It should be a Sonebraèn. We can't know if it's his sister, but who else would it be?"

Unable to contain his excitement, Gregor exclaims, "It's Aileen! I know it is."

Cunung tries to temper the boy's expectations, "Gregor. We can't be sure. Just don't get upset if this isn't her."

Gregor insists with conviction. "It's her."

Cunung appears worried for Gregor, pausing momentarily before shaking his head in resignation. "Okay, Gregor."

Niko and Jas approach the trio, and Niko asks, "So, what now? Should we keep going? Do we know what we're walking into?"

"Maybe, Dar? Not the friendly kind. It could be Ssthraza down here. Probably not Goblins this deep," Cunung muses. A frown crosses his face before he adds, "If it's anything else, this will be a recovery, not a rescue."

Jas inquires, "Any idea how many we may have to deal with?"

"Not yet. If we're lucky, it'll be a minor post," Cunung replies.

"And if we're not?" Jas presses.

Cunung sighs deeply.

"Could be a city. If so, we'll have to reevaluate our situation. We won't risk sneaking into a Duerrodar fortress with these two."

Gregor interjects firmly, "I'm not leaving Aileen."

Cunung responds with a stern reminder, "You promised me, Gregor. Down here, you listen and obey without question."

"I'm not leaving Aileen," Gregor insists.

Cunung shakes his head slowly, then turns to Jas, "We'll figure it out, Jas."

With a grin, Niko chimes in, "I think the boss is getting soft these days, Jas."

"You might be right," Jas agrees.

Despite the comment, Cunung can't help but smile. He shoots his friends a warning look. "Keep talking. You'll find out."

He then points to the device in Jas' hand, "Your toy seems to work."

Jas boasts, "I'm telling you, those little guys are smart. I don't know how anything they make works, but some of their toys are *exciting*." He emphasizes the word exciting to suggest that this is rarely good.

Leading the group forward, they follow the pinging of the peculiar device.

"Can you make it shut up?" Cunung asks.

"Dunno. I can try." Jas fiddles with a knob, and the device suddenly emits a puff of smoke. The pinging stops, replaced by a blinking light from the device's center.

Jas offers Cunung a shrug.

"That'll do. Let's go."

CHAPTER FORTY-THREE
READY TO GO

Unadorned stone benches flank a sturdy table hewn from the same solid rock. Weathered by time, these benches provide a humble place for Sonebraèn and Taumkin to gather. A group huddles around the table, talking in hushed tones about the breach in one of the upper branches of the mine.

Aileen, Seònaid, all of the Taumkin, one of the Sonebraèn men, and two Sonebraèn boys stand on the far side against a wall. Each one expresses anticipation and fear as they watch the others prepare to leave.

On the other side of the room, Edoric rubs his hands excitedly. His voice is barely above a whisper, "They're breaching the tunnel now. Once it's clear, we make our way out of here."

William thinks momentarily before asking, "Anything else we need to handle before we go?"

Edoric says, "I'd say pack your bags, but I'm pretty sure we're all wearing everything we brought."

Leona shakes her head, her eyes filled with sorrow, "I tried talking the girls into coming with us, but they both refused."

Edoric glares at the group huddled together against the wall, "I don't understand. What's their problem anyway?" His eyes flash disdain.

Leona sighs, "It's that redhead. She keeps saying her brother is coming, and the blond girl believes her."

William frowns sympathetically, "Pity. The girl must be touched."

Leona agrees, "Aye, poor thing. Strange though, I almost believe her myself."

The man nods soberly.

Leona continues, "Now she has others believing her. All the Kin want to stay now."

Edoric's glare intensifies, and his voice drips with disdain. "Well, it doesn't take much to fool their kind."

Leona concedes, "That may be, but she's even managed to convince Doren to stay here with his boys."

The man stares at her without expression, "Made his choice. I won't blame him, but I can't say I understand it. We have a chance to escape from here right now. That's the truth."

The woman smiles and nods enthusiastically, "Foolishness. Trust some girl who says she saw something in the dark."

They both look toward the group huddled against the wall. The harsh lines on Leona's face soften. She speaks with a voice cracking on the verge of tears. "Will they be safe when those things find out we're gone?"

William shrugs and shakes his head, "Truthfully? I doubt it. What can we do though?"

"It's a shame. The girls seem so sweet." Leona laments.

Edoric laughs, "You're welcome to stay with them."

Leona's eyes widen, 'No, I didn't say that. Just a sad situation, is all."

We hear footsteps rush from one of the entrances to the mines.

A young Sonebraèn boy named Cornyn emerges. "They broke through the wall. Sure enough, it's hollow! Can we go now?"

Edoric smiles at the young lad, "Sure boy, let's get out of here."

The teenage boy sprints back to the entrance to the mine. Within a second, he's out of sight. His footsteps echo for a moment longer until he's out of earshot.

Edoric motions for the others to come along and heads for the entrance, "Sure you won't be joining us then?"

Aileen nervously looks between the members of her group, but none seem intent on leaving. Edoric and William walk toward the tunnel.

Leona pleads with the girls, "Oh, come on, girls."

When no one joins them, Leona turns and follows Edoric and William into the mines. The three are soon lost from our view.

Seònid looks into Aileen's eyes, "Aileen, I hope you're right about this."

Frowning, Aileen replies, "For their sake, I hope I'm wrong."

The slaves who have chosen to wait for Gregor walk toward the empty table and take seats. No one speaks. Everyone looks into the darkness of the main exit from which Khuz and Gom will return.

CHAPTER FORTY-FOUR

LITTLE REMORSE

The small chamber is at the end of a long, narrow shaft. It measures four span in width. One wall holds an entrance into the chamber. The opposite wall is marked with an opening freshly cut into the stone. Rubble is heaped against the wall on each side of the opening. A trail through the debris forms a path that has been cleared for people to walk through.

A teenage boy rushes to a congregation of half a dozen men and a boy. Cornyn looks eager to investigate the new tunnel, a recently discovered passage that could potentially lead them to safety. "How's it look? Has anyone been inside yet?" The boy runs past the group and looks into the darkness beyond the tunnel they are currently occupying.

Rory replies, "Not yet. Wait for the others. Are they all coming?" He's a middle-aged man with greying hair and a receding hairline. His face is etched with worry. His stained and tattered clothes hang from his thin frame, a testament to years of hardship. The grime covering them tells a story of untold years below the surface.

Cornyn shakes his head. "It looked like the girls are staying. Those kin, too."

The man sighs, clearly exasperated, "If I live another hundred years, I'll never understand."

Cornyn can't hold in his excitement over the escape attempt. "I can't wait to see what's inside there. I wonder how far we are from the surface?"

Rory nods and grins, "It's running in the right direction. That's a good sign."

Footfalls approach.

Leona, Edoric, and William appear from around a corner in the tunnel and approach the small chamber.

Edoric assesses the small group of escapees, "Is everyone ready to go?"

"Yes, just waiting for you. None of the others had a change of heart?" Rory looks hopeful that others are coming.

Edoric is exasperated. His growing irritation threatens to blossom into a full-blown rage: "They're all bought into the idea that the girl saw her brother coming to rescue us. There's a strange madness about it."

William nods. "She's convincing." He offers.

Edoric's had enough. His fury begins to spill over. "It's a little too convincing if you ask me. If I thought it would save the others, I'd..."

Leona replies in shock, "You'd do nothing! She's just a poor girl."

"You realize that girl is likely killing the whole group? I'd be doing them all a favor." Edoric realizes he's crossed a boundary and tries to justify his thoughts. The tension in the air is palpable as the group grapples with the girl's influence and the implications of Edoric's words.

William looks Edoric over. He can't be sure if Edoric is just frustrated or if he is suggesting that he would kill Aileen. "She's just a confused girl, Edoric. Relax."

Edoric tenses up and starts to reply but cuts himself short. He realizes there is nothing to gain from this argument. Finally, he spits, "Let's get out of here." The group moves forward after deciding to search the new tunnel for an exit.

Edoric takes the lead and steps into the tunnel that cuts perpendicular to the one they just came from, "Come on, everyone."

Edoric steps into the passage and disappears from view. One by one, the group follows, starting with Leona, the Sonebraèn men, and the boys. William enters the tunnel last.

Before William walks out of sight, he shakes his head mournfully. He looks back and whispers, "Ao, keep you all."

William ascends the sloping path and disappears out of view.

CHAPTER FORTY-FIVE

KNOCK-KNOCK

The passage slowly rises toward the surface of The Dark Below. There is just enough room here for two adults to squeeze in and walk side by side. Most have chosen to take this passage as a single file. Two of the boys near the back of the group walk side by side and talk among themselves. Leona and Edoric likewise walk together and lead the group forward.

William is alone in the back. He remains aloof and silent. His face is ashen, and his eyes are full of remorse. Occasionally, he looks behind him as he guards the group's rear.

Cornyn excitedly throws his hands into the air and bumps into his friend Jesse's shoulder. Laughing, he throws an arm around Jesse's shoulders, "I can't believe we're finally going home!"

Jesse, another adolescent boy with blonde hair and blue eyes, asks, "Yeah! Do you think we missed our birthdays?"

Cornyn shakes his head and looks at Jesse, "You sure know how to ruin a party, Jess. I hope not."

Jesse laughs apologetically, "Sorry, I wonder how long we've been down here."

Knocking rings through the tunnel as the group walks through the passage. Everyone pauses for a moment and looks around nervously. The group continues walking slowly and cautiously for several more seconds.

"How far are we from the surface?" Leona asks. She scans every corner of the sloping tunnels.

Edoric chuckles to himself, "You think I know? How'd you get down here?"

Leona replies with sadness, "Raid on our little mountainside village. Those nasty Dar killed most of us in the middle of the night."

"How long did it take to get down there?" Edoric asks.

Leona takes several seconds to ponder the question, "A long time. I fell asleep at one point on the way down."

"It'll take at least as long to return."

The ominous knocking rattles through the tunnel once again. The stone shakes a bit after the sound, and a loud creaking is heard among the stone and soil. Dust and debris break loose from above and pepper the group.

Thankfully, it's fine debris, and no one is hurt. Everyone stops moving and looks around. Once Leona is convinced they are okay, she says, "I hate being down in this pit."

"It's okay. We're going home," Edoric says. He places his hand on Leona's back and tries to reassure her.

She doesn't take comfort in his touch but does her best to smile.

The group continues to press on.

CHAPTER FORTY-SIX
A DOOMED EXPEDITION

The passage narrows to about a span; everyone forms a single file. The tunnel begins to slope steeply upward, around a 60-degree incline. They scramble forward on their hands and knees.

William shouts, "I hope the others are okay. I wonder what those Dar will do when they find us missing."

Edoric shakes his head from the front of the group. His breath is heavy from the climb, "Well... it won't be pretty..." Edoric pants as he speaks, "But they should have thought... of that before..."

Edoric reaches a point where the tunnel flattens above. He takes the opportunity to stand upright again and recover his breath, "Before they decided to stay behind." Edoric continues to pant but recovers his breath as Leona rises to the flat landing.

William's voice quakes as he hurls his words toward Edoric in a rage, "Couldn't care less, could you?" Edoric's callous demeanor has pushed William to the point where he's ready for a fight. William aggressively ascends the sloping passage.

Noticing William's anger, Edoric calls back down the tunnel, "It's not that. The reality is they chose to stay. It's their fault."

William shakes his head with a look of disgust.

At the landing, the passage widens to three span. As people reach the top, they begin to form a huddle.

Edoric begins to survey this new area and notices a light coming from a nearby opening. "What's this?" He walks to the gaping opening, looks in each direction, and plans the group's next move.

A massive chamber opens up to a grand slope in either direction. It is a vast cylindrical passage that has been gouged into the ground from above—the opening curves down into the chamber floor around twenty span over a curve. On the left, the grand chamber rises. Light streams down from the opening, a clue that the slope may rise to the surface. The tunnel descends toward the right into an abyssal darkness that seems to glare back at Edoric with hatred.

Edoric shudders briefly and looks back to the left and up, "I think we found our way out. I see sunlight!"

"I want to see!" Leona stands upright and sprints to his side.

Edoric flashes a grin at Leona, "Really?"

Leona bubbles over, "Yes!" She can't contain herself and suddenly breaks into skipping steps around the chamber.

Edoric laughs and exits the landing, "Come on, everyone, let's go!"

Several group members, including the two boys and William, are still climbing toward the landing from below.

The ground is moist gravel as a diminutive stream babbles down the tunnel's center toward abyssal darkness. Sunlight pours down into this massive chasm carved into the mountain. Light filters through dust floating in the air, forming a green and grey haze all around the area. The roof of the passage was sundered long ago, and vegetation crawls down into the hole from the edges far above. Edoric and Leona are the first to scramble down into the grand passageway.

Another four men scramble down into the colossal gap. Edoric, Leona, and the four men wander toward the light as they explore the route toward liberty. Everyone is eager to reach the enormous opening where the roof is torn away. They follow the tunnel into a gaping chasm in the mountain.

A cavernous wound in the mountain reveals a group of half a dozen people. They are mere ants from this distance. The group of Adam begins to rush toward the exit. A harrowing roar shakes the mountain. Debris and dust fall from the tunnel's ceiling over the group. The falling soil and stone pepper them all. One of the men's legs is crushed beneath the weight of a falling stone.

Amid his cries of pain, the others stop, turn, and rush to help him.

Everyone has reached the top of the tunnel now. William pants from the effort of his climb. A terrible roar shakes the mountain. The faces in the room are etched with terror as William rises. He motions back toward the tunnel leading down. He ushers everyone toward safety, "Come on, everyone! Hurry!"

We hear the first terrible step of some monstrous, unknown thing.

Leona screams from the massive chasm.

Edoric cries out in panic, "Run! Everyone run!"

"Where? Where?" Leona wails helplessly.

There is a pause before Edoric desperately calls out, "Back to the... no, run out! Get out!"

Leona screams again.

A tremendous footfall

shakes the mountain

More debris

falls on the group

boys disappear

down the shaft

Men scramble

down the pit

Thunderous footsteps

unceasing

-

gust of wind

rocks everyone

abomination

approaches

-

gaping hole

blackness

a moment

horrific shape rushes past

Everyone screams.

Leona lets out a blood-curdling howl, "Nooo..."

Another dreadful roar cuts off her cries.

Thunderous noises mix with more screams.

A crash forms a sea of audible nightmares. An explosive snap brings the screams to an abrupt end.

The cacophony of terror crescendos.

Its volume falls into silence.

A sinister pause follows.

The sound of wings popping open breaks the silence. There is a whoosh as they gulp air. Something massive takes to the skies.

A blast of wind fills the tunnel. The last members of the group scramble down into the sloping passage and away from this place of horror.

Chapter Forty-Seven

Taking Flight

Aileen, Seònaid, and the others all sit at the stone table. A solemn aura hangs in the air. The world feels grey. The vibrance of life is drained away. Everyone is silent. They contemplate an uncertain fate. Doren, a man in his early fifties with a weathered face and dusty blonde hair, rests his head against the table. He lifts his head, and stoic grey eyes scan the room. They are filled with a lifetime of experience. He pushes against the stone platform and stands to face the others.

Doren looks into the space above the group, "Those Dar should be back soon." Doren's boys stand up on each side of him and put their arms around the man as if to comfort him.

Aileen and Seònaid sit near the center of the table. Aileen ponders, "How bad will it be?"

Doren hesitates to speak. He thinks for a moment but finally answers, "I hope they don't kill us all."

Aileen winces and offers apologetically, "I'm sorry."

The man smiles, "It's okay, girl. We made our own decisions." The kindness in his voice makes it clear that he doesn't blame her for the situation.

Footfalls, barely audible at first, grow louder. The sound echoes through the silence. Someone is running, and the group's fear intensifies.

Aileen has a concerned look on her face. "Is that them?" She asks.

Doren shakes his head, "No... it's coming from the shaft."

The boys from the doomed expedition pour into the dining area, followed by the men. Doren's face is full of surprise. "You're back? What happened?"

Jesse has to take a moment to catch his breath. His eyes are wide and dilated, and the boy is sweaty. Finally, he composes himself enough to answer, "Something terrible! We didn't see it, but we heard it."

Doren throws his head back and asks, "What? You're not making sense."

It's all bitter confusion until William cuts through the noise and chaos, "Something came out of the darkness and..."

William pauses a moment. He shakes his head and continues, "The others are gone. Dead. We didn't see it, but we heard their screams."

Aileen cries out, "No!"

William tries to comfort Aileen, "I'm sorry dear, they're gone."

The new arrivals collapse into the benches along the table. Doren is still trying to process the implications of William's words, "They're gone?"

William again tries to explain, "It was like the world itself came up to take them."

Cornyn emphatically adds into the rising mass of voices, "I've never heard anything like it."

The room is full of riotous and dissenting voices. The conversation breaks into a roar. As the confused murmur crescendos, a familiar voice silences the hall.

Gregor's voice cuts through the cacophony, "Aileen!"

Aileen looks up for a moment. When she recognizes her brother, she leaps from the bench and rushes toward him. The two embrace for a moment. Cunung steps forward and beckons for everyone. His voice is urgent and commanding, "Hurry, everyone! We don't know how much time we have to escape!"

William responds with a shocked smile as wide as his face: "Bless my eyes, it's a boy! Is that her brother? Did she really see him?"

Cunung glances at the man. Confused, he reinforces the need for urgency: "What? Come on, now!"

Everyone springs into action, their desperation fuels their speed as they run toward Cunung, who points them down the tunnel. As the group begins their desperate sprint back to where Cunung emerged, the distant sound of footsteps grows louder. The sound comes from the opposite direction of the intersection.

A group of twelve Duerrodar turn the corner. Khuz and Gom are in the group's lead and point at the escapees. Most of the Duerrodar are dressed in the fashion of the guards, Khuz and Gom. One Duerrodar, Xuduok, wears filthy robes that may have once been purple or crimson. His robes are adorned with plates and hides. A gray stole, three span in length and a finger in width hangs from his shoulders. Zuuk runes on the stole glow orange in the dark tunnel. The stole seems to move of its own volition in the stagnant air of the passage.

Khuz shouts in Zuuk, "Tuokek! Kxo Xuth!" - "Slaves! Get them!"

Cunung acts without hesitation and turns over a large barrel near the entrance. It crashes to the ground and partially blocks part of the tunnel through which the Dar must come.

"Run!" Cunung cries out, but the group is already in motion.

Only Aileen, Baldwin, and Gregor remain with Cunung as he barricades the hall to prevent the captors from entering.

Cunung looks down and realizes the kids aren't moving, "I said run! Go!"

Aileen, Baldwin, Cunung, and Gregor join the race down the timeless halls.

Chaos floods the long passageway as slaves and liberators pour down the corridor and away from the Duerrodar pursuers.

The clapping of bare feet as they race for freedom fills the air. The thunder of heavy Duerrodar boots pummeling the stone floor overshadows the sound of the escapees' flight.

CHAPTER FORTY-EIGHT

STONE AND FURY

Jas and Niko lead the sprint away from the mining camp from the front. The Sonebraèn men push forward the younger boys. Seònid follows these closely. Next up are Taumkin men and children. Aileen, Gregor, and Baldwin follow with a gap of about fifteen span between them and the Taumkin.

At the back of the group is Cunung. He does what he can to slow the pursuers behind them. A rack of curiosities goes sprawling toward the ground as Cunung throws it down. The passageway twists through the treacherous Dark Below, a labyrinth of tunnels and caverns. The chase passes intersecting tunnels that join from the left or right of the stone hallway, a constant reminder of the danger. A portion of the tunnel continues straight for twenty spans.

Xuduok's guttural voice begins chanting from a distance in Zuuk, "Gour buro zo kxugo ruu!"

A fist-sized chunk of stone breaks from one of the walls flies through the air and strikes Cunung in his lower back.

Cunung cries out in pain with the harsh blow, "Hnnffff..." The wind is knocked out of him with the force of the blow. He gasps for air. Cunung slows his sprint to a walk as he tries to regain his breath. Cunung risks a glare over his shoulder and meets Xuduok's wicked grin.

Baldwin is the first to notice Cunung's struggle. Without hesitating, he turns and rushes back to the man's side. Gregor senses the absence and turns to join him. Cunung's voice strains with pain. He shakes his head in disapproval but cannot speak as the boys help him run. Cunung finally gasps and draws a breath: 'Go! Leave me! Go on!' He pleads, his voice full of determination.

Baldwin pleads with his newfound mentor, "No! You're coming with us!"

Cunung presses them away and forward, "I said go!" He grabs his side but manages to quicken his pace once again.

Aileen, Baldwin, and Gregor lead Cunung as they race to catch up with the others. The passage takes another turn, and they lose sight of the Duerrodar pursuers. Cunung's voice calls ahead with humor and caution, "They have magic, rock-throwing guys!"

Niko chuckles, "Of course they do!"

Cunung calls out to the fleeing escapees, "Run faster!"

Gregor grins despite the danger. His eyes shine with a mix of excitement and fear.

Baldwin looks at Gregor and grins. His sarcasm is evident: "You are enjoying this!"

Gregor shrugs, "Sorry!"

Baldwin shakes his head, but his grin broadens a bit.

Aileen calls to her brother, "I knew you were coming to save us."

Gregor is puzzled, "Really?"

Cunung urges the kids to run, "Let's get out of here first, okay?"

As the passageway turns, everyone focuses again on escaping from the Dar. The tunnel opens into another straight passage, much longer than the last. The air here is heavy with the scent of damp soil, and the sound of hurried footsteps echoes off the stone walls. The area is dotted with majestic natural columns of stone, where stalactites and stalagmites have met and fused together, creating a breathtaking sight amid the desperate chase.

The tunnel widens to around three and a half span. Several tunnels intersect along this straight path. The end of this long, straight section can be seen in the distance. It narrows to a span before disappearing off to the right. A passage connects to the right immediately before it tightens midway down the straight path.

Cunung has caught up to Aileen, Baldwin, and Gregor. The Dar emerge into the straight section of the tunnel, their heavy footsteps ominously echoing behind them. The more heavily armored Dar rush into the hall first, followed by Xuduok, who immediately halts and strikes the ground hard with the haft of his great hammer. Again, his voice thunders in Zuuk, "Gour buro bxukh..."

Cunung shouts, "Here we go again..."

Xuduok slams the haft of his hammer again to the ground, "Buro bxukh ro..."

Niko runs into the narrow opening and leads the front of the group toward the surface. Jas stands where the tunnel narrows and encourages the escapees to run faster. Cunung guides the three children to hide behind a stalagmite, fully expecting to be pelted by more stone missiles, "Get to cover!"

Xuduok again slams the heavy hammer down onto the stone floor. The ground begins to quake as debris shakes free from the ceiling and peppers the group. As soon as the ground starts to quake, the Duerrodar guards cease their pursuit. Evil grins spread like a contagious disease across the guards' faces.

The voice of Xuduok resonates through the ancient halls, "Uk ukxo bhu kxugo ruu!"

One last time, the haft of the great hammer strikes the ground at the declaration of "ruu".

The quaking grows far more intense until, finally, between Jas and Cunung, the ceiling splits, and the roof collapses.

Cunung shouts, "No!"

CHAPTER FORTY-NINE
ALTERNATE PASSAGE

The tunnel collapses between Jas and Cunung. Aileen, Baldwin, Cunung, and Gregor are trapped away from the others. Their hearts pound as they desperately scan the chamber for any way forward.

Gregor looks to Cunung for an answer, "How do we get out?" Gregor's eyes plead for hope.

Ominous laughter haunts them as Xuduok admires his work. Cunung looks toward the passage that turns to the right and out of the collapsed tunnel. Cunung points toward the remaining passageway, "There! Go!"

Their hearts pound, and adrenaline surges. Everyone sprints for the side passage, their only hope of escape. Within seconds, the protagonists have once again slipped from the sight of their deadly foes. The Duerrodar guards again charge after them as Xuduok resumes the race to catch their prisoners. This new passageway twists and turns even more than the last.

"What now?" The question comes out through heavy breaths. The chase is beginning to wind the children.

Cunung answers with resolve, "No idea. At least we're still going up."

Baldwin becomes increasingly concerned, "Are we okay?"

Cunung shakes his head with a frown, "No. Keep running!"

The passage opens into a wider area. The group finds themselves in a carved chamber likely mined out by the Dar. Petroglyphs adorn the room, and ancient symbols are etched into the walls. They are reminiscent of those within the alcove where Baldwin, Cunung, and Gregor encountered the Goblins. They rush into a long, straight tunnel with no intersections.

"Oh no. This is bad." Cunung realizes there's nowhere to hide from sinister Xuduok's dangerous incantations are resounding

The tunnel floor is smooth and flat, suggesting this area was designed as an underground road. The Duerrodar arrive in the passage behind them, and Xuduok's deep, guttural laughter chases the group down the hallway.

"Nubro, tuokek." - "Hello, slaves."

Again, the Dar cease their pursuit. This time, they slam their weapons on their shields or the ground in unison and chant after the fleeing group. The Duerrodar guards chant in unison, "Khu vu!"

The group turns their heads to look at their pursuers.

Xuduok slams the great hammer's haft down hard on the stone floor.

Cunung shouts in a panicked voice, "Run!"

The three younger protagonists turn in unison and sprint with all they have left. Cunung takes a single step closer to the Duerrodar. His face bears the weight of desperate thoughts. He reaches for a pouch. His other hand massages the bruise where a stoney missile struck him.

Xuduok again begins to weave dark energies, "Gour buro bxukh..."

At the end of the hall, an entrance to another section of these caverns appears. This finely carved entrance is in the same general style as the petroglyphs that adorn the walls.

Cunung produces a small steel shot. He closes his eyes and lifts the shot over his shoulder. He prays as he prepares to throw the missile. A small steel shot, around the same diameter as a thumb's length, holds their only hope of survival. Cunung's eyes snap open with a deadly look of focus.

"buro bxukh ro..." Again, the heavy haft of the hammer slams down upon the floor.

Gregor's eyes widen as he breathes life into the thought, "Wait, do they live there?"

Cunung shouts, "You think I know? Keep running!"

The laughter continues and grows more audible as the Dar guards slowly walk forward. They appear in no rush to apprehend their prey, and their confidence in the magic of Xuduok is noted. The crash of the hammer's haft upon stone rings through the cavern.

The ancient corridor quakes.

Dust and debris fall from the ceiling between the Dar and the group.

Cunung's body twists forward

  the sphere takes flight

    spiraling in a deadly arc

  toward Xudouk's head

Xuduok continues

foul conjuration

"Uk ukxo bhu kxugo ruu!

missile strikes

runepriest's nose

a sickening crunch

he sprawls backward.

Xuduok topples as his hammer slams into the floor. The great hammer crashes into the ground with the sound of mighty thunder. The ceiling splits, the roof tumbles to the ground, and the tunnel collapses between the Dar and Cunung.

The thick dust and debris filling the chamber obscures the group. The air is heavy with the smell of dirt and stone.

Aileen, Baldwin, and Gregor huddle together as dust fills the passageway, and the roar of the collapse continues. Dust fills the hall, making vision almost impossible. The three wear long faces drawn into frowns that convey the crushing emotion of loss.

Baldwin whispers in a broken voice, "Oh no, Cunung..."

Several tense seconds pass as three young protagonists stare hopelessly into the haze.

A choking sound comes from within as Cunung emerges from the debris cloud. He collapses to the ground beside the children—faint light streams in from further ahead in the tunnel. Cunung continues to choke on dust as he tries to regain his breath. His arms are crossed. His elbows rest upon his knees.

Finally, after several long moments, Baldwin breaks the silence.

"Cunung! We thought you were gone!"

Cunung shakes his head, his eyes full of exhaustion and determination. 'Yeah, well... Guess you should give me more credit.' His words are a mix of bravado and vulnerability. They reflect the inner struggle to maintain his composure in danger.

Gregor smiles, his voice full of gratitude and relief, 'Thanks for saving us, Cunung. Can we go home now?' His question is a plea for safety and normalcy, a desire to escape the danger they find themselves in.

For the first time, Cunung's stoic expression trembles, his facade of strength crumbles. He appears broken, his usually confident demeanor replaced with a look of despair, "You know the way out?"

"No," Gregor admits.

Cunung nods with finality, "Neither do I."

Cunung rests his head between his arms and looks at the ground.

He sighs heavily, and then his shoulders begin to heave as he struggles to suppress tears.

Chapter Fifty

One Way

Cunung sits with his back to the wall. The cloud of dust is gone. The hall is silent. The occupants are painted gray with debris from the collapse. Baldwin walks over and stands quietly beside Cunung, who struggles to breathe.

After several long seconds, Baldwin breaks the silence, "Cunung? Are you okay?"

Cunung thinks, shakes his head, and his voice trembles. "I am sorry, Baldwin." Fear and regret hang in the air.

"We'll be okay, right?" Baldwin asks in a voice tinged with uncertainty. His eyes betray a fear of the unknown that lies ahead. Cunung remains silent. Baldwin presses, "Cunung?"

Cunung stands and brushes some dust off his chest and shoulders. "I won't lie to you. We are in trouble."

Gregor and Aileen both walk closer.

Cunung continues, "I should never have let you two come with us. I am sorry, Gregor."

Gregor looks at Aileen and smiles, "I was going either way. You kept us safe."

"Thank you, Gregor." Cunung's voice is full of renewed determination, "We need to be careful. I had a plan. I had contingencies. None of them accounted for this." Cunung looks back and forth between Baldwin and Gregor, "I need your help getting us out of here."

Baldwin and Gregor both nod their heads. Aileen looks at Cunung and tries to comfort the weary warrior, "Thanks for helping them find me." The young girl's small gesture pours fire on the great man's spirit.

Cunung turns his gaze to Aileen and smiles, "When we first arrived, one of the men said you saw us. You said you knew we were coming here? What did you mean?"

Aileen shrugs and tries to collect her thoughts, "I saw the three of you rescue me. I saw us escape."

Cunung persists, "Saw us?"

Aileen thinks for several moments and then continues, "It's hard to explain. I was singing, and there were lights. I could see you in the lights and knew what I saw was truth."

Cunung has a curious expression. He begins to ask a question but stops himself short.

Cunung shifts the conversation to a different topic: "There is only one way to go. We should start moving."

He takes the lead, and the group begins walking in the only direction that isn't currently collapsed. With its white bricks, the hall starkly contrasts the dusty tunnel they just escaped. The craftsmanship, visible even through the layer of dust, is breathtaking.

Gregor is awestruck. His eyes scan all directions, "I can't believe those things chasing us built this."

"Are you so sure they did?" Cunung asks.

Gregor doesn't reply, but his expression shows he is contemplating the question.

CHAPTER FIFTY-ONE
THE GRAND STAIR

The ancient stonework ascends in a long series of stairs.

Twenty-seven steps, followed by a landing some three span square. The vaulted ceiling rises four span in height.

"This place is beautiful, whoever built it." Baldwin's eyes are wide with wonder. The landing is occupied by a pair of stone guardians flanking the walls on either side. Statuettes carved in the manner of the room they encountered above the Goblin's lair.

Aileen recalls a distant memory, "Yes, it is. I haven't seen this place before."

Cunung casts a knowing eye upon Aileen and smiles, "Should we be surprised?"

Aileen shrugs, "No, I don't suppose so."

Cunung laughs, "There's more to you than I first suspected, Aileen.."

They continue up another set of stairs at the far end of the landing. The pattern repeats: twenty-seven stairs. "It's just that I don't feel afraid here. Not like the mines." Aileen continues. Her face glows as she takes in the beauty of this place.

Cunung cautions her optimism, "Stay on your guard. There are worse things than those Duerrodar down here. Beautiful things can be dangerous."

Aileen nods, "That's true. Have you heard of the Naoischlatt?"

Baldwin shoots her a glance, "Not now, Aileen!"

Cunung laughs, "It's okay, Baldwin. I have heard of it, Aileen. Yes, she is beautiful and dangerous."

"Yes!" Aileen beams a smile.

On another landing, a pair of statuettes and guardians flank each side of the landing as they guard some ancient hall lost to time.

Gregor winks at Aileen, "Did that one move?"

Baldwin's eyes go wide as he stares at the statue in anticipation.

Gregor's lips widen into a smile as he watches his friend.

Baldwin stops moving, and Gregor breaks into laughter.

"Gregor, why'd you do that?" Baldwin looks slightly hurt and just a little angry.

"Sorry, Balds. It was funny." Gregor cuts off the laughter as he realizes the words might have hurt his friend.

"Sorry, Baldwin, it was. Let's save the jokes for another time, though, Gregor." Cunung says, trying not to sound too harsh to either boy.

"Okay, Cunung, I'm sorry." Gregor frowns at himself, and the group continues. Yet another set of stairs, twenty-seven by count.

"What do you think is at the top of these stairs?" Gregor wonders out loud.

Cunung replies, "I would not dare guess."

"Something bad or good?" Baldwin asks.

Cunung tries again to avoid answering the question, "Baldwin, sometimes it is best not to risk mention of either good or ill."

"Really?"

Cunung sighs and continues, "I have pondered whether I have summoned misfortune." Cunung seems distant; his eyes drift to an unreachable faraway time, "I have regretted that I may have chased hope away." Cunung's voice quakes as he wipes away a single tear.

Aileen seems to understand Cunug's pain, "You loved her."

"Not enough." Cunung avoids getting into details.

The ancient halls fall silent once again as the group reaches the top of another landing. This landing is much larger than the last two. The ceiling flies up at least nine spans in height.

The near side of the landing is again three span in width, but it is trapezoidal. The sprawling landing extends nine span from the stairs to the far wall, nine span wide.

A series of twelve stone guardians occupy this room. Three rest on either side of the door, and three lines each of the walls on the side of the great landing.

An imposing arched doorway about five span in height occupies the center of the far wall.

Gregor audibly gasps with awe, "Wow."

Cunung nods, "Guess this is it."

Baldwin's eyes fall upon the great door at the far side of the chamber, "I don't want to open that door."

Cunung shrugs. He looks around the room and, when he sees no other exit, suggests, "We don't have a choice."

Aileen looks tranquil. She expresses joy as she replies, "I feel safe here."

Again, Cunung looks at Aileen with a raised eyebrow.

"Good enough for me. Stay back here." Cunung approaches the archway with practiced caution. The door handles rest at a low level, considering their great height.

Cunung takes the handles in each hand and pulls hard.

The doors swing open easily.

Cunung gasps and stumbles backward, half a step in surprise, as the doors reveal a vast underground forest.

Cunung exhales, his eyes wide with astonishment, "Not a city."

The three children rush to the doorway to see what's beyond the door.

CHAPTER FIFTY-TWO

XUNA'S GARDEN

A brick road leads through the doorway to a thick forest of towering mushrooms. These rise eight to ten spans in height. The ground is a lush carpet of moss and lichen, a vibrant contrast to the towering mushrooms that seem to whisper secrets as they dominate the landscape.

Water laps against a shore somewhere in the distance.

Clouds slowly swell near the area's roof. They roll as an unseen source feeds them.

Cunung, Gregor, Aileen, and Baldwin enter and walk along the paved path toward the surreal forest.

Scales shimmer in the dappled light for a moment. A lizard-like form darts behind a group of mushrooms that tower four to seven spans into the sky, its presence a chilling reminder of the unknown dangers lurking in this surreal forest.

Gregor points to the creature and exclaims, "Did you see that!"

Everyone stops and looks at Gregor. Cunung puts a firm hand on the young boy's shoulder and turns him away, "Try not to look too closely."

Gregor looks up to Cunung and asks, "Why?"

Cunung shrugs with his hands, "It is a Pebble Gnawer."

Gregor casts a confused look at Cunung.

Cunung realizes that Gregor has no idea what he's talking about and laughs. "Sorry, it's a small basilisk."

Gregor has never heard of basilisks. "A what?"

Cunung takes a deep breath, "Basilisks are like lizards but more dangerous. That one was small, but some Basilisks have the power to turn you to stone if your eyes meet."

Gregor's eyes grow wide with fear and curiosity at the mention of the basilisk's dangerous gaze.

Cunung suggests caution. "I didn't see it that well, so I'm not certain, but to be safe, I wouldn't look directly at any others."

"Okay. Heads down." Gregor's eyes are open wide, and he looks at the ground.

Baldwin laughs and ponders, "Why are they here? No, wait... Why are we here?"

Cunung laughs, "Don't worry, we're probably not close enough to see their eyes anyway."

"Would it attack us?" Gregor asks as he continues walking down the path, focusing on the ground straight ahead.

Cunung's voice is low and cautious as he answers. "If that's what it was, we're probably safe. They're not aggressive. It's more afraid of us..."

Baldwin shakes his head before cutting off Cunung mid-sentence, "Nope."

Cunung laughs again.

Baldwin smiles in apology for the interruption.

"We'll be fine," Cunung reassures, his voice a beacon of confidence.

He resumes walking toward the forest, the others following him closely. "Just be careful and stick close."

Baldwin nods his head slowly, his eyes wide.

Baldwin is a little nervous, but he's slowly coming around to this adventure, "You know, it isn't so bad here. I don't know what I expected, but this forest isn't it."

Cunung looks genuinely proud of the progress Baldwin has made.

Cunung leads, and the three children are close by.

Baldwin is directly beside Cunung.

Gregor and Aileen walk together right behind them.

Aileen scans the great forest. She turns to her brother and asks, "Pretty, isn't it, Gregor?"

Gregor smiles at her and reflects, "Yeah. Yeah, it is."

Baldwin joins their moment, "Hey, Aileen?"

"Yeah?"

Baldwin continues, "I was worried about you, and I wouldn't want to have to find you again..."

Gregor laughs, "Yeah!"

Baldwin laughs a little less enthusiastically, "Yeah, but I'm... I'm glad I could help Gregor find you. I'm glad you're okay."

Aileen smiles at Baldwin, "Thanks..."

The conversation ends abruptly when a loud **thump** of heavy boots begins to trudge along the path behind the group.

Cunung whispers, "They found us. Let's go."

He leads the group off the path and into the woods, but it's too late.

Unknown shouts in Oldar A'Bhaketh, "Kho!"

Realizing it's too late for subterfuge, Cunung shouts, "Run!"

The group sprints into the woods as their hearts pound with fear and adrenaline. Cunung is in the lead, his mind racing with thoughts of escape, and the others follow close behind, their breaths coming in ragged gasps. Heavy boots are in pursuit, but the group is increasing the distance from their pursuers.

The mighty fungi of the underground wood speed past as the group sprints.

The skies begin to empty in a torrential downpour as the clouds can no longer contain their swelling mass. The storm is a mixed blessing as they find it almost impossible to see where they're running, but the beating rainfall masks the sounds of their sprint. The forest suddenly opens onto the shore of a deep pool, an underground lake.

Gregor's voice trembles as he motions to run into the water, but Cunung grabs him with a firm and unyielding grip and holds him back, "No! Look!"

Ten span out the water boils, and steam rises from its surface.

Cunung, "We'd be cooked alive if we went in here."

They turn to find another way, but it's too late.

Seven Dar form a semicircle around the group; four have crossbows trained upon them—one of their number steps forward, a heavy axe in hand. In guttural broken Volspechen, a language familiar to Cunung from the northern reaches of the empire, he speaks, "Adam, here? Why did you run?"

Cunung answers in a determined voice: "We're trying to find our way home."

Thedda is still speaking in Volspechen. "We will see." He motions to the other guards in his patrol group.

Thedda, now in Oldar A'Bhathekh, "Kho vak den." - "Take the Adam to our home."

The heavily armed guards, their eyes cold and unyielding, step forward and grab the characters. They disarm Cunung and begin marching them through the woods.

─────────────

Back on the paved path, the sound of heavy boots follows the four toward an uncertain fate.

Thedda marches in a lead position with Cunung at his side.

Cunung's weapons have been taken, but otherwise, the detainees have been allowed freedom.

Aileen, Baldwin, and Gregor follow close behind Thedda and Cunung.

The remaining guards follow behind in three rows of two.

Thedda's eyes hold Cunung sternly as the Dar continues in Volspechen, "Why are you here? Tell me. You are spies."

"No. We're lost."

Thedda scoffs at the suggestion in broken Volspechen, "Vak do not live here. Do not travel here. Do not get lost here. You are spies."

Cunung shakes his head, "No. These children were kidnapped."

Thedda looks at Cunung with suspicion still, "No. You came to steal. Vak, uh... no, Adam, you are a thief?"

Cunung sighs, "No, we're not thieves. The children were stolen. Duerrodar..."

Thedda stops marching and looks at Cunung, "Kiner! Here?"

Cunung seizes the opportunity while he has Thedda's attention, "No. Not here. Beyond the door."

"I will take you to see Dutha. He will know the truth." Thedda turns back and continues, leading them down the road.

Ahead to the left and up a hill is an outpost cut into the wall's stone.

Cunung asks, "You speak Volspechen."

"We trade. Our metals are good. Your food is acceptable. You have good hides." Thedda almost smiles for the first time since the pair have met.

Cunung nods with a relieved smile.

Thedda gives a less severe look, "Our brew - very good."

Cunung laughs, "Not today."

Thedda joins Cunung's laughter.

Gregor whispers, "Look at that place..."

Aileen nods, "It's beautiful."

"Yeah, it is. I never thought..." Gregor recalls a time long ago. A thousand made-up stories, and now he's here in a place he only imagined but never believed existed.

Aileen smiles, "I know. I never believed you either, Gregor."

Baldwin laughs, "I'm glad I came, Gregor."

Gregor throws an arm over his friend's shoulder, "Me too Balds. Me too."

The guards march them into the outpost.

CHAPTER FIFTY-THREE
DATH A'BHORSI

Cunung stands in a stone chamber flanked by guards on either side. The room is adorned with fine pelts and rich tapestries, creating a sense of luxury in an otherwise austere environment. A large desk occupies the room's far end, and a stout Brunoldar stands behind it. There are no chairs within the chamber.

A pair of simple war hammers hang on the wall behind the Brunoldar. These symbols serve as a display of the Dar's authority and power in this realm. Dutha's eyes scrutinize Cunung. He wears a squinting gaze reminiscent of a wolverine carving through the soil to dig up prey. His questions are sharp, probing, and full of suspicion. "Why are you here, Adam?"

The Dar speaks slowly and pauses between each word. The deep voice resounds in the small room. Hidden beneath the stern tone is a warmth and kindness in Dutha's voice.

Cunung compliments the Dar, "You speak well."

This was a mistake. The stoic Dar brushes his words aside with a hint of anger, "Do not try to flatter me. Why are you here?"

Cunung winces before he tries again, "I came to rescue those children."

Dutha slams a fist into the stone desk, "You came down here to rescue them? How did you get here?"

Cunung remains steady and confident. "We spent months seeking the girl. We found her in a Duerrodar mining camp. It was beyond the great door in your forest." Humility proves to be a much better approach than flattery when dealing with the stoic Dar.

Dutha's eyes open more fully at the mention of Duerrodar. "Near?"

Cunung shakes his head, "No. Not near."

Dutha nods and relaxes again. Cunung may win the Dar over to his side. "Good. Continue."

Cunung obeys. "We found her. Somehow, she was unguarded, so we rescued her."

"Unguarded?" Dutha laughs. "Of course she was. Where would she go?"

Cunung ignores the comment and continues, "As we left, the Duerrodar returned. We tried to escape, but one of them knew geomancy."

Dutha's interest grows, and his eyebrows furrow into a frown, "A Runepriest?"

Cunung thinks momentarily and responds in the affirmative, "Yes, I think so."

Dutha again nods, "Dangerous."

Cunung recalls the painful bruise on his lower back: "Yes. He collapsed the tunnels. We couldn't go back home."

Dutha nods. "Where will you go now?"

Cunung raises a hand to stroke his beard before replying. "We want to return home. We're lost. Can you help us?" His voice pleads.

Dutha thinks for a long moment. Finally, the elder answers. "You will stay while I consider what we will do."

Cunung nods, "Thank you."

"Go to the children. You are free but may not leave our outpost, Dath A'Borsi. I will summon you when I have made a decision." Dutha motions toward the exit.

The two guards turn and escort Cunung from the room.

The three children are huddled together near a stove, providing only light in this cell. The room is designed to hold prisoners, but even this simple prison cell is less oppressive than the mining camp of the Duerrodar.

Baldwin holds his hands near the fire and asks, "Do you think they will help us?"

Aileen shrugs, "I don't know."

Baldwin frowns.

Gregor smiles at his friend and tries to encourage him, "Don't worry, Baldwin. I think they'll help us. They didn't seem like the others."

Baldwin grins, "Yeah, they didn't try to kill us yet."

Gregor laughs, "That's not what I mean."

"I know. I think you're right. I feel it." Baldwin smiles broadly at Gregor as the cell door swings open. It is Cunung. Baldwin's face lights up with joy and relief as he leaps up and rushes toward his newfound mentor. "Cunung!"

The others are close behind. Cunung's smile is radiant. His voice is full of a newfound sense of freedom and hope, "You are free."

Gregor cheers at the words, "Great! Are we ready to go home?"

Cunung laughs, "Not that free. We can look around, though."

"Better than sitting in the dark," Aileen says. Her curiosity is piqued. She peers beyond Cunung into the streets, eager to explore the mysteries of the underground city.

Cunung pats his belly, "Want to find something to eat?"

Baldwin nods, "I'm starving!"

Aileen jumps and claps her hands together excitedly, "Me too."

Cunung motions behind him. The group walks toward the exit.

CHAPTER FIFTY-FOUR

RELUCTANT ALLIES

Cunung sits at a stone table. Thedda sits beside him. Aileen, Baldwin, and Gregor share the opposite side. A platter with smoked meat, cheese, and fruit occupies the center of the table. Steam still rises from the meat.

Cunung looks at Thedda across the table, "Thanks for showing us around."

"I had no choice. Dutha gives orders; I follow orders." Cunung finds it hard to tell whether or not this is an attempt at a joke by the stoic Dar.

Cunung smiles, "Regardless, thank you."

Thedda nods and tears off a large strip of roasted meat before starting to chew it. Cunung struggles to connect with the stoic Dar, "Do you know how far we are from the surface?"

Thedda looks confused, "Surface?"

"Outside? Above? Where do our people live?" Cunung points up.

Thedda nods, "Oh, Vak home? The surface. It could take weeks to get there."

All three children sigh. Their expressions turn to disappointment, and they become more broody. Cunung nods, leans back, and crosses his arms, "Thanks, Thedda." His voice carries a hint of resignation. Thedda nods and continues to eat. After a moment, everyone resumes their meal in silence.

Cunung asks, "Anything we should know about the forest outside?"

"Fungi, bats, and lizards are bad for food. The berries are good unless they are green. All mossfruit is good. Duskstag is very good." Thedda smiles and points to the roast before them.

Cunung thinks for a moment before he continues to press for information that might help the group survive in the forest: "Is there anywhere to find water?"

"Three streams toward the surface. On the far side of the garden is a large lake, Uth Athua. If you travel straight from Dath A'Bhorsi, you will see another lake, Dath Athua. That is the lake where we found you." Thedda speaks as juice from the roast drips down onto his long, full beard.

Cunung nods, "Thanks again, Thedda. Anything dangerous that we should avoid."

Thedda stops eating and nods, "If you see dead fungi or lichen, there is danger near." A pair of guards approach from behind Thedda. Hearing these guards draw near, Thedda offers a final tip, "Do not try to swim to the far shore of the great pool. There are many dangers near the surface."

A firm hand claps Thedda from behind. Thedda turns to the guard standing behind him to see a Brunoldar guard. The guard speaks in Oldar A'Bathekh, "Kxo Dutha." - "Dutha is ready."

Thedda looks back toward Cunung, "Dutha has considered your case. Are you ready, Vak?"

Cunung nods.

Everyone follows the guards as they head out of the small market and away from the half-finished meal.

Cunung again stands before Dutha in the grand chamber. Its walls are adorned with intricate carvings, and the ceiling vaults high above as if to touch the sky. Incense burns within a brazier upon Dutha's stone desk—wisps of smoke curl between Adam and Dar. Dutha stares deeply into Cunung's eyes. Dutha's voice conveys uncertainty: "I have considered your situation. You may leave, but we offer little more than your freedom."

Cunung's voice is full of gratitude, "It is enough. Thank you, Dutha."

Dutha returns a nod. He focuses intensely on the swirling smoke of the brazier and takes a deep breath: "Duerrodar are kiner. They are fallen, dangerous, and evil, but they are kin. You intended no harm to them."

Dutha looks from the smoke back to the eyes of Cunung, "Thank you."

Cunung queries, "Can I have my equipment now?"

Dutha shakes his head, "Your weapons will be returned when you leave. I will ask the merchants to treat you fairly for my reputation among the Adam. Please share that we have treated you with kindness when you return."

Cunung nods, "Thank you."

Dutha asks, "When do you leave?"

Cunung's voice is tinged with hope, "We will rest and leave when we awaken."

"May you see home soon. You may leave." Dutha raises a hand to summon his guards. They approach and escort Cunung from Dutha's chamber.

Cunung walks among the stalls of the simple market. The three children walk alongside him.

"Dry rations." Cunung takes dried cakes of minced meats and drops them onto a table where a merchant stands. Cunung produces a pouch and begins to count silver coins. He offers the merchant three coins, but the Dar merchant shakes his head and extends a hand with five fingers raised. Cunung scoffs and rolls his eyes but takes another two coins from the pouch and pays for the provisions.

As he packs away the food, Thedda approaches. "This is for you."

Thedda hands Cunung a stone tablet. Cunung takes it and replies, "Thanks Thedda."

Thedda explains, "Dutha inscribed it. It is a map of Xuna's Garden. It is simple, but I hope it will help you."

Cunung nods and smiles, "You have been kind to us. I hope we meet again. Be safe, Thedda."

Thedda nods, "You be safe, Cunung."

Cunung and the children turn and leave the market.

CHAPTER FIFTY-FIVE

HOMEWARD BOUND

The cell door is open. The children are asleep. Cunung enters the cell, "Ready to go home?" Slowly, at first, the children begin to rouse.

Gregor's heart pounds with anticipation. He rises to his feet and strides towards the open door. His voice is unburdened as he speaks with newfound freedom, "Yeah. Let's go."

Baldwin wakes up and joins the rest of the group as they leave the prison.

They stand at the gate out to the pathway down the hill and into the garden. Dutha and Thedda join them. Thedda holds Cunung's armaments, ready to present them as they leave the outpost, "I am sorry for the cramped quarters."

Cunung smiles, "It was fine. We slept in safety."

Thedda offers Cunung his katzbalger, knife, and a pouch of various other items. Cunung takes his effects and nods.

Dutha motions toward the great forest, offering a final warning, "Tread carefully, Adam. Should we meet again, let it be under better circumstances."

Cunung smiles, "Be well Dutha."

The group leaves the outpost. The heavy gate grinds closed behind them.

They walk back down the hill toward the wood.

Chapter Fifty-Six

A Gift for Art

They follow a stream that boils as magma flows underneath. The wood is densely populated with broad and tall mushrooms that rise and block the view of the ceiling, creating a surreal canopy. Their faces are etched with exhaustion, yet they continue their march undeterred along the stream.

Aileen rubs her belly and asks, "Do we have more berries?" Her voice is tinged with weariness.

Cunung shakes his head. He retrieves a fist-sized melon and offers it to Aileen. "No. Sorry. I have another mossfruit if you'd like it."

Aileen grimaces, "Gross, I'll look for more berries."

Cunung laughs at the comment and shares her opinion of the strange melons. "Must be an acquired taste. Not my thing either."

Gregor longs for home. "How long has it been since we left Dath A'Bhorsi?" He asks.

Cunung thinks for a moment before offering an estimation: "My guess? Fifteen to twenty days? It's hard to tell without seeing the skies day or night. I think we have to be close. The map shows this stream leads right to the exit."

Baldwin posits, "I hope this is the right stream."

Cunung shakes his head. "That is an unfortunate possibility."

The sky unleashes fury as a downpour begins. Raindrops drum on the mushroom canopy and splash in the boiling stream, beginning a symphony of nature's music.

Gregor shouts over the rain, "I was enjoying the rain when we got here, but I think I've had enough."

Baldwin shouts over the rain, "We could rest under one of these mushrooms. May help us stay dry."

Cunung nods in agreement. They all huddle together under the protective brim of a towering mushroom near the bank of the stream. A magma vent flows under the stream, causing the water to boil.

Aileen tries to remain positive, "At least the water keeps it warm here."

"Yeah. I should enjoy the place. I can't imagine we'll ever see it again. I'm just tired." Gregor takes a deep breath and looks around at the place's grandeur.

Cunung agrees, "Someday, I think you'll look back at this fondly. You may even miss it."

Baldwin nods and thinks, "You like to draw, right Gregor?"

Gregor nods and smiles, "Yeah, but I'm no good."

"Sure you are! You should draw this place." Baldwin declares with incredulity.

Gregor huffs, looking for a reason to avoid the suggestion, "I don't have anything to draw with."

Cunung reaches into a pack and retrieves a leather-bound tome and a long stick of coal, "Take care of it, Gregor. It cost me enough."

Gregor's eyes widen as he accepts the gift, and his voice is full of gratitude and wonder. "Thank you."

Cunung smiles and nods, "Going to rest. Don't sneak off anywhere. Oh, and have fun, Gregor."

Gregor sits beneath a towering mushroom and sketches the bubbling stream and the forest.

CHAPTER FIFTY-SEVEN
SETTING A TRAP

The rainfall calms and the wood grows silent and serene.

Cunung rises and walks alongside the stream, "Going to scout for a bit."

Baldwin rushes to Cunung's side, "Can I come?"

"Sure, come on." Cunung looks grateful to have some company.

They move further up the stream, out of view of the camp. Cunung stops abruptly and points to the lichen-covered soil near one of the mushrooms. This mushroom has a lower-hanging cap. The soil is disturbed in a large oval shape as if something was digging recently. Cunung points where the lichen is torn apart and whispers, "That's a scrape. There must be duskstags near."

Baldwin whispers, "What is a duskstag?"

Cunung shrugs and mutters, "Never seen one, but that was the roasted meat back at Dutha's place. It can't be worse than mossfruit."

Baldwin nods, "What do we do?"

Cunung thinks momentarily, then removes his pack and digs through it. First, he pulls out a piece of charcoal, like the one he gave to Gregor. Cunung breaks off a small piece and hands it to Baldwin. He then breaks off another piece for himself and returns the rest to his bag. Cunung whispers, "Crush some of that and use it to cover your hands."

Baldwin whispers, "Okay."

Baldwin and Cunung crush some charcoal into a fine powder and rub it into their hands. Cunung retrieves a roll of heavy twine, draws his knife, begins to unroll lengths that are several span each, and cuts them off.

After completing five of these, he hands two to Baldwin, "Now, crush up more and rub it all along the rope."

Baldwin asked in a hushed tone, "Okay. What does this stuff do?"

Cunung smirks, "It keeps them from smelling how bad you stink."

Baldwin chuckles.

Cunung whispers, "I'll show you how to set one of these, but you're responsible for your own. Deal?"

Baldwin whispers, "Deal!"

Cunung whispers, "Make sure if you have any questions to ask them."

Baldwin watches as Cunung ties a long loop in one end of the rope.

Cunung then unties it and hands the rope to Baldwin, "Can you do that?"

Baldwin tries to tie the slipknot.

Cunung whispers, "Loop it twice more before you go back under and tie it there."

Baldwin adjusts the knot, and it slides easily back and forth. Baldwin looks up at Cunung with a wide grin.

Cunung whispers, "Good work. Tie the other end off to the base of this mushroom."

Cunung pats the round stalk that rises from the mossy ground. Baldwin walks around the tree's base, then loops the end around the other part of the rope and ties it tight.

"Okay! Now what?"

A Gnoghl, a doglike humanoid, hears the voices of Cunung and Baldwin. It has short grey fur and wears leather, fur, and bone armor. It carries a wicked-looking cleaver. The weapon is marred with rust and broken in at least three places along the blade, with crude modifications designed to inflict additional pain.

Its ears perk up, and it begins to sniff the air, then lick its jaws. It slinks carefully beneath the mushrooms, drawing closer and closer to the two Adam, who are focused on the snare. It almost crawls along on all fours when it scurries behind a mushroom from which it can spy on the characters.

Cunung finishes cutting a slit in the bottom of a mushroom cap and hands Baldwin his knife.

"Take this. The last thing is to hang the snare."

Cunung presses a part of the loop into a tight slit near the base of the mushroom cap.

He places more of the loop into another slit near the edge of the cap.

The rope hangs open, forming a loop centered above the scrape.

Baldwin, "Will it work?"

Cunung, "Don't know. Never tried catching a deer with a mushroom."

Cunung smiles at Baldwin, "Think you can handle setting two more?"

Baldwin, "Yeah!"

Cunung points to the other bank, "I'll set two over there. You set a couple here."

Baldwin, "Great! Just put them anywhere?"

Cunung shakes his head, "No, no. See how the ground is all messed up here? That's a scrape. Look for mushrooms like this."

Baldwin, "Okay!"

Cunung, "Another good spot would be a mushroom that looks like something has been stabbing it or cutting into the side."

Baldwin nods with a great smile.

"Let's stay close to each other. Thedda said it could be dangerous here." Cunung wades across the water, and the two begin walking upstream, looking for a place to set their snares.

The Gnoghl slinks behind them as if stalking its prey.

CHAPTER FIFTY-EIGHT

PREDATOR AND PREY

Gregor and Aileen talk under a large red and orange mushroom cap. One of the nearby streams meanders past the two siblings. This part of the forest has a serene majesty that helps them relax as they talk about the events that occurred the day Aileen was taken. Baldwin and Cunung sleep nearby.

Aileen giggles, "What did she say?"

Gregor chuckles as he fondly recalls his mother's fearless confrontation with a burly man, "There's nothing wrong with that baby! We are going to find her now!" The memory of her unwavering courage brings a warm smile to his face. Behind them, a patch of grey slides behind one of the nearby trees. The Gnoghl slinks through the shadows of the wood. Yellow eyes glint from the shadows as the Gnoghl watches them from afar.

It licks its maw occasionally but seems to have no interest in testing the perimeter as long as the group is together, especially with the armed and seasoned veteran so near. It scrapes its claws restlessly on the surface of the mushroom stalk. Its snarls are barely muffled. The tension in the air thickens as it waits for the perfect moment to strike.

Aileen responds with a shocked smile. "Really?"

Gregor exclaims, "Yes! She hit him in the forehead with her spoon twice when he argued that we might not find you!" Aileen's laughter fills the air, a sound that Gregor has missed dearly. Her voice trembles with emotion, "I miss them both."

Gregor looks at Aileen and nods.

Cunung stirs. He opens his eyes and sits up. He tosses the blanket aside and rises to greet the siblings. The ethereal glow of fungi filters through the dense canopy. The bluish-green light casts dappled shadows on the forest floor and Gregor's face as he speaks. "They miss you, Aileen. I can't wait to get home and see their reactions,"

Cunung walks over to the children, and they look up. "Unfortunately, they'll have to wait a little longer. I'm glad you two are having fun. Did I miss anything while we were resting?"

Gregor says, "We heard a splash, so maybe there are fish here. We heard something walking upstream as well. Maybe a duskstag?"

Baldwin and I should check the traps. Think you can wait a little while before you sleep?"

Gregor nods with a smile. "Yeah! We're having fun catching up anyway!"

Cunung walks back over to Baldwin and nudges him with a foot, "Get up, lazy kid."

Baldwin groans. He slowly opens his eyes. With all the speed of a slug as it crosses a garden, he sits up with another groan: "Why..." The question is rhetorical and comes out over several seconds.

Cunung rolls his eyes. "Come on, let's check the traps. We might have venison later." Baldwin immediately perks up.

"I'm awake!" Baldwin leaps from the makeshift bed. The pair walk out of sight upstream to check the traps.

The Gnoghl flashes an evil glare through narrowed, jaundiced eyes.

CHAPTER FIFTY-NINE

HUNGRY

The scrape is the same as they left it. The loop still hangs from the mushroom cap, and the area appears undisturbed. Cunung says, "Gregor heard something this way. If it was a duskstag, it couldn't have been the one that did this. Do you want to head back or check the snares upstream?"

Baldwin excitedly declares, "Let's check them out. I'm hungry!"

Cunung smiles at Baldwin, and they continue upstream.

Gregor and Aileen stand beside the stream.

A scratching noise draws their attention to the far side of the camp. They turn to see the Gnoghl standing in the camp. With a long finger, it tests the sharpness of a cleaver held in the other paw. Panting breath becomes a peal of evil laughter as the creature enjoys finally having its prey alone.

With a bark, it lunges at the children.

Gregor pushes Aileen forward, dodges the creature's lunge, and sprints after her, "Run!"

The Gnoghl's motions are serpentine as it flushes the two children out of the camp and away from the stream. Snapping bites and cleaver strikes pursue Gregor as he leaps back and forth, trying to delay the creature and protect Aileen.

"Take that!" Aileen throws a mossfruit at the creature. It bounces harmlessly off its arm as the beast keeps running. The Gnoghl amuses itself as it herds them along. The Gnoghl doesn't direct precise strikes at the boy; these clumsy jabs press the young boy toward the creature's sinister whims. If it wielded a staff, it might appear to be shepherding the children.

Away to a place where it can play with them. Alone.

Gregor flees after Aileen. "Baldwin, help!"

Chapter Sixty

Cut loose

Baldwin stands beside the first snare he set. Cunung is on the far side of the babbling stream. His silhouette slowly fades in the distance as he walks toward his snare. Baldwin looks discouraged. There are fresh carvings on the side of the mushroom, but his rope lies trampled in the soil.

Baldwin whispers, "It must have fallen. I could have caught it."

A pair of competing voices reach Baldwin's ears in stereo.

Cunung shouts, "We got something!"

Gregor shouts, "Baldwin! Help!"

Baldwin doesn't hesitate. He drops the dagger and draws the shortsword he has hidden for so long. At this moment, he looks like a younger version of Cunung. Baldwin is gallant in defiance of his age and previous fears.

He charges off in the direction of Gregor's voice, "I'm coming, Greg!"

Cunung approaches the snare and sees a large doe struggling with the rope. He smiles and whispers, "It's okay, girl. It's okay."

Cunung shouts, "We got something!"

Baldwin yells, "I'm coming, Greg!" His voice echoes through the still air.

Cunung utters an oath under his breath. He draws his katzbalger in a flash and rushes to the rope with a heavy sigh.

He cuts it, freeing the deer. Finally, he turns, sprints back to the water's edge, and begins to chase after Baldwin.

Cunung shouts, "What now?"

Chapter Sixty-One

The Chase

The chase is a heart-pounding battle of agility and speed as they rush across flat ground. The Gnoghl is a relentless predator. Its blows exhibit the creature's cunning. They direct Gregor's motions and force him to continue along a path of the Gnoghl's choosing. Gregor would be dead if he wasn't dodging with every ounce of his strength. Otherwise, Aileen and Gregor might realize the trap being laid for them.

The Gnoghl forces Gregor further and further into the woods. Aileen continues to run but looks for any way to help Gregor. She throws stones or debris at the creature and taunts it whenever possible: "Leave him alone!"

Gregor backs into the stalk of one of the plentiful mushrooms, "Run, Aileen! Run!"

Aileen frantically warns Gregor, "Look out!"

A cleaver strike misses Gregor's head by a finger's width and bites deep into the flesh of the mighty stalk. The blade sticks fast in the trunk.

Aileen beckons for her brother, "Come on, Greg!"

Gregor ducks under the Gnoghl's struggling arm and rushes toward Aileen. They hurtle further into the wood, trying to buy distance as the creature struggles to remove its weapon. As the woods part, the pair is confronted by a stone wall of the cavern. They hear the beast crashing toward them. They turn right and continue their flight, following the stone wall.

The Gnoghl bursts from the woods and swings the jagged cleaver with wild abandon. Its hideous laughter chops at them from behind, "Kakalakalaka!" It cackles and snarls as it chases them alongside the path between the fungi and the vaulting stone wall that looms over them all.

Aileen throws another stone toward the beast, "Be careful, Gregor!"

It strikes the creature in the eye, causing it to cry out in fury. Gregor ducks again to avoid a wildly aimed blow from the enraged beast. Foam and spittle spray the young boy as the creature rages behind him.

The creature slows its pace and begins its sickening laughter anew. It is low, rasping that might be described somewhere between a man snickering under his breath and a dog panting as it plays with a toy.

The lake looms just ahead—an unforeseen obstacle to escape.

Aileen and Gregor are already on a peninsula that abuts the stone wall beside the lake. A cutback turns right and leads along the water's edge, but the children are focused on avoiding the Gnoghl's wild attacks and miss their opportunity to follow the water. They find themselves trapped in a short path that ends where the lake's water laps gently against the beach.

The Gnoghl hunter advances slowly toward the trapped children. Its intent is clear and terrifying. Gregor stands between the beast and his sister. He tries to look threatening. The odds aren't in Gregor's favor, but he stands in defiant courage. They retreat, but Gregor refuses to give up hope in their shrinking space.

"Gregor! Be careful!" Aileen's voice inspires her brother. He clutches his walking stick firmly in his hands. Gregor holds it before him and tries to make himself look more threatening as he takes another backward step toward the water. The Gnoghl takes a quick strike, hitting the stick sharply. Gregor's fingers tingle with the vibration of the blow.

It continues to toy with its meal. The flat of the cleaver easily presses the staff to one side. Gregor snaps the staff back and takes a swing with it. The creature steps into the blow and grabs the end of the wooden staff with its wicked claw.

The Gnoghl wrenches the staff away and throws it into the water as Gregor screams, "No!"

Aileen calls out, "Greg!" Her eyes are full of panic. She doubts the visions she saw as she sank into the pool.

The creature froths a snarling growl. It is a mockery of laughter.

CHAPTER SIXTY-TWO
Almost Hero

Sprinting footsteps.

Baldwin charges from the wood and leaps into the creature from the side. It squeals in shock as the blade of Baldwin's sword digs deep into its hip.

Baldwin smiles in victory.

Gnoghl steps back

looks down

short blade stuck

bone plate – leather armor.

Gnoghl grins

cruel hate

brutal strike

Baldwin's cheek

the cleaver

Baldwin - spirals

collapse

heap

Aileen screams, "No! Baldwin!"

Gregor collapses to his knees, "No! No! No..."

The last word is a cry of pain. A whimpering, hopeless sound. Not so much words as a song of pain and distress.

It wasn't spoken; it escaped.

CHAPTER SIXTY-THREE

OUTMATCHED

The creature steps toward Baldwin as if to finish what it has started. Cunung bolts from the woods. He spends only a moment surveying the scene. Cunung takes a protective stance over Baldwin's body, "Try it."

Baldwin groans.

Aileen's hands cover her mouth. She is terrified for her dear friend. She grabs Gregor's arm and whispers, "He's alive!"

Gregor doesn't notice. His face is in the muddy soil of the beach.

The Gnoghl charges

cleaver flies

  man steps to side

   striking twist

  the Gnoghl's wrist

   beast cries in rage

man turns the blade

  creature lunges

   hacks at man

-

Cunung steps to the side

his motion belied

harmless beast passes by

veteran dips

katzbalger tip

deep into its thigh

Blood starts to drip

beneath its foul hip

enraged and back turned

wound more severe

the legend is clear

no effort was burned

-

Aileen interrupts the furious melee with a shout. "Be careful, Cunung!"

-

Gnoghl turns

faces Cunung

emits a slow growl

for a moment

snarl becomes

crazed barks

these match

wild strikes

it charges.

-

Cunung weaves

between three blows

carefully measures

distance

a final swing

a glancing blow

Cunung's arm

below the shoulder

Cunung winces.

creature raises

cleaver high

above its head

-

Cunung ducks low

steps close

foul breath

plants feet

rises from

low stance

katzbalger tip

beneath ribs

he rises

blade slides deep

creature's chest

eyes open wide

for a moment

-

        Drops the cleaver

       swipes at hands

     topples backward

   slips down

 lies crumpled

in mud

Cunung withdraws his blade and rushes to Baldwin, "Baldwin, you okay?"

There is no reply.

Gregor weeps into his hands.

Aileen's eyes are wide with concern. Her lips quiver.

CHAPTER SIXTY-FOUR

SPACES IN BETWEEN

Time moves slowly. Baldwin stares at the soil—his head bobs. Cunung lifts Baldwin and throws him over his muscular shoulder. The man's voice seems distant. "It's going to be okay, Baldwin. We have you. Stay with us."

Cunung sounds broken. He's certainly not convinced his words are true.

Gregor pleads with Cunung for his friend, "Is he going to be okay?"

Cunung tries to reassure Gregor. "He's okay, he's okay."

Aileen is talking through tears. "Oh, Baldwin! Please be okay!"

They all seem impossibly distant.

Baldwin rises and falls with Cunung's steps as he turns and follows the wall away from the lake.

Cunung calls the children to action. "Don't let him fall asleep."

Sounds are muffled.

Baldwin's eyes blink slowly.

Everyone runs, but time slows.

Aileen's voice seems distant, "Stay awake, Baldwin!"

Baldwin's eyes close again.

It is dark for a moment. Silent. Peaceful.

A light appears. The silhouette of a man stands in the light.

A voice soft but close, "Baldwin, why are you afraid?"

Baldwin's eyes open.

The world continues bouncing along as Cunung carries Baldwin along.

Everything is desaturated; color has left the world.

Still, there is no sound—only the Voice.

The Voice, soft but very close, "Baldwin? Why carry your fear?" It is deep and calm. It resounds within Baldwin's spirit. The Voice brings with it warmth.

Baldwin looks confused and very weak. He whispers, "I don't know."

The Voice speaks again, "You don't have to be afraid."

Baldwin's eyes close once again, but the world becomes brighter as they close.

A silhouette cast in light appears.

There is a sound. A crashing of waves. A strong breeze.

Baldwin's lips don't move, but his voice whimpers, "I... I am afraid."

The Voice continues, "Did the wound hurt?" The Voice is the hope of a warm fire burning on a frozen winter evening. It is the strength of a mother bear who fights for her cubs.

Baldwin's voice continues, "No."

The Voice presses, "Did your fear?"

Baldwin's voice seems resigned now, "So heavy."

The Voice seems to understand. It is patient as it continues, "A burden you should never bear."

Baldwin's voice slowly grows more resolute, "I'm sorry."

The Voice asks with love and concern, "Why are you afraid?"

Baldwin's voice now sounds full of might, "I don't know."

The Voice seems genuinely pleased, "Your days are set in order. Do not carry your fear. You are loved, Baldwin."

The wind rises in volume. It stops. Complete silence follows.

The light fades away.

CHAPTER SIXTY-FIVE

TIME TO GO

Cunung carries Baldwin on his shoulder. He jogs as he searches for an exit from The Dark Below. "Come on, we have to get him out of here! He needs help!"

Gregor looks at Cunung as they run. He turns his eyes toward his friend for a moment. "Baldwin! Please be okay!"

Cunung asks, "Is he awake?"

Aileen, "No! No! Baldwin, wake up!"

Cunung continues jogging forward. Baldwin bounces like a rag doll against Cunung's back. "Do you see the exit? We have to be close."

Gregor strains to look, "No, not yet."

Cunung decides he must occupy the children's minds. "Could you both try to find it for me?" He wants to protect them in case Baldwin doesn't survive.

"We will!" Aileen shouts as she and Gregor sprint ahead of Cunung, looking for any signs of an exit from this place.

Cunung continues to run and pats Baldwin on the back, "You were brave, Baldwin. So very brave. Please stay with us."

———————————————

Gregor and Aileen run ahead of Cunung. They look for any sign of an exit.

They see a sloping ridge rise from the stone face ahead at last. It cuts back on itself and might easily have been missed in their haste. Gregor sprints up the path toward daylight.

Aileen shouts, "Found it!"

Aileen turns up the path and catches up with Gregor. They must slow down on the treacherous trail. The sloping pathway turns back on itself several times, and each cutback could become a deadfall for the unwary.

———————————————

Cunung races up the path and turns onto the sloping ascent out of the wood.

He carries Baldwin up the path. Like the kids, he must slow to avoid falling, "Hold on, Baldwin. We're almost out of here. We're getting you to help."

Cunung quickens his pace after every cutback up the trail.

CHAPTER SIXTY-SIX

EAGLES CRY

A dark, cavernous nook lies at the base of a mountain. Small animals play nearby in the golden radiance of the Greater Light. It's midday, and birds sing in the still air. Footsteps from within the opening interrupt the symphony of nature. Gregor clambers out of the opening, then turns and helps Aileen climb over a pile of stones that block the entrance.

They look around in wonder as their eyes adjust to the new light.

Gregor exclaims, "We made it!"

"It's beautiful." Aileen gasps.

Behind them, we again hear the sound of someone approaching.

They turn and watch Cunung arrive. He steps over the stones and carries Baldwin out into the daylight.

Aileen looks around in wonder, "Cunung, where are we?"

Cunung looks around at the beautiful scenery, "I have no idea."

An eagle cries in the distance.

CHAPTER SIXTY-SEVEN

BASE OF THE MOUNTAIN

Gregor looks to Cunung. The young boy's eyes look old. They are hatched with red veins, and his face is stained from mud and tears. His brow is furrowed with lines that etch his face with worry. Cunung gently places Baldwin on the soft grass. The boy is pale and unconscious.

Gregor asks, "What now?"

Cunung removes his cloak and gently wraps his young protege in it for warmth. His voice is determined: "We need to prepare for the night. I don't know how far we are from civilization. Do you two mind gathering branches? We need lots of them."

Aileen and Gregor both nod. Aileen adds, "We'll do it. Is Baldwin going to be okay?"

Cunung's expression is grim. "I don't know, but it's bad. We need to get him warm. I'm sorry."

The concern in Gregor's voice grows, "Is there anything else we can do?"

Cunung thinks for just a moment, then replies. "Let me know if you spot plants with dark green leaves and flowers shaped like bells. If you hear water, do the same. We need to clean the wound and keep it from getting infected."

Gregor nods.

Everyone starts to gather branches, leaves, vines, and anything else they can find. It displays their resourcefulness and adaptability in the face of adversity.

Cunung cuts a few saplings down and lashes together a makeshift raised bed.

CHAPTER SIXTY-EIGHT
A CERTAIN PEACE

Gregor's wise, aged eyes shine in the dim light of a burning candle. His smile beams with an understanding of the trials and struggles you've experienced. Gray hair wreathes his head like a crown. He continues sharing their adventures with you, "That's how we escaped from the Dark Below. Although, at the time, we had no confidence that we had escaped at all. We were certain Baldwin was dead, or at least dying."

He pauses for a moment. His eyes drift up and off into some distant place as he battles with time to retrieve some long-lost memory. With a heavy sigh and a frown, he overcomes his age-old adversary to retrieve the captive thought, "Still, a certain peace descends upon us in the most hopeless of situations. So, we continued to make preparations for whatever might come. It must have been early in the morning because..."

CHAPTER SIXTY-NINE

FIRE AND WATER

A makeshift raised bed lashed together from small saplings rests in the center of the clearing. Cunung is starting a fire with logs from an old, rotted-out tree nearby. He blows hard several times into the tinder placed beneath several logs until a flame blazes to life, "Yes! Finally!"

Cunung stands and steps back. "Gregor, can you keep an eye on this fire? Don't let it die."

"Yes, sir, I'll watch it." Gregor is already admiring the warm flame.

Cunung looks to Gregor with a pained expression, "Thanks. I need to find water. Keep an eye on Baldwin and your sister, too. You're in charge now. I'm sorry."

Gregor smiles at the man who rushed in and offered so much help on the worst day of his life. "It's okay. Thanks for keeping us safe."

Cunung cautiously makes his way out of the camp. Gregor walks over to Baldwin and pulls the cloak that Cunung left around his friend. He then places a hand on Baldwin's head. He looks down at the deep wound and whispers, "Thanks, Baldwin. You saved us."

———

Cunung walks through a wooded area. He notices something on the ground. He stops, kneels, and digs it up. He holds up a small garlic bulb and smiles, "Beautiful."

The man rises and continues to make his way through the woods, traveling another hundred span. He hears water flowing across the stone. It's a gentle sound in the distance, but it seems to invigorate Cunung. He hastens toward the sound.

Cunung breaks through the undergrowth and discovers a stream flowing from the mountains. He grins and turns in the direction of the camp before stopping himself. He turns back and fills a bladder with water from the stream. He rises and heads back to the makeshift campsite.

CHAPTER SEVENTY
MEMORIES OF HOME

Aileen sits beside her brother at a burning campfire. Baldwin rests on a makeshift bed on the opposite side of the glimmering flames. Aileen looks deeply distressed, "Gregor?"

Hearing the pain in her voice, Gregor looks at Aileen with concern. "Yeah, sis?"

Aileen asks, "Is Baldwin going to be okay?"

Gregor shakes his head. He doesn't want to lie and is afraid of the answer, "I don't know. Cunung seems to know what he's doing. I hope so."

"I'm scared." Aileen's eyes brim with tears.

Gregor nods, "Yeah, me too."

Baldwin groans from the other side of the fire. Aileen and Gregor rush over to his side, but it's clear that Baldwin is still unconscious.

Aileen's voice cracks as she speaks. A flood of emotion wells: "I miss Mom and Dad. I'm afraid we might not see them again. Where are we?"

Aileen cries. "I want to go home. I want to go home, Gregor. I miss Lily. I miss Belly."

Gregor is shocked. He has never seen Aileen crumble like this before.

He has no words.

He reaches over and hugs her. Gregor is trying to be Aileen's strength. He tries not to cry, but it's a noticeable effort as the lines around his eyes and mouth curl and quiver, "It's okay. It's okay, sis."

Aileen manages to get her tears under control, but she continues to struggle to stifle her sniffling.

After several long seconds, footsteps approach the clearing. Aileen quickly pulls it together. The siblings rise, and Gregor turns to face Cunung as he walks into the camp.

Cunung holds the bladder high in the air, full of water. "Look what I found!"

Gregor wipes his eyes on his sleeve and replies, "Water! Is it close?"

Cunung nods, "Not too far. The terrain is a little rough, though. Going to be tough carrying Baldwin."

Aileen struggles to compose herself. She has her back to Cunung so he doesn't see her so upset.

Gregor looks around the campsite and asks, "Do we need to move our camp there?"

Cunung smiles and settles Gregor's concerns, "I have a better idea, but we'll settle down for the night. Let's clean up Baldwin's wound."

Gregor sighs with relief. "Okay, what can I do to help?"

Cunung looks past Gregor toward Baldwin. The young boy looks pale, and Cunung's growing concern is clearly evident. "Did you find any of those plants?"

"No, sorry." Gregor frowns.

Aileen runs over to a pile of debris she pulled earlier in the day and retrieves something from within, then she rushes over to Cunung, "Are these the ones?"

Cunung smiles at Aileen, "Those are the ones! Great work, Aileen!"

Aileen hands Cunung the bundle of flowers.

Cunung takes the flowers. He kneels and wraps Aileen in a great hug, "Thank you, Aileen. This might help Baldwin's pain. Let's crush it and mix something to keep him from getting worse."

Cunung takes the plants to a large stone and tears the green leaves off the stems. He throws the rest of the plant away.

Cunung hands Aileen a smaller stone, "Can you crush these leaves for me? I need to prepare the garlic."

Aileen takes the stone and uses it to crush the leaves. "I can!" Aileen looks excited once again at the prospect of helping.

Gregor chimes in, "Anything I can do?"

Cunung points to his pack on the other side of the camp near Baldwin, "Yeah, there's a white cloth in my pack over there. Can you grab that and bring it over?"

Gregor runs to the pack as he replies, "I'll see if I can find it!"

Cunung walks to the other side of the large stone and retrieves the garlic bulb. He begins to break off the individual cloves, bruise each with a round stone, and remove the skin.

Once all the cloves have had their skin removed, he crushes them with the stone until it's a pulp. He scoops the pulp onto his knife's blade and carries it over to Aileen. "How's it looking?" He asks.

Aileen shrugs. "Okay? Is this good enough?"

Cunung looks at the messy pile of goop she's created from the leaves. "Looks great, Aileen."

He scoops the green pulp onto his blade and mixes it into the garlic. Gregor runs over with a piece of cloth mesh. "What is this for? "

Cunung takes the cloth from Gregor. He places the mixture from his blade into the fabric and then ties it together, "It's a poultice. It will relieve Baldwin's pain and prevent the wound from getting infected. It should buy us time to find help."

Cunung pours a little water onto the makeshift bag and rubs it together in his hand. He walks to Baldwin and rinses the wound with water.

Baldwin groans in pain as the water touches the wound but doesn't wake. Cunung gently places the poultice over the wound. He shakes his head with a frown.

"I hope he's going to be okay," Aileen speaks in a voice of deep concern.

Cunung nods at her. The mighty man's eyes are filled with gentle comfort, "I do, too, sweetheart. Let's leave him alone for now."

The three rest beside the campfire opposite Baldwin.

Chapter Seventy-One

Cunung's Story

The sun sets on the campsite as they finish preparing a series of lean-tos. Beneath each structure is a short, raised bed made from saplings and vines leashed together. Each lean-to faces the campfire and the mountain base to help keep the wind out.

Baldwin's bed is covered in foliage in addition to the cloak Cunung shared with him. Cunung weaves some vine into Baldwin's lean-to and steps back. Cunung walks to his pack and retrieves a small pouch. He opens the pouch and dabs a finger in some waxy substance. He rubs it into his neck, hands, and wrists. "Are you two still getting bit?"

Gregor shakes his head, "Nah, that helped a lot. Thanks."

"I'm still hungry." Aileen's vocalizes everyone's thoughts.

Cunung nods at Aileen, "Still have that mossfruit."

Aileen makes a face.

Cunung smiles and nods, "Do you want to try cooking it over the fire?"

Aileen raises her eyebrows. "Will it make it taste better?"

Cunung shrugs and chuckles, "I doubt it, but it couldn't be much worse. Want to give it a shot?"

A smile spreads across Aileen's face. She nods enthusiastically at Cunung. The man is lost in his thoughts.

Cunung walks over and sits on a makeshift log bench near the fire. The siblings join him.

He takes his knife and peels the fruit. He cuts it into sticky pieces. These pieces are set upon a nearby cloth, and the sticks are used to skewer the fruit. They roast it over the flame. After a minute, Aileen's mossfruit turns golden brown, and she retrieves it. She blows it to cool it, and we see a trail of smoke from the cooling fruit. Finally, she pops it into her mouth and chews it up.

"Hot, hot, hot!" Aileen swallows it and smiles, "Yum!"

Cunung chuckles. "Is it good?"

Aileen looks at him as if the man has gone mad and shakes her head vigorously. "No. I was pretending."

Cunung and Gregor laugh.

Aileen thinks for a moment before she offers, "It's a little better. I can eat it."

"That's something." Cunung pulls his piece back and eats it, "I've had worse." He smirks at Aileen, and she giggles.

Gregor changes the subject, "Hey, Cunung, you've seen a lot of scary stuff, right?"

Cunung nods.

Gregor smiles and asks, "What's the scariest creature you've encountered?"

Cunung thinks for a moment, "Probably us—the Adam. We are unpredictable. Some of us are good, but some are very evil. For instance, have you heard of Kwylun?"

Gregor nods.

Cunung thinks for a moment and then continues. "He probably looked like anyone else but almost destroyed us all."

Gregor's eyes widen with the idea. "Yeah, that's true. I just..."

Cunung smiles at the boy. He realizes that Gregor wants to hear about adventure and monsters. Gregor wants cool monsters, not some boring idea that a raving madman almost destroyed the world.

Cunung laughs to himself and continues, "Nah, I get it. Ever heard of the Graelaidh?"

Aileen and Gregor both smile and lean in to hear more.

Gregor shakes his head. "No! What is that?"

Cunung wears a broad grin as he continues, "So, ten or twelve years ago, Niko and I were in a pack led by Pyotr. Back then, I was just a pup like Jas."

Gregor and Aileen plunge into Cunung's yarn. Gregor prompts the storyteller to continue, "Yeah?"

Cunung obliges, "Well, we were tasked to figure out why this wealthy merchant had never come home. Officially, people thought he'd just taken off, or maybe his wife had offed him, and Nachtulfen usually doesn't get involved in these kinds of things."

Gregor again prompts. "But???"

Cunung ignores the question and continues. "Yeah... but this time, something seemed off. Lots of other weird stuff was going on, and we got pulled in because some inquisitor, I think his name was Jerol, said it felt a lot like the lead-up to the Mage Wars."

Gregor's eyes are wide at the mention of this.

"Wow." The voice belongs to Aileen.

Cunung goes on, "Exactly. So, when an inquisitor brings up those events, that gets our attention. Lots of people were going missing. He was right about that, but it wasn't some rogue mage."

Aileen and Gregor sit at the edge of their seat as Gregor asks, "What was it?"

Cunung laughs to himself. "I'm getting there. One thing we noticed about all these disappearances was they were all central to one area, an old, abandoned mausoleum. It belonged to a wealthy family that had all died out. We go to check out this creepy old place in the wild."

Aileen again interrupts the storyteller, "It sounds creepy enough!"

"It was. I remember we showed up, and the doors to this mausoleum were just gone. I don't know if that was just time, tomb robbers, or if the things in there had done it, but that was the first thing that set off alarms in my head."

Aileen and Gregor are hyper-focused on Cunung's retelling.

"Yeah, that's spooky!" Gregor sits at the edge of his seat, his hands clenched into tight fists.

Cunung chuckles. "So, we started to head in, and I remember the closer we got, the colder that place seemed. There was a strong wind at the entrance, and I remember we all stopped and looked at each other because it was blowing out from the inside. Naturally, we showed up after dark because that's how we tend to operate, and I just wanted to go home."

Aileen looks concerned for the people in Cunung's story, "What happened?"

Cunung sighs.

"I wish I could say we bravely ran in and took care of business, but Pyotr threw a torch into the darkness, and just for a moment, we saw this thing moving about. It looked like a man, but it was made of whirling dust. Its black eyes glared at us. We got out of there. We just ran back to the public house. We made a plan and sealed it in there the next day."

Cunung gazes into a place far in the distant past.

Gregor looks surprised at the conclusion, "That's it?"

Cunung nods.

"That's it. It's a Graelaidh, and we didn't know how to kill it. So we trapped it. Now that rich merchant is buried down there with the thing. I guess he heard stories about the rich family's tomb and had gone to try and take some of the wealth for himself. Instead, he lost everything. What about you, Gregor? What's the scariest thing you've ever met?"

Gregor's eyes meet with Cunung's own, "Besides you?"

Cunung laughs, "Sure."

Gregor shrugs, "Just those goblins."

"Hi?" Cunung says with a smirk

Gregor rolls his eyes, "I was alone! They were scary to me!"

Aileen seems confused," Hi? What does that even mean?"

Gregor quickly shuts down the question. "Nothing. What about you, Aileen?"

Aileen thinks for a long moment.

"That thing that hurt Baldwin. I did see a scary cat, but it was in a cage."

CHAPTER SEVENTY-TWO
A Pleasant Surprised

The embers of the campfire smolder in the early morning. Cunung is awake. He stands over the remnants of the fire and kicks dirt over it to smother it. Baldwin groans and then cries out in pain.

Cunung rushes to Baldwin, "Baldwin! Baldwin, are you okay?"

Baldwin whimpers," It hurts! It hurts! It hurts!" His hands cover the deep wound and his eye.

Cunung replies, "You're going to be okay. Can you sit up?"

"I can't see!" Baldwin suddenly realizes that he can't open his eyes.

Cunung claps the boy on his shoulder to get his attention. "Baldwin, can you sit up?"

Baldwin holds his eye with one hand and uses the other to sit up in the lean-to. Cunung helps the young boy to get into a seated position. "It hurts so bad that I can't open my eyes." Baldwin's eyes pour tears.

Cunung offers the boy some water from the bladder, which is about half full now, "Here, take a drink. We made it out."

"Wait, we're out? As in, outside?" Baldwin's excitement is palpable.

Cunung smiles at the boy's sudden enthusiasm. "Yeah! We're outside!"

Baldwin again whimpers in pain. "Oh, it hurts so bad. Where are we?"

"We're still trying to figure that out. Think you can stand up?" Cunung reaches over to try to help Baldwin.

Baldwin feels Cunung's touch and shifts, trying to get leverage to rise. "Maybe? I can't open my eyes, though. They are killing me."

Cunung thinks for a moment. "We have to make our way out of here. You need help. If you can walk, we can lead you out. Otherwise, I will have to leave Gregor and Aileen with you."

Baldwin nods. "No, I'll be okay. My legs seem fine; it's just my eye. It hurts so bad."

"I know, I'm sorry. Your eye should heal quickly. I'm sure that's little comfort right now." Cunung reaches out again and takes Baldwin by the arm to steady him. Baldwin stands with help from Cunung. Gregor turns over in his bed. He lazily opens his eyes and then briefly shuts them again.

A few seconds pass. Gregor bolts upright and charges out of his lean-to. "Balds!!! Whoah..." Gregor trips and sprawls out across the ground in a heap. He quickly picks himself up. "Balds! You're awake!" Gregor rushes over and hugs his friend.

Baldwin groans in pain. "Aeiiigh... Hey Gregor."

Gregor steps back and looks at his friend with disbelief. "Are you okay?"

Baldwin nods. "I can't see. I can't get my eyes open."

Cunung looks over where Aileen is sleeping. "Can you get your sister up, Gregor? We should start looking for help."

Gregor rushes over to Aileen's lean-to and shakes her. Aileen is groggy and fusses. "Gregor, stop."

"Aileen, wake up! Baldwin is awake."

"Greg... Baldwin?" Aileen opens her eyes and rushes from the lean-to. "Baldwin! Hey!" She hugs Baldwin. Gregor joins her and offers to help Baldwin walk. Baldwin puts an arm over Gregor's shoulder, and the four head off toward the stream Cunung discovered the day before.

Gregor exclaims, "Hey, Balds, Cunung told us some stories last night. You should hear them!"

Aileen says in her spookiest voice, "Scary stories."

Baldwin is unphased. "Yeah?"

Gregor laughs, "Yeah! They were great!"

Baldwin nods and smiles, "Huh, I'll have to ask him later."

Aileen is pleasantly surprised.

CHAPTER SEVENTY-THREE

CLEANING THE WOUND

As they walk alongside a stream, great tears pour from Baldwin's eyes. Gregor guides Baldwin along the bank, but Baldwin stumbles and trips over the brush from time to time. Baldwin groans in pain from the wound in his face and eye, "It hurts so bad. How long is it going to be like this?"

Cunung shakes his head, "I don't know Baldwin. As soon as we figure out where we are, we'll find someone to help you."

Baldwin cries out in frustration, "It just hurts. Why did this happen?"

No one answers.

Gregor stops and tries to point out yet another obstacle to his friend, "Be careful; there's a vine here. Big step."

Baldwin struggles to get over the large vine. Once across, the group continues along the stream. Cunung stretches out a hand to halt the group. "Hold up. Listen." The group stops walking for a moment, and everyone listens. Baldwin groans again. In the distance, a dog can be heard barking.

Gregor has a curious expression, "Dogs?"

Cunung nods. "Yeah. It could be wild, but it could be..."

Gregor leans his head back and snaps a finger with the realization. "Somebody hunting?"

Cunung grins. "Maybe. Let's hope so."

The group presses forward. Baldwin's leg gets caught on a branch. He tumbles down and scrapes his knees and a hand.

Gregor is pulled down to one knee with his friend. He tries to stand up and help Baldwin. "Oh no, are you okay, Balds?'"

Baldwin fights free of Gregor and walks in a tight circle. "I'm done, I'm done, I'm done! Just leave me alone. Oh, it hurts so bad."

Cunung frowns and steps over to the young boy. He places a hand on Baldwin's shoulders. "It's okay, Baldwin. I know you're hurting. We can't leave you. We can take a break here."

Baldwin sighs apologetically. "I'm sorry. It just hurts so much. Oh, my eye hurts so much."

Everyone gathers around and sits together.

Gregor frowns. "I'm sorry, Baldwin. You saved us, though."

Baldwin doesn't respond. He holds his eye and breathes deeply.

Cunung gets some fresh water from the stream. "Can I take a look? It might be good to rinse the wound again."

Baldwin tries to pull his hand away but can't remove it. Cunung pulls it away and looks at the wound with concern. He pours some water down over the eye to rinse the wound.

Baldwin winces and draws a deep breath, "Aeigh!"

"All done. See if this helps." Cunung hands Baldwin the poultice. Baldwin presses it into the wound and winces, "What is it?"

"Just something we mixed up. It should prevent the wound from getting infected and help with the pain. We can rest for a minute, but we need to get moving again soon and find you some help."

Baldwin frowns but nods in agreement.

Chapter Seventy-Four

Little Fish

The weary group makes slow progress along the stream. The dog's distant and intermittent barking constantly reminds them of the dangers they've faced.

Aileen suddenly points at the water, "Look! A fish!"

Cunung looks over and sees a blue and silver fish swimming upstream alongside the group, "That little guy doesn't belong near Riverview."

Gregor looks at the form swimming in the stream with curiosity. "I've never seen one like that before. It's pretty, though."

"It is. I've caught a lot of those in my life." Cunung looks puzzled for a moment before speaking. "Good eating, but they don't belong in Beaumont. The waters are too warm for them." He starts to say more but catches himself. He points into the distance. A tremendous wooden bridge crosses high above the stream.

Gregor looks up into the great chasm they are approaching. He follows Cunung's gesture, and his eyes light up, "It's a bridge!"

Cunung adds, "It's a road."

Gregor looks at Cunung and shrugs. "Okay?"

Cunung explains, "Roads lead somewhere."

The sight of the bridge lifts the group's spirits; they try to hasten toward it but are soon forced to slow their pace again. Baldwin needs help keeping up. "Thanks for putting up with me. I'm sorry," his voice is full of gratitude and guilt. Gregor looks at his friend with a reassuring smile. He shakes his head, "Balds, you don't need to apologize. You're my best friend, and you saved Aileen and me!"

"It was courage in action." Baldwin tries to smile through the tears at Cunung's compliment before the man jokingly chides, "Don't ever do that again."

Aileen tries not to giggle.

The banks slope toward the bridge, and reaching it from their position in the chasm below seems like a hopeless climb. "Up isn't looking very safe, is it?" Cunung asks with a voice full of exhaustion and determination.

Baldwin wonders aloud, "What do you mean?"

Gregor looks at his friend with concern. "Baldwin, the bridge is towering above us in the sky. We might need to climb some. Can you make it?"

Baldwin shrugs with a frown. "Gregor, you are my eyes. Can I?"

Gregor looks to Cunung, who shakes his head. "Don't worry, Baldwin, we'll get you up there. Let's take the slope for now. It's steep, but if we keep following the bank here, we'll have to climb straight up."

Gregor nods and leads the group. He turns left and follows the sloping path upward and into the towering heights toward the bridge. The path is steep and treacherous, but he navigates it with a surefootedness that inspires confidence in the others.

Cunung refills the bladder with fresh water and then follows the others in the group.

CHAPTER SEVENTY-FIVE
HUNTING FOR HELP

They stumble through thick brush. Baldwin tries to keep his spirits up even as his face contorts with anguish with each step. It's clear he's in severe pain and struggles to continue. Every step is a testament to his determination. Despite the poultice, his eyes stream tears. Cunung resumes the lead position and carefully monitors the others as they move forward.

They reach level ground, and the brush clears. Cunung stops the group. "Look! We're on a trail."

Aileen and Gregor look around and smile. Baldwin can't open his eyes but tries to muster a smile.

The group continues down the trail until it opens to a T-intersection with a road. Gregor looks exhausted, but the sight of the road brings them hope: "We made it! Which way should we go, though?"

"Let's head for the bridge. It's bound to lead us to help." Cunung's words fill the group with renewed hope as they turn right and start their journey toward the bridge.

Aileen runs out onto the great wooden bridge and turns to look over the edge, "Wow! Look how high up we are!" The wind whips through her hair. The sound of rushing water echoes in her ears from below, adding to the moment.

Gregor leads Baldwin up onto the bridge. "Come away from there, Aileen."

She replies, "Okay, but look! It's so pretty up here!"

Gregor turns his head and scans the horizon. "Yeah, it is."

"I wish I could see it," Baldwins adds with regret.

Gregor comforts his friend, "It's okay, Balds, we'll bring you back sometime."

Cunung catches up and resumes his position leading the group. Aileen runs along beside him. "I think I know where we are. It's hard to believe, though." Cunung thinks aloud. Aileen looks at him with a curious expression. "Why?" He thinks for a long time before he answers in a somber tone. "If I'm right, we are far from your home. Much farther than should be possible."

The group reaches the bridge's halfway point when the barking resumes; this time, it's very near. A pair of dogs run onto the bridge and rush toward the group, their intentions unclear. Cunung takes a defensive stance in front of the group. He draws his katzbalger and stands between the dogs and Aileen. Gregor leads Baldwin behind Cunung.

Before the dogs reach Cunung, a man and woman dressed in brown and green clothing walk onto the bridge. The man whistles, and the dogs come to heel. The man is named Alfons, and his wife is Sigi. They are a pair of hunters from the nearby town of Gryfburg.

Sigi cries out to her animals, "Hold Ulva! Hold Erma! Don't eat the poor folk alive!"

The hunters rush toward their dogs.

Cunung sheathes his blade as the dogs halt, and their owners hurry over. "We need help. Do you know where we are?" Cunung asks in a haggard voice. Alfons answers with concern, "Yes! You're just outside Gryfburg! Is everyone okay?"

Baldwin breathes a deep sigh of relief.

Gregor waves at the couple. He shouts, "My friend is hurt! It seems bad!"

Alfons looks at his wife and says, "Sigi, get help! I will follow with them!"

Sigi commands the animals, "Ulva, Erma come!"

Sigi turns and runs back toward the town. The dogs stand, turn around, and follow Sigi as she runs back across the bridge to look for help.

Chapter Seventy-Six

Welcome to Gryfburg

The high bridge near Gryfburg towers over the valley below. It is a massive landmark that spans the Thaumerin River, some fifty span below. Aileen and Gregor lead Baldwin along the high bridge near Gryfburg. Alfons and Cunung walk in front as they head toward the edge of the bridge.

Cunung asks with a curious expression, "You said you are from Gryfburg. In Ostenplatz?"

"Yes, of course." Alfons replies.

Cunung looks puzzled and concerned. Alfons notices Cunung's expression. "Is something bothering you?" Cunung thinks for a moment before he responds, "Sorry, Alfons. Everything is okay. I'm glad we ran into you."

"You seem capable. I am sure you'd have made it to Gryfburg without our help." Alfons remarks before asking, "Where are you from?"

"Originally? Gottleibt, but my home now is Ulfreich." Cunung smiles at the man.

Alfons nods as he replies, "That isn't too far."

Cunung laughs. "Yes! We are very nearly neighbors."

Alfons joins the laughter. "Yes! You should visit more often! No doubt you would be invaluable in the hunts."

Cunung wistfully remarks, "Perhaps. I rarely have the luxury of being near home, but I hope someday to return."

"Oh?" Alfons looks curiously toward Cunung.

Cunung responds, "Yes. My work keeps me busy. Lots of travel."

Alfons nods. "I see." Alfons thinks for several long seconds before asking, "Cunung, what happened to the boy?"

Cunung takes a deep breath. "The children are lost. I am trying to help them get back home. A creature hunted and attacked us. It struck the boy while he was trying to protect his friend. We thought it had killed him for a moment."

Alfons whispers, "Poor child. It doesn't look good. I am afraid it might be infected."

"Yes. I share your concern. I tried applying a poultice of garlic and heather, but we didn't have much to work with. Your wife went to get help?" Cunung looks ahead to see if he can spot her on the horizon.

Alfons tries to comfort the man, "Kaleia, our healer, will know how to treat his wound. It's good you were nearby—a few more days and there might not be much hope for him."

"I know." Cunung's voice bears an unmistakable weight of guilt as he looks behind him at the wounded child. Because of the pain, Gregor and Aileen have to carry most of Baldin's weight. Somehow, they manage to move him along. Cunung shudders to think of what might have happened had Alfons not found them.

Alfons breaks the silence. "Well, I am glad you found us. You say those children are lost? Where is home for them?"

Cunung shakes his head, "Riverview in Beaumont."

Alfons laughs but realizes Cunung isn't joking. "Really?"

Cunung nods.

Alfons speaks with a voice of disbelief. "How long have they been lost? How did they get so far from home?"

Cunung is in deep thought but finally shrugs and responds, "We've traveled less than a month." Cunung doesn't want to continue down this line of questioning. He is sure they couldn't have traveled such a great distance in so little time.

Alfons looks curiously toward Cunung, "Less than a month? Meaning you don't know?"

"Unfortunately, it was hard to track the days. We were underground." Cunung searches for a reason that they might have traveled longer than he realizes, but he can't find any. A look of disbelief washes over Alfons' face. "You are a mysterious fellow. I sense you leave much from your tale."

Cunung nods, "Sorry, I can assure you, there are good reasons."

The old hunter seems to find the answer acceptable. "It's okay, my friend. I sense you mean no harm to my people or those children."

Cunung smiles.

Baldwin shouts from behind the men, "How far?"

Alfons responds, "We are near my young friend. I am sorry you must travel wounded."

Baldwin doesn't respond, but he tries hard to smile through the tears that continue to stream through the blood-caked poultice and down his face. Gregor carries most of Baldwin's weight, but it's nowhere near the guilt of dragging his friend into this situation. "Thanks for staying with us, Alfons."

Alfons seems grateful that they discovered the group, "Of course. We are getting you help, young man."

Alfons resumes his conversation with Cunung, "So, you are traveling on foot to Beaumont? Another two or three months, then?"

Cunung seems perplexed by the situation. The distance they've traveled would be impossible across level terrain. Moving through the twisting corridors of the Dark Below, the distance is impossible. "I had hoped so. The terrain will prove challenging, and we will need supplies. I didn't realize we were so far from the children's home. It may be some time before we may even leave."

Alfons is intrigued by Cunung's answer. "Again, you surprise me. Where did you think you were?"

Cunung seems reluctant to answer. He hesitates momentarily, then stammers, "I thought we were near Riverview."

"Riverview in Beaumont?" Alfons laughs again before noticing Cunung's demeanor. "Are you serious?"

Cunung nods.

Alfons is shocked, "How? Why would you think that?"

Cunung stops walking and looks at the man. "We were near Riverview when I found them."

Alfons ponders the timeline and distance involved. He decides to ensure he understood, "Less than a month?"

Cunung replies with a nod, "Yes."

"I find this hard to believe." Alfons gauges Cunung for several seconds.

Cunung agrees, "So do I." Cunung and Alfons begin walking again.

The group is approaching Gryfburg's limits. Gryfburg is much larger than Riverview but a relatively small town. Sigi and Kaleia appear, running back toward the group from the town gate. Each of the women brings fresh water with them. They run to the group, where Sigi stops to speak with Cunung and Alfons. Kaleia runs past the men to the children and immediately begins to look over Baldwin.

"Welcome to Gryfburg. Kaleia is going to help the boy." Sigi shares her water with Cunung, and Kaleia hands hers to Gregor. Kaleia pulls Baldwin close and gently looks at his wound, "The wound is hot. Let's go to my house. I can treat him there."

Inside Kaleia's home is a central room that serves as an office. A desk on one side of the room is near a closed door, and behind the desk is a small chest. In the center of the room is a small bed where Baldwin rests. Along the walls are many shelves filled with herbs, ointments, poultices, and other exotic ingredients helpful to a healer's work.

Kaleia hovers over Baldwin. The others are seated on couches near the door, which exits her home and goes to the garden outside. Two windows are on opposite sides: one above and behind a sofa and the other between two bookshelves.

"The drops should help with the pain in your eye, young man. It will hurt, but only for a moment." Kaleia opens Baldwin's eye with one hand and squeezes a cloth in her other. A single drop of some liquid falls from the fabric and lands in the boy's eye.

As it lands, he takes a deep breath but smiles immediately, "It doesn't hurt!"

Kaleia warns, "The medication won't last long, but it will help. I warn you, I can't give it often."

"It's okay, thank you!" Baldwin hesitates, clenches his fist in anticipation, then tries to open his eyes. "I can open my eyes again! I can see! It doesn't hurt!"

Gregor can't contain himself. He leaps up and runs over. Kaleia smiles and doesn't interfere. "Baldwin! You're okay!"

Baldwin looks at Gregor and smiles, "I can't believe it doesn't hurt!"

Gregor smiles, and the boys hug for a moment.

"You're courageous, young man. In any case, it would be best if you tried to rest. You still need to heal." Kaliea touches Baldwin's forehead and eases him back onto the couch. Baldwin nods and closes his eyes, trying to relax. Kaleia turns to the others, "It is good that you found your way here. The wound is severe, and I am very concerned about the infection."

Aileen runs to the healer and hugs Kaleia, "Thank you."

Kaleia seems apprehensive about Baldwin's condition. "We still have a long way to go. Can you please leave us? I will do what I can, but I need some time. If you are able, please return around dusk." Everyone stands up. Cunung nods and opens the door. He turns his head before leaving and looks to Kaleia, "We're running low on coinage. I can work to repay you."

Kaleia shakes her head. "We can figure something out later. Go, I will take care of the boy." Cunung smiles at her. "Thank you."

Everyone leaves through the door and follows a trail through the garden, back to one of the dirt roads through Gryfburg.

CHAPTER SEVENTY-SEVEN
HELPING HORST

The garden behind the home is well-tended and would be beautiful in early spring. Alfons and Sigi have laid out frames to cover the spinach, cabbage, and other vegetables that Alfons has planted for the winter. They have also set aside a tidy area and established soil to grow garlic bulbs.

In the background, Sigi plays a game with Aileen and Gregor. Their laughter echoes through the garden. Cunung tells Alfons, "I'm low on money and have little to barter. I need to find work to prepare for our journey. Do you know anyone who could use some help?" His voice carries with it a hint of apprehension. Alfons shoots a curious look toward Cunung. His eyes narrow with keen interest, "Perhaps. Tell me a bit about yourself, Cunung. What do you offer?"

Cunung shrugs and responds, "I'm a decent hunter. I can scout, clean an animal, and set traps. I'm good with most weapons. I prefer spears, but I can also use a sword or bow."

"You described most of the men in this town." Alfons thinks for a moment. In the background, Sigi stands with her eyes covered, counting to ten.

"I have an idea. A friend had a tough year. He's a trapper who wants to compensate for some setbacks before winter. He might be willing to pay, but only if you get him results."

Cunung nods, "That's fair. I'm in no position to negotiate."

Alfons laughs and replies, "Keep that between us. Let's visit Horst. He will be pleased to meet you."

Gregor hides in a nearby bush as he listens to the conversation. Gregor takes a keen interest in Cunung and Alfons as they prepare to leave. The two men pass beyond Gregor's view. Sigi taps Gregor on the shoulder. "Found you!"

Gregor jumps at first. He laughs and climbs from his hiding place. "All right, my turn to hunt."

Horst's home stands amidst a dense forest. It is a simple shack on the outskirts of Gryfburg. A trail leads toward the town through the yard—the only indication of a path to his home. Alfons leads Cunung down the narrow path toward the shack and calls out.

Alfons calls, "Horst. Are you home?"

Behind the shack, movement can be heard—a man with long white hair steps around the corner. He holds an axe. "Alfons! It's good to see you, friend. I'm just splitting some logs for the months ahead. What brings you to my home?"

Alfons smiles and approaches Horst with an outstretched hand. The two men shake hands. Alfons motions to Cunung and introduces the men: "Hello, Horst. I want to introduce you to Cunung. He's an expert woodsman, a master scout, and a trapper. He can help you turn this year around."

Cunung offers an outstretched hand, and the two men greet each other. Horst nods with a frown, "It's been a tough year. I could certainly use help. I may have something to offer once my fortune turns."

Cunung looks at Horst and gestures back toward the town of Gryfburg, "You have relationships with the people here. If you need the help, I am willing to take payment once you can arrange to sell what I acquire."

Horst looks at Alfons and laughs. "I like this man, Alfons." Alfons nods with a broad smile and responds, "He brought three children here safely from Riverview. He seems capable."

Horst raises an eyebrow. "You are from Riverview, Cunung?"

Cunung shakes his head. "No, Ulfreich. I was traveling when I met them." Horst seems astonished, "Beaumont is a long way from home. Why would you bring children here?"

"Someone kidnapped one of them, a girl named Aileen. Her brother needed help, so I went to find her. The boys were determined to join me. When we rescued her, we had arrived here." Something about the situation bothers Cunung.

Horst nods and seems curious. After a moment, he leaves his thoughts and opens up to Cunung. "I see. I need your help, Cunung. Something's been taking our traps. Fewer traps mean fewer animals are taken. My men and I have lost many wages this year. I'm in no position to turn away someone willing to prove himself. Can you do some scouting today?"

Cunung smiles and responds. "I can and will."

Horst sighs with relief. "Thank you, Cunung. Come back in the evening and let me know what you find."

Cunung nods.

Cunung calmly investigates the woods. He scans the ground around him and whispers, "Something's off."

He stops and kneels to look closer at the forest floor. There is a patch of disturbed soil. He touches it, pulls back his hand, and then rubs his fingers together. He stands up as oil-covered dirt falls from his hands. Cunung looks around as if expecting to catch someone, or something, stalking him. Cunung notices an area of disturbed vegetation and walks toward it.

He follows a trail of impressions in the soil. Circular holes that head deeper into the wood.

Cunung continues to follow the trail of strange prints. A few hundred feet down the trail, he hears a strange noise repeat.

Whir... tick... ***thump.***

Whiiir... tick... ***thump.***

Whiiiiir... tick... ***thump.***

Something heavy moves through the trees. Cunung places a hand on the katzbalger at his side and unsheathes it—a bronze shape glints in the sunlight just ahead.

Cunung steps into a clearing and sees the object, perhaps a creature, more clearly—a spherical central body with bronze legs that extend like a spider's. The contraption is about a span tall. It continues to whir as it wheels about to face Cunung.

Cunung takes a defensive posture as a funny-looking humanoid rushes between them. "Stop! Don't hurt her!" the humanoid faces Cunung pleadingly. Cunung's heart races as he takes a deep breath and looks at the person speaking to him. His hand still has a firm grip on the katzbalger.

Cunung looks shocked, "Me? Hurt that?"

The diminutive figure looks aghast. "*That*, as you so rudely put it, is Xtr-Nk. *She* is my friend and my creation. Please do not hurt *her*! Please!" He pronounces Xtr-Nk as Excetera Nak. Cunung narrows his eyes, lowers his blade, and takes a more neutral stance.

The creature breathes a sigh of relief, "Thank you."

Cunung asks, "Who are you?"

"I am Kl'kn. Your people call us the T'nKrnl; I am by trade a tinker." He pronounces Kl'kn as Keliken and T'nKrnl as Tin Kernel.

Cunung sighs. He sheathes his blade. "What are you doing here? How long have you been here?"

Kl'kn thinks for a moment. "I've been here a few months. I had to leave home, and I've been searching for parts to keep X running."

Cunung points to the robotic automaton and asks, "X?"

Kl'kn nods, "It's a nickname I developed for her. It's great! It increases efficiency by 80% each time I use it! Of course, I usually have to explain what I mean, but that will work itself out over time."

Cunung's eyes widen, and he nods. He then whispers, "Where is Jas when you need him?"

Cunung focuses on the metallic being behind Kl'kn. "Did you build X? That's impressive. She looks pretty beaten up, though."

Kl'kn nods enthusiastically, "We traveled from Barak A'Dun here. The terrain was rough, and we encountered many enemies along the way. There was wear and tear and aggressors! X was a dear. She protected me! Sadly, she was hurt in the process. I've been scrounging spare parts to help. I have been acquiring what I need to patch her up."

Cunung grins as the gears click in his mind. "You've been *stealing*." He corrects.

Kl'kn looks shocked and hurt, "Stealing? No! I have been repairing my friend!"

Cunung rolls his eyes and continues, "You mentioned *scrounging*. What kinds of things have you been *acquiring*?"

Kl'kn thinks momentarily and responds, "Nuts and bolts here and there. Mostly from rudimentary devices that have just been abandoned out here."

Cunung laughs. "Mind showing me?"

"Of course!" Kl'kn throws a level hand out horizontally and motions down with the hand as he commands, "Sit X." Xtr-Nk whirs and clicks as she kneels and crouches before Cunung and Kl'kn. The pair walk near her. Kl'kn points to an iron bolt on the side of the automaton.

Cunung looks closer at the bolt. "Where'd you *acquire* it from?"

Kl'kn thinks for a moment. "Just some wooden boxes lying around in the brush. They're just lying around abandoned out there, so when I find one, I take it apart and store the scrap at my camp nearby."

Cunung rubs his eyes in disbelief. "Let's take a look."

Kl'kn smiles, "You want to see my camp? Okay, come along, X."

The pair walk off further into the wilderness. The automaton rises on its legs and follows.

Piles of wood and metal clutter about Kl'kn's camp. In the center is a bedroll beside a prepared fire site. A strange popup lean covers the bedroll.

Cunung looks shocked at the great piles, "You've been busy."

Kl'kn nods. "Yes. Poor X took a beating to an Obviin. A monstrous beast! I was afraid she wasn't going to make it. I was able to patch her up, though. Good as new!" X sputters and backfires. "Almost as good as new."

Cunung looks through all the debris scattered around. "All this wood and the metal bits here."

Kl'kn looks up with an enthusiastic smile, "Yes! That's what I disassembled to acquire the parts to repair X."

Cunung picks up some of the boards. "There are ten or more traps here."

Kl'kn is puzzled. "Traps? Is that what those were? Seventeen, to be exact. Odd. Who would be setting traps around here?"

Cunung is amused at the short creature. "Trappers. A friend named Horst and his family. They might like to meet you."

Kl'kn's jaw drops. "Oh. I didn't mean to break their traps! I just wanted to fix X up."

Cunung smiles and shakes his head, "I get it. You were helping your friend. Can you stop stealing their traps now?"

Kl'kn gives a big nod. "Of course! I'd never steal. I may have to *acquire* parts to finish repairing her, though."

Cunung shakes his head. "*Acquire*? You mean buy them, but not from Horst's traps, right?"

Kl'kn smiles and nods again. "Of course! Unless I need the parts."

Cunung sighs and tries again. "You can't keep stealing from the traps, Kl'kn."

"I'd never steal! I *recycle*!" Kl'kn looks hurt.

Cunung pleads. "Please only *recycle* other people's things with their permission."

Kl'kn finally concedes, "Fine."

Cunung sighs in exhaustion, ready to move on. "Let's introduce you to Horst and his family."

Kl'kn smiles. "Yes, I would like that very much! Guard here, X. I can help fix their traps. I will not be taking any more apart. That is a certainty of approximately 82.178293% likelihood." Cunung and Kl'kn head out of the campsite. X begins to patrol the camp. "Unless it is *necessary*."

Cunung surrenders with a sigh.

CHAPTER SEVENTY-EIGHT

STALKER

K l'kn and Cunung arrive at Horst's home late in the evening. A fire burns inside his shack. Cunung calls out for the man. "Horst. It is Cunung. I brought someone to meet you."

"I've never had so many visitors in a single day." Horst opens the door and steps outside to greet Cunung.

Cunung flashes a grin, "Good evening. I've discovered what happened to your traps."

Horst seems excited, "That's great news!"

Cunung motions to the diminutive being standing beside him. "This is Kl'kn." Horst looks confused but smiles and nods to Kl'kn. "Hello, Kl'kn." Horst turns again to Cunung. "You said you know what's happened to my traps?"

Cunung sighs and nods. "Kl'kn is what happened. He didn't know they were traps and used parts of them to repair his friend."

Kl'kn looks apologetic. "I didn't realize they belonged to you. I can help repair them."

Horst is furious, "Help repair them? We've lost months because of you! Why? What were you thinking?"

A shadowy female figure moves through the woods in the distance, unseen by the three men. She draws close enough to listen to the conversation and hides among the trees.

Horst is a strong man. His fists are clenched in rage, and the veins of his muscular neck pulse as his face reddens. His jaw clamps tight, but somehow, he restrains himself as he speaks. This restraint speaks volumes about his character.

Kl'kn pleads, "I'm sorry. I was trying to save a friend."

Horst unclenches his fists and takes a deep breath. He turns around and puts a hand over his face. Several seconds pass in silence until he speaks again with a calmer tone. "I understand trying to help a friend. Will you help me now? My family could die over the winter if we can't restore the harm you have caused."

Kl'kn nods, "I didn't mean to cause you any harm! I will do everything I can to help!"

Horst nods. He turns back to face the T'nKrnl and offers a subdued grin. "Thank you. It may be too late, but we will try to recover from the hardships of this season."

Horst thinks for several seconds before he adds, "Let's not spread the news that you are responsible, little fellow. I don't know how some of the men might take it."

Kl'kn nods at Horst, who extends his strong arm in an offer of friendship. Horst's hand consumes Kl'kn's small hand as they shake in agreement. "I will bring your materials here with Ex in the morning, and we will fix everything."

Horst resigns to make the best of their situation. "Be careful out there, Kl'kn. Thank you, Cunung."

As Horst mentions Cunung's name, the shadowy figure slips into darkness.

"Thank you, Horst. I'll scout early tomorrow morning. Once Kl'kn repairs the box traps, I'll help place those. We can turn things around now that we've figured out the problem." Cunung looks at Kl'kn as he speaks the word problem, causing the tinker to blush.

A shadowy figure moves through the darkness. Her skin is covered in grey and black robes. She moves with impossible speed and grace.

She whispers to herself as she sprints through the dark wood. "Cunung has returned. She will be so pleased." The voice is soft and beautiful in the darkness. It is alluring and toxic, like a fresh, crisp apple tainted with strychnine.

The figure never slows as it weaves through the dark forest.

Cunung walks down a path through Gryfburg in darkness. Homes line the path on either side. Rushlights burn in some windows, but the streets are relatively empty. Cunung makes his way down the dirt road. The only light along his path is from the Lesser Light.

Cunung looks around and shudders. "It's a good thing the Lesser Light is bright tonight." Cunung reaches Alfons' home and turns to walk up to the entrance. He taps on the door and waits for an answer.

Alfons' voice calls from the other side, "Who is there?"

Cunung answers, "It's me, Alfons." He looks around nervously as if he senses someone watching.

The door opens, and Alfons smiles at Cunung. "How did it go?"

Cunung flashes a wry smile at Alfons, "Well. I found the problem. He has agreed to solve himself." Alfons looks puzzled, but Cunung laughs. "I'll introduce you two tomorrow. How are the kids? Is Baldwin here?"

Alfons nods. "Aileen and Gregor are well. We waited for you to visit Baldwin. Are you ready to go, or would you like to eat first?"

Cunung thinks for a moment before he answers. "I'm tired, and a hot meal is tempting, but I'd like to check on Baldwin first. Perhaps he could join us for dinner."

Alfons smiles at Cunung. "I hoped you'd say that. Come in. Let's get the others."

Everyone now stands on the path through the herb garden outside Kaleia's home. She answers the door and smiles. "You are late."

Gregor asks optimistically, "Can we see Baldwin?"

Kaliea nods and welcomes the group into her home. "Of course, step inside."

The group walks into the room and sees Baldwin sitting up. A bandage crosses diagonally from his left eye, where he took the blow down to below his right cheek and under the jaw. It wraps tightly and covers most of his face.

His left eye is covered. A bundle of some concoction causes the bandage to bulge out over it. "Hey, Gregor! Good to see you!"

Gregor runs into the room straight to Baldwin. "Hey Balds! How are you feeling?"

Baldwin smiles. "It hurts, but it's much better than it has been. Kaleia says the eye should stop hurting in a few days, but the wound will be sore for a while."

Aileen joins the conversation, "Baldwin! Hey! I'm sorry about your eye."

Baldwin grins at Aileen. "It's okay. Besides, someday, this will be an awesome scar, huh?"

Cunung laughs. "Calm down, Baldwin. You need to grow up some more before you start thinking about having good-looking scars."

Baldwin rolls his eyes and answers with a shake of his head, "On our way here, did you say I was brave?"

Cunung smirks, "I said don't do it again."

They laugh.

Cunung seems ready to get going. "Want to grab dinner?"

Baldwin replies with timidity, "I ate with Kaleia, sorry. Can I still come? It would be fun to spend some time together."

Cunung tries to encourage the boy. "We'd be grateful if you did."

Gregor agrees excitedly, "Yes!"

Everyone heads toward the door. Alfons invites his friend Kaleia along. "Kaleia, would you like to join us?"

Kaleia thinks for a moment but declines with a frown and a shake of her head. "You go ahead. I ate with Baldwin and need to plan some treatments for tomorrow."

Everyone leaves. Kaleia waves goodbye and shuts the door to her home.

Outside a small tent that looks like it belongs in a carnival, a campfire illuminates the silhouettes of two figures inside. A pair of young female voices speak with each other. "I am confident it was Cunung." It is the woman who stalked Cunung near Horst's home.

The other voice speaks. She appears to be the leader. "If you're lying, sweetheart, I will kill you. Slowly." The words come out with a soothing calm that belies her dangerous nature.

The stalker replies, "It was him."

With a sense of finality comes a response from her mistress. "Gryfburg. My sweet little puppy has come home at last. Thank you, Jezharielalynne."

CHAPTER SEVENTY-NINE
A Visit with Alfons

It's dark. A rooster crows in the distance. The entrance to The Jolly Gryf, a public house in Gryfburg, is illuminated with a reddish glow as the first rays of the Greater Light begin to peak over the horizon. The sky burns into life with reds, violets, and blues as golden radiance carves through the darkness.

The door to The Jolly Gryf opens, and Cunung steps out onto the porch. He pauses on the porch, rubs his eyes, and stumbles down the stairs. He walks down the main path, turns left, and heads toward Alfons' home. His mind is still foggy from sleep.

Cunung strolls up the path toward Alfons' house. One of the bushes in front of the home shakes as Gregor hides in it.

Cunung heads past the bush that conceals Gregor but continues toward the house. He smiles once he's past the young boy who lies in ambush. Cunung pretends not to notice Gregor. Instead, he continues to walk, his steps light and carefree, as though utterly oblivious to Gregor's presence.

Unable to contain his excitement, Gregor leaps from the bush and playfully touches Cunung with his stave. "Argh! He got me! He got me!"

Cunung, in dramatic fashion, feigns death. Gregor exclaims, "Aww, you saw me."

Cunung rises from where he fell and casts a cunning grin at Gregor, "It was a nice try, Gregor. I thought I'd play along. You're going to be a very stealthy hunter someday. This isn't that day." Cunung turns and smiles at Gregor. "You're up early."

Gregor nods wistfully, "Yeah! I was waiting for you. Can I go with you?" Cunung rolls his eyes, and the hint of a smile plays upon his lips.

"Didn't you have fun with Sigi yesterday?" Gregor tries to sound grateful for Sigi's excellent hospitality. "It's not that—Sigis's great. Going on an adventure with you is incredible, though!"

Cunung laughs and blushes slightly, "Oh yeah?"

Gregor nods. "Besides, I won't learn much playing hide and seek."

Winking at Gregor, Cunung quips. "You didn't learn much about hiding anyway."

Gregor briefly feigns being hurt by the words, "Hey!"

Cunung acquiesces, "Fine, you can come. Think Aileen wants to join us?" Gregor throws his head back with a smirk. "Pfft, she'll be fine here."

Cunung shakes his head sarcastically. "I need to speak with Alfons. Would you like to come with me, or would you prefer to try and set another ambush?"

Gregor shrugs. "I'll go with you. You'd be expecting it this time."

Cunung laughs.

The two head over to the door of Alfons' house. Cunung knocks on the door.

Cunung and Alfons sit at a table. Each man has a steaming cup of some dark liquid.

Alfons blows air over the top of his mug as he attempts to cool it more quickly so that he can drink. "You impress me, Cunung. I was very concerned about Gryfburg. Without Horst's contributions as a trapper, this would have been a very harsh winter, and many would have died. You brought a lot of hope to us."

Cunung smiles, "Glad I could help."

Alfons looks at Cunung thoughtfully. "Please reconsider staying here with Sigi and me. The children have missed you these past few days. Please stay here in the evenings." He speaks pleadingly as a grandfather might toward a beloved grandson.

Cunung shakes his head, "You're too kind, Alfons. I'll try to stop in more often. You know it's already crowded with the children. Besides, I've paid to board at The Jolly Gryf for the rest of the week."

"It's a nice place, but you should have saved your money." Alfons seems slighted by Cunung's refusal.

Cunung sighs. "I don't mean to offend you, Alfons. We're desperately low on funds, and I appreciate your offer. If I can't catch anything for Horst, we'll soon discover how crowded your house can get."

Alfons laughs. "It will be fine."

Cunung decides to change the subject. "I need a spear."

Alfons looks puzzled, "What?"

Cunung repeats his query. "I need a saufeder. I can use a sword, but am much more proficient with spears. Spears are better for hunting, anyway."

Alfons raises his head in understanding. "Ahh, I see! I don't own any. Wait, have you spoken with Evorik? He runs the smithy on the other side of Gryfburg."

Cunung nods, "I haven't. I'll find his place. Thank you, Alfons. I should go visit him now."

Alfons sighs and frowns at the sudden departure. "Won't you stay for breakfast with Sigi and me?"

Cunung shakes his head. "I need to get into the woods before it gets too late. Besides, if I start eating Sigi's cooking, I'll eat until I am worthless to anyone here."

Both men laugh.

Alfons agrees, "She can cook."

Cunung nods and rises from his seat. "Come on, Gregor."

Gregor runs over to Cunung. Aileen rushes after him, "Wait! Can I come too? Please?"

Cunung looks at her brother, "What do you think, Gregor?"

Sensing his sister's disappointment, Gregor looks at Cunung pleadingly. He hesitates between his desire for a quiet adventure and

Aileen's excitement. "I wanted to spend some time with you alone, Cunung."

Aileen frowns, turns around, and walks away with a broken expression.

Gregor huffs and rolls his eyes as he acquiesces. "She can come. I know how much she loves an adventure."

Aileen turns around and rushes back toward Gregor, practically bouncing with every step. "Thank you, Gregor! I love you!"

She hugs him, but his body sags as he refuses to hug her back. "You're just trying to get on my good side," Aileen says excitedly as she hugs him. "Yes!" The three head toward the back entrance to Alfons' home.

Cunung calls into the dining room, "We'll be back around midday, Alfons."

CHAPTER EIGHTY
THAT LOUSY HAMMER

Baldwin lies on the bed in the heart of Kaleia's infirmary. His body is covered in sweat, and his skin is fiery red. He tosses and turns, caught in the grip of a relentless fever. Kaleia hovers nearby, her face etched with concern.

She presses her hands against his forehead.

Kaleia mutters to herself, "The fever has grown worse."

She rises and walks to one of the shelves. She retrieves a mortar and pestle and several herbs. She takes these to a standing table and begins to crush them. There is a knock at the door. Kaleia opens it. Gregor stands at the entryway. "We are going with Cunung to scout. Would Baldwin like to go with us?"

Kaleia smiles at Gregor. "It was nice of you to think of him, but he's asleep now. He has a fever, and I am a little worried about him. Could you check on him when you return this afternoon?"

Gregor's eyes widen at the news of Kaleia's concern. "Is he okay?"

Kaleia looks somber. "I hope so, but the wound is severe. Go and enjoy your morning. If he's feeling well, I will send him to visit Alfons when he wakes up."

"Thanks, Kaleia." Gregor turns to leave. The door closes, and Kaleia returns to work on the curative mixture.

A man with short black hair arranges his equipment and prepares for the day. He wears a heavy smock and casually carries a crate full of scrap metal toward a furnace. The man is the owner of the smithy, Evorik. Above him is a wooden sign, charred and covered in soot. The shop's name, *That Lousy Hammer,* is inscribed on the sign.

Evorik runs the forge with two of his childhood friends, Jud and Timmer. He hired his friends to keep them out of trouble. The name of the workshop came about one morning when the mischievous duo bailed on work because they were hungover.

Evorik brought a miniature anvil to the street outside the men's home and began to pound steel until they woke up. The pair stumbled outside and yelled at Evorik, "Knock it off with that lousy hammer!" Evorik dragged them off to the workshop. He took inspiration from their complaint to name his shop as a reminder to the two friends never to risk another hangover on a work night.

Cunung approaches the man with Gregor and Aileen in tow.

Evorik sets the crate down and turns to face his visitors. "Good morning! I haven't opened the shop yet. If you have something in mind, I'm happy to discuss it."

Cunung approaches the blacksmith, "Do you have, or can you make a saufeder? Something sturdy?"

Evorik laughs. "Going hunting? You'll find only a few boar around here. I suppose that only makes the hunt more enjoyable."

Cunung chuckles to himself and nods.

Evorik thinks momentarily before replying, "I don't have anything on hand, but I can prepare something for you if you have a few days. It'll cost twenty silver coins in weight."

Cunung sighs and shakes his head.

Sensing the trepidation, Evorik queries, "Is something wrong? It's a fair price. You'll love the quality, my friend."

Cunung winces and hopes that he hasn't offended the man. "It's not that. The price is excellent, but I'm low on coins. I only have thirteen silver and twenty-two copper to my name. I'm working with Horst to earn my way. I plan to do some hunting to supplement the traps." His resourcefulness shines through his words and wins Evorik's respect.

Evorik's face lights up with a broad smile. "Ah, Cunung! Welcome to Gryfburg. I have heard of you from Horst. I'll let you have it for the cost. How about eight silver?"

Cunung smiles and shakes his head in wonder. "I don't know what to say. Yes, of course. Thank you."

Evorik beams a smile at his newfound ally. "No, thank you, Cunung! I'll have it ready to pick up in two days. I know how busy you've been since you got here. You'll find it hanging over there if I'm away when you stop by. Feel free to pick it up at any time."

Cunung looks like he's in shock. He retrieves the coins from a pouch, walks over, and pays Evorik. "Thanks, Evorik. I'll see you soon."

Cunung and the kids leave the workshop and head toward the forest.

Gregor grins at Cunung mischievously, "Someone's getting a reputation."

Cunung laughs and shrugs.

"I didn't think we would get such a late start." Cunung scans the forest floor and then points at the trunk of a great oak tree. "That's something you want to look out for." Gregor and Aileen walk over to look at it. They rub their hands along an area of the trunk where the bark has been scraped away.

Gregor turns his attention back to Cunung after inspecting the deer rub. "What's this?" Cunung's smile widens at the boy's curiosity.

"It's a deer rub. Bucks scrape their antlers against the trees, wearing down the bark. It's a sign of a good hunting spot."

Gregor smiles with bright eyes. "Oh! That's interesting!"

Cunung smiles back at the boy. "Yeah, it is. You're a smart kid, Gregor. You should share all the things you're learning."

Gregor wears a curious expression, "Share it?"

Cunung taps the side of his head. "Yes. I believe you could be a great teacher someday. Just a thought."

Gregor nods and thinks to himself.

Aileen cuts in with a quip, "His head's big enough already." Cunung laughs at Aileen's commentary. She notices his attention and says, "I want to hug the deer."

"They can be dangerous." Cunung reaches over and pulls a sapling down as he teaches them how to set a trap.

Cunung leads Aileen and Gregor back to Alfons' house for lunch. They turn the corner. Alfons opens the front door to greet them. "Welcome back! We've been waiting for you three. Guess who else is joining us for lunch today!"

Baldwin peeks around Alfons from inside the doorway. When he sees Gregor, he runs past Alfons and walks down the path with his friend. "Hey, Gregor! Did you catch anything?" Gregor shakes his head no. "Balds! Not yet. We just set them up. Are you feeling better?"

Baldwin takes a deep breath and nods. "A little. Kaleia said the fever had returned. She gave me something green and nasty." Baldwin makes a gagging face. "It helped. I do not want any more of that stuff, though. Did you see any deer?"

Gregor shakes his head. "Uh, no. Cunung showed me how to set a snare, though!"

Baldwin looks excited, "That's great! I can't wait to get back to Riverview. We'll have a new hobby for Old Gloamwood!"

Gregor smiles and nods.

Alfons welcomes everyone as they arrive at the doorway and enter.

The children sit on a rug in the corner of Alfons' dining room. Alfons and Cunung rest beside each other on pillows at a low table.

Alfons looks grim and whispers to Cunung so the children can't hear, "Can you turn this year around for Horst before winter? There are only a few weeks left before the snow arrives."

Cunung shrugs. "It's hard to know. I have only had two days to scout. It's late Autumn. If the deer are plentiful, they'll be active." Cunung thinks for a moment and shakes his head. "Unfortunately, we missed early Autumn, but I feel good about our prospects."

Alfons nods, satisfied with Cunung's answer. "You should check in with Horst after lunch. I bet he's eager to hear from you."

CHAPTER EIGHTY-ONE
A Lot of Traps

Horst towers over Kl'kn and watches the small figure work. Cunung walks toward the pair. Upon seeing Cunung, Horst waves. "Cunung! Come and see what our friend has done these past few days!"

Cunung quickly walks to the pair and looks down to see Kl'kn's handiwork. The T'nKrnl is inside one of the cages. He inspects it from within. A bronze dome-shaped device is affixed to a corner on the top of the cage—a transparent sphere and an antenna rise from the dome.

Kl'kn holds a wrench and tightens a bolt inside the cage. He finishes and crawls back out. Kl'kn stands. "Good afternoon! Do you want to see it in action?"

Cunung nods.

Kl'kn retrieves a long rod to trip the mechanism and triggers the trap. The sphere begins to glow a radiant yellow, and a familiar pinging sound comes from Kl'kn's toolbelt.

Kl'kn retrieves a familiar-looking device that pings repeatedly. The sound increases in pace as the device nears the trap. "This brilliant device will alert you the moment a trap is triggered! You may use it to lead you toward the trap." Kl'kn looks at Cunug to make sure he understands.

Cunung nods, and Kl'kn continues, "Once you have reached a distance where visual contact is possible, the luminance of the device should guide you directly to it. Remarkable, isn't it?"

Horst wears a broad grin. "What do you think, Cunung?"

Cunung looks at the device Kl'kn holds. It seems familiar. "I've seen something like this before." Kl'kn throws his hands into the air indignantly. "Impossible! This is a proprietary design; only my brother and I have legal rights to use it!"

Cunung shrugs with a grin. "Maybe someone *acquired* it?" Kl'kn glares at Cunung. Cunung ignores the evil look and continues, "A friend of mine had a device similar to this one. We used it to find Aileen." Kl'kn thinks for a moment. "I wonder. Never mind, we don't have time for endless speculation. What do you think?"

Cunung takes a closer look. "It looks interesting. The 'enhancements' may help, but only if I get the traps out there. Are we ready to start setting them up?"

Horst nods to Cunung. "Yes. I will stay here with Kl'kn and help him finish repairing the traps. My eldest son, Wigand, is preparing a cart we loaded earlier. He will help you set the traps out. Follow this path; he should be almost ready to go."

Horst points down a path toward a large shed. Cunung walks to the shed. As he arrives at the far side of the shed, Wigand harnesses a mighty white horse dappled with grey to a cart bearing five of Kl'kn's modified traps.

Cunung waves. "Wigand?" Wigand finishes tightening the last of the straps and turns to Cunung." You must be Cunung. It is good to meet you."

Wigand extends a hand, and the two men greet each other. Cunung asks, "Ready to set these traps?" Wigand smiles and nods." Let's get to work. Thank you for helping us."

The cart pulls alongside a worn patch of ground where the leaves and weeds have been scraped away to reveal soft soil.

Cunung throws up a hand to halt the cart. "Hold. Let's set one out here." Wigand pulls the reins on the horse he's guiding, and the two men take the second to last trap from the back of the cart. The Greater light hangs low in the sky.

Cunung asks a question he's been contemplating since they set out for the day, "Wigand. I am curious. Why does your family use these heavy box traps instead of snares?"

Wigand smiles. "We sometimes use snare traps, but only one or two. This region is infested with Schraega. Thrashing deer might attract them. Deer feel more secure in the box traps, so the risk of attracting Schraega is much less."

Cunung looks suddenly concerned. "Wigand, there may be a problem. I've been setting snare traps." Wigand laughs. "I'm sure it will be fine. How many can one man set in two days?"

Cunung bites his lip and cringes before he replies. "Thirty-seven."

Wigand looks surprised. "Thirty-seven?"

Cunung nods.

Wigand smiles. His eyes are wide in shock, and his smile is tinged with a bit of trepidation. "That is a lot of traps."

Cunung nods. "Yes. I was 'helping'. Let's set this one up and head back to your house. I'll return and start taking them down before dark."

Wigand laughs and agrees, "That may be wise."

Cunung and Wigand unload the large box trap and drag it into place. Cunung shakes his head and laughs under his breath while they work. "Schraega. Things keep getting better."

Wigand laughs. "Does such excitement always follow you around?"

The men have set the trap near the disturbed soil. Cunung opens a pouch and pours corn into the middle of the trap.

He turns back to Wigand with a big grin. "Yes."

The men lead the cart back toward Horst's house, with the last box trap still loaded onto it.

CHAPTER EIGHTY-TWO
NIGHT LIGHTS

Alfons and Sigi are in their cozy dining area. Aileen, Baldwin, and Gregor gather with the couple. They settle on soft cushions around a low table. A simple yet inviting meal awaits—a loaf of freshly baked bread, ripe fruit, and a succulent herb-roasted chicken.

Baldwin's heart sinks as he scans the room for Cunung. The absence of his newfound mentor weighs on him, and he can't help but feel a sense of loss. "Was Cunung planning to join us for dinner?" he asks, his voice full of disappointment.

Alfons frowns, "I'm sorry, Baldwin. I don't know. He has been swamped since you arrived."

Baldwin looks at the older gentleman with pleading eyes. The corners of his lips turn downward in a frown. "I haven't seen him since we arrived," he admits, his voice filled with sadness and longing.

Gregor pats Baldwin on the shoulder. "Sorry, Baldwin. We tried to get you this morning, but Kaleia said you shouldn't come with us."

"It's not your fault. I hate this stupid wound." Baldwin looks dejected. Sigi half-smiles at Baldwin, concern visible in her eyes. She cuts some of the chicken and places it onto one of the wooden trenchers with bread and fruit slices. Sigi hands the plate to Baldwin. "I'm sorry, Baldwin. I wish Cunung could be here with us tonight. I hope this meal brings you some comfort."

Baldwin takes the trencher and smiles at Sigi. "Thanks, Sigi. It smells incredible. What kind of fruit is this?"

"Late plums from our orchard. I hope you enjoy them." Baldwin grins and licks his lips. "I've never had a plum, but I love apples."

Sigi smiles. "You might like them. Taste and see."

Baldwin picks up one of the purple wedges and takes a bite. "Mmm! This is great!" Sigi begins serving everyone else in the room. Once she has set a place for each person on the low table, Alfons asks, "Shall we bless the food and pray for Cunung?"

Sigi nods.

Gregor thinks for a moment. He smiles and asks, "Can we please? Thank you."

"Father, thank you for our meal and for Sigi, who prepared it for us. We are grateful for your provision. Please protect our friend, Cunung, and bring him back to us safely."

Alfons looks up and smiles at the children.

Wigand leads the cart up the path toward the family's homes. Meanwhile, Cunung runs toward Horst's shack. Beside the shack, Horst cuts firewood. He turns to greet Cunung. "Welcome back Cunung."

Cunung skips the formalities of a greeting. "I'm sorry. Listen, I may have made a mistake. I didn't realize there were Schraega in this valley. I must disable the snare traps I've been setting out there."

Horst laughs a deep, rich sound that rises from his belly. "I'm sure it will be fine, my friend. You couldn't have set out more than a dozen since you've been here, right?"

Cunung grimaces slightly as he states, "Thirty-seven. I was concerned about the coming of winter." Horst's jaw drops. He puts a hand over his mouth in shock. Cunung notices that he has Horst's full attention and continues, "I'll take care of it now. I'm sorry."

Horst is flabbergasted, "Yes. Go, my friend. Thank you."

Cunung looks at the sky. Before he turns to leave, he asks, "Do you have a lantern? I may not have time to retrieve mine, and it may be a very late night."

Horst points to the large shack where Wigand is steering the cart. "Wigand can get it from the tool shed over there. Hurry."

Cunung races toward Wigand and the shack.

Cunung makes his way through the forest. He tries to move quickly, but it isn't easy through the brambles. He reaches a small clearing and looks for the snare he set earlier. He finds it and hastily pulls the sapling, which releases the trap. He slowly allows the sapling to reach its full height.

Beads of sweat roll down Cunung's face and drip from his chin. He's been at this for some time. "Twenty-eight. That should be enough for tonight. I'll get up early and check the rest. No way they'll all catch something."

Cunung has been working hard and looks exhausted. He turns and heads for the nearest trail back toward Gryfburg. He hears voices softly singing at night and quickly snuffs out his lantern. He begins to walk toward the voices. After a few seconds, lights can be seen floating through the trees.

Cunung whispers to himself, "What's that?" He tries to move closer quietly.

As he draws near the trail, he sees a group of slender figures ride toward Gryfburg mounted on smooth grey horses. The song's language is unrecognizable but sounds beautiful and haunting in the darkness.

A solitary figure leads the procession. Behind this figure is a line of eight others who follow in two columns. All share in the song. Voices of both males and females. Cunung steps quietly onto the trail behind them. As his feet touch the ground, every train member spreads out, draws weapons, and turns their mounts to face him. The motion is so graceful that it appears choreographed.

The leader dismounts and steps through a hole made by the others, holding a long, curved blade extended toward Cunung.

Four other similar silver blades are ready to engage him. Half of the procession are torchbearers, each carrying a silver blade. The remaining four each hold a bow with an arrow readied.

The leader's horse remains perfectly still. A testament to its discipline. Her voice breaks the still night air. "Who are you? Why have you been watching us? Don't think we haven't noticed you."

Cunung shakes his head. "I am heading to Gryfburg. I have been working late."

The leader sheathes her blade and pulls her hood back. Pale skin and dark hair appear from beneath. The moonlight strikes her hair, burning it with a silver light. Moonlight washes over her skin and reveals runes that glow vibrant blue from beneath the surface of her skin.

The sight catches Cunung off guard. He takes a deep breath. "Lumanesti? Here? My name is Cunung. I serve the Nachtulfen and Chancelmir. You are?"

She looks Cunung over and appraises the man's prowess. "I am Ilurien. You may accompany us on our journey toward Gryfburg. We will travel there tomorrow."

Cunung moves toward the procession leader. Two sentinels sheath their blades. The other two guards lower their blades and move directly behind Cunung and Ilurien as the ranks reform behind them. "Working? What kind of work keeps you so late?"

Cunung still bears a blush and looks at the ground in shame. "I've been setting traps. Well, triggering them." Ilurien smiles at Cunung. "Triggering them? Isn't that the job of the prey?"

Cunung doesn't lift his head but can't help but laugh at himself. "Yes, normally." Ilurien remains intrigued by the odd man she has discovered prowling around the woods. "And whoever laid these traps won't be upset?"

Cunung squirms as if caught in one of his own snares. "No. That was me as well." Ilurien has an amused expression. "You are a strange man, Cunung, who serves the Nachtulfen and Chancelmir. Why would you do this?"

Cunung laughs and then, with a sigh, continues, "It is a long story."

Ilurien laughs. It is soft and warm in the flickering torchlight. "Then you should begin now. We only travel a little farther tonight."

Cunung bows and replies, "Thank you, Ilurien. This tale started when I overheard a young boy frantically searching for someone to help find his sister."

Ilurien seems impressed by the man's candor and demeanor. "Interesting. Please continue."

Ilurien and her cohort have set up a campsite along the road near Gryfburg. Her horses are tethered to the trees in a clearing. White silken tents decorate the area. Blue pennants fly from the top of each tent. "You are welcome to stay with us. We have room."

Cunung smiles at the elegant Lumanesti. "Thank you, but I will go on to Gryfburg. I need to meet with my friends in the morning. I will let them know you are coming. It has been good to meet you, Ilurien."

Ilurien smiles at Cunung and nods. "I hope that we will see you tomorrow." Cunung bows to the Lumanesti. "I have much to do to help prepare for the coming winter, but I hope to see you as well."

He turns and leaves the camp to make his way back to Gryfburg. Once out of the torchlight, he reignites his lantern and continues.

Cunung walks down a dark path toward The Jolly Gryf. It's very late, and he looks exhausted. He reaches the perimeter of the light provided by the Jolly Gryf's lanterns. He extinguishes his lantern and continues walking toward the steps.

He wearily climbs the stairs and enters the building. The doors close behind him.

Somewhere deep in the forest, a snare is tripped in the darkness. A deer struggles to escape before the forest again falls silent.

A box trap is triggered. The light blinks on, and the deer panics as it struggles, banging against the box trap. A second and then a third box trap snaps shut. Each time, the light spooks a trapped deer until the forest is alive with the sound of deer crashing against wooden frames, trying to free themselves.

The deer settle, and the forest slowly falls silent yet again.

Until the night breaks into a din of goatlike screams, which echo through the night, only growing in intensity.

CHAPTER EIGHTY-THREE

THE OBVIIN!

I t's black. A familiar voice cuts through darkness and dreams. "Cunung." Cunung groans. Again, the voice voice squeaks, "Cunung, get up! Cunung. Cunung! Wake up! Cunung, wake up now! I need help! Cunung!"

Cunung slowly opens his eyelids. Kl'kn stands in the dim light of a dying fire from the fireplace in the common room of The Jolly Gryf. Kl'kn is shaking Cunung to wake him up.

Cunung is... *displeased.* "Kl'kn? What? What's going on."

"It's the Obviin! They've found me!"

Cunung floats somewhere between dream and reality. "The what?"

Kl'kn is in a panic. The Tn'Krnl's eyes flash wildly about the space. "The Obviin! They must have followed me from Barak A'Dun when I fled from T'kTkn. Oh, I have been so foolish. I should have known they'd never give up when they tried to kill me. I thought I was safe when X defended me, but..." Cunung cuts the tinker off, "Wait, you think the Obviin have come from Barak A'Dun to kill you?"

Kl'kn is shocked, "What else makes sense?"

Cunung takes a deep breath from the bed and tries to restrain his anger. After several long moments, he responds, "Most things? Do you realize how far they would have traveled to get here?"

Kl'kn thinks for a moment. "Haven't you heard their screams? They surround the valley!"

Cunung sighs. His resistance is fading. He decides it's better to get up and face the day than to face Kl'kn's silly assault. "What? You're not making any sense." Kl'kn is in a frenzy, "They're here, Cunung! Everywhere! Come outside, and I'll show you!"

Cunung's voice is full of resignation, exhaustion, and frustration. He is determined to help his newfound friend. "Fine. Let's go see what trouble you've stirred up now."

Cunung gets up and heads for the door.

Cunung and Kl'kn rush outside the Jolly Gryf and down the porch steps. Xtr-Nk is faithfully waiting for Kl'kn at the path. She begins to follow him as soon as he comes into her view. They reach the path, and Ilurien can be seen making her way toward the town square. In daylight, her pale skin contrasts her dark robe and black hair. Her piercing violet eyes focus on Cunung as she approaches. "Cunung. We have to talk."

Cunung's nerves are frayed. His sleep has been fitful and fleeting. The day is off to a terrible start. "Busy morning."

Ilurien ignores the quip. "The Schraega frenzy."

Kl'kn is relieved. "Schraega? Is that what the horrible screams were?" Ilurien responds dismissively, "Yes."

Kl'kn smiles. "Oh! Thank goodness, I thought that was an army of Obviin coming to kill me!" Ilurien is becoming perturbed. "No, Schraega are much worse." Kl'kn is thrilled. "Yes, but they aren't trying to kill me!"

Cunung and Ilurien look at the T'nKrnl with shock. Cunung shakes his head. "How bad is it?" Ilurien motions toward the woods with her hand, "We've heard at least ten distinct voices from our camp near Gryfburg."

Kl'kn nods, "The screams woke me up this morning. I'm so glad it wasn't Obviin. Thank you, Ilurien."

Ilurien turns from Cunung and glares at the short Tn'Krnl. Her voice is measured but decidedly full of anger. "You do understand that the Schraega may kill us all?" Kl'kn is too relieved to notice her wrathful glare. "Oh yes, of course! But it's not Obviin. I thought they were going to kill *me*."

Cunung cuts in again before the conversation devolves further. "I'm going to wake Alfons. He knows Gryfburg and can help us get this information to the right people. Kl'kn?"

Kl'kn cuts a curious look at Cunung, "Yes?"

Cunung's gaze pierces Kl'kn. "Stay with me and try not to cause any more trouble." Kl'kn blushes but nods. Ilurien cuts in, "I'll go with you. In case Alfons has any questions."

Cunung smiles at the Lumanesti princess. "Thank you."

The three rush off toward Alfons' house. Xtr-Nk faithfully follows the trio.

Cunung sprints toward Alfons' house and knocks on the door. He waits a few seconds and strikes the wood again. Movement can be heard from inside. Alfons arrives and opens the door. Kl'kn, Ilurien, and X arrive. "Cunung? What's going on? Is something wrong?"

Cunung points toward the woods. "The valley is alive with Schraega's screams." It takes a moment for Alfons to process, and when reality sinks in, Alfons looks serious. "The Schraega are in a frenzy."

Cunung nods.

There's a commotion from behind Alfons. Gregor runs through the room behind Alfons and bursts through the doorway. "Hey Cunung!"

Cunung greets the young boy but tries not to allow distractions. "Good morning, Gregor." Gregor suddenly notices Kl'kn and Ilurien. "Whoah. What are you?"

Kl'kn's eyes pop open in shock, "Have you no manners, boy?"

Gregor blushes, "Sorry, but I've never seen a... We've never met before. Hi, I'm Gregor." Kl'kn seems slightly less insulted. "That is a little better. I am Kl'kn. A T'nKrnl."

"Cool." Gregor fails to hide his astonishment. Ilurien seems to find this adorable. She speaks first in her native tongue, Ithwei, "Anu menwe en'Gregor." She repeats in perfect Saeldring, "Good morning, Gregor."

Gregor's eyes are giant orbs. His mouth is wide open. "Wow."

Cunung grows more irritated and tries to get the conversation back on course. "Gregor, this is Kl'kn and Ilurien. Everyone, this is Gregor. Yes, Alfons, it seems they are in a frenzy." Gregor doesn't take the hint and continues speaking with Ilurien. "Hi Ilurien. It's good to meet you."

Cunung gives Gregor a sharp look. Ilurien winks at Gregor and gently places a delicate index finger across her lips, indicating they should remain quiet for the moment. Gregor nods enthusiastically. Cunung turns his attention back to Alfons, who asks, "Cunung, will you see if you can uncover what caused this?"

Cunung agrees with Alfons' proposal. "Yes. Warn the townsfolk to prepare, Alfons. I'll be quick. Kl'kn, go to Horst and see if he has any thoughts."

Kl'kn runs off to find Horst.

Cunung turns to the Lumanesti, "Ilurien, will you help defend the town."

Ilurien nods. "Yes, I will summon my company."

"Be careful, everyone." Cunung rushes off to investigate.

Free from restraint, Gregor turns back to Ilurien and asks, "What is a Schraega?" Smiling, she answers, "Come with me, Gregor. I will explain along the way."

Gregor and Ilurien run back toward Gryfburg.

CHAPTER EIGHTY-FOUR
THE OLD BEAR

L umanesti hastily pack their belongings. Ilurien tightens the saddlebag containing her gear. The screams of Schraega continue to echo through the forest.

Gregor stands nearby. "Anything else I can do to help?"

Ilurien smiles but shakes her head. "No, thank you, young Gregor. We have time for questions now if you still have any." Gregor beams a smile. "What's a Schraega?"

Ilurien nods. "Ah, yes. Dangerous creatures. If one were standing still in thick woods, it might be mistaken for an Adam. Until it moved."

Gregor is enthralled. His eyes lock with Ilurien's own. "Make no mistake, the Schraega is a deadly foe. They move with swift, leaping strides. Carried along on legs like a goat, they rush with little concern for their safety."

A threatening scream pierces the air from somewhere nearby.

Gregor looks over each of his shoulders, "Are you scared?"

Ilurien smiles at Gregor. Erohuil, the lieutenant in her company, joins the two. "Ene ishil eth ibhuilen, in'elwe." - "The company is prepared, my lady."

She nods at her lieutenant. "Let us return to Gryfburg and see their defenses, young Gregor. Will you ride with me?"

Gregor looks at her with amazement. "Yeah! I've never ridden a horse before!" Ilurien points to a stirrup. "Place your left foot there and step up." Ilurien holds Gregor's hand and helps him onto Nibhiel, her mighty steed. She softly whispers to the animal, "Anu il'envi." It remains calm and sturdy as a statue while the young boy climbs onto his broad back. Once Gregor is seated, Ilurien effortlessly climbs onto her creature. "Are you ready?"

Gregor nods. Ilurien clicks her tongue once and strikes the reigns. Nibhiel surges forward. The company follows her toward Gryfburg.

Kl'kn runs down the path toward Horst's shack. "Horst! Horst!"

Horst is talking with his son Wigand near the large shed. They both turn and head toward the shack to meet Kl'kn. "Kl'kn, is everything okay?"

Kl'kn is in his usual panic, "It's Schraega! Cunung said they were frenzied!"

Horst nods. "Yes. I was talking to Wigand about them." Kl'kn points toward his camp in the woods, "I heard them! I thought they were the Obviin. I'm so glad it wasn't."

Horst looks confused. "I don't know what Obviin are, but Schraega are deadly creatures, Kl'kn."

Kl'kn tries to pull Horst into his mania, "Oh, the Obviin are terrible! Mighty and with great big heads like a bull!" Horst isn't so easily distracted. "Kl'kn! Not now. Where is Cunung?"

Kl'kn apologizes, "Sorry, Horst. He went to scout out what happened."

"Good. Can you help us gather our things? We are heading to town to help prepare the walls for raids." Horst shakes his head and sighs. "This is a nightmare."

Kl'kn is visibly upset. "Yes. I hope I didn't cause this trouble."

Horst laughs under his breath. "Don't blame yourself, Kl'kn. I know you are trying to help. I will gather my family, and we can return to town."

Kl'kn smiles at Horst.

A box trap is broken in the clearing where Cunung and Wigand ended the previous day. Wooden splinters, soaked in blood, litter the ground. The bronze dome is flattened. The transparent orb lies shattered on the loamy soil. The only trace of the deer is a bloody trail that leads off into the woods.

Cunung kneels and sifts through the shattered pieces of the trap. He then picks up the device that Kl'kn had attached to the traps. "We can't win."

Cunung stands back up and heads off to check the other traps.

Alfons walks quickly down the streets of Gryfburg. He comes to a grand manor near the center of the town, turns into the path leading to the house, walks up the steps, and heads right in. He walks to the unoccupied desk of the Bürgomeister and picks up a large, silver bell on the ornate desk. He begins to ring it. The manor fills with the loud clanging of the great bell.

After several seconds, Alfons stops. Movement can be heard from down a long hall. The voice of the Bürgomeister echoes, "I'm coming, I'm coming! Just don't ring that infernal bell again!" Alfons cries out impatiently. "Hurry! It might be an emergency!"

Heavy footsteps echo down the hallway, and an older man plods toward the office. He holds his head and stumbles toward the lobby. His motions suggest he was up late drinking. "Alfons! What is all this about? What do you mean this might be an emergency? It either is or isn't! I was dead asleep, and with all that noise, I may very well have ended up just plain dead!"

Alfons throws his hands into the air, "The day is young. Wait to count it as a missed opportunity. The Schraega are in a frenzy."

The Bürgomeister gasps. "What? Are you serious, Alfons?" Alfons frowns and nods. "Yes. You should rally the landholders and have them prepare a defense." Bürgomeister Urso sighs. "I doubt that's necessary."

"At least bring them into the main square. Just for a day or two to be safe." Alfons pleads for the townsfolk. Urso tilts his head back and raises a long, bushy eyebrow. "And just live here?" Alfons glares at the man. "Yes, for a day or two. In the safety of the walls, just like you are currently doing."

Urso huffs. "Oh, you can't be serious."

Alfons balls his hands into tightly clenched fists. He stares angrily at the man who should be taking responsibility for the people of Gryfburg, but his rage goes unnoticed. "I am. I'm going to see the constable." Urso throws his arms into the air and lets out an exasperated sigh. "Fine! I'm going back to bed!"

The old Bürgomeister stomps back down the hallway.

Alfons angrily shakes his head. "Miserable old beast. Never cared for anyone but himself."

With that, he turns and stomps out of the office.

CHAPTER EIGHTY-FIVE

UNVEILING THE UNKNOWN

Alfons crosses the street with urgency. His eyes are fixed on the constable's office, only a block away. A figure in a chain shirt emerges in the distance, striding purposefully towards the square.

Alfons waves him over and continues past the office. "Constable Weibald! I need your assistance!"

The man notices Alfons, waves, and heads down the street toward him. "Hi, Alfons. What's this?"

Alfons rushes to meet the man. His voice trembles with urgency. "The Schraega have frenzied. The valley is alive with their screams!"

Constable Weibald looks grim, "Why? What happened?"

Alfons shrugs, "We don't know. Cunung has gone to investigate. He's the man who has been helping Horst." The constable decides, "I'll check on the families to the east. You check on the families on your side of town. Let's convince everyone to spend the night in town."

Alfons nods and grins at the constable. "Thank you, constable. I will. I told crusty-butt in there the same thing. I think he's been drinking, the worthless old coot."

The constable laughs under his breath. "Has anyone ever told you you have a fiery temper, Alfons?"

Alfons bats down the accusation with a swipe of his hand. "Bah. Let's go rally the townsfolk before we get raided."

Both men rush off in opposite directions.

Urso has finally roused from his slumber and recovered from his hangover. His face is etched with anger and frustration. Alfons, Evorik, and Jud, one of Evorik's assistants, stand nearby. Urso paces the street in the heart of Gryfburg. His steps are heavy and thunderous. He moves like an enraged bear. "This should never have happened, Alfons. Who is responsible for this chaos? I demand answers!"

Alfons's voice brims with frustration. "We're still in the dark, Urso. A man named Cunung has gone to investigate." The old bear's steps falter, his anger palpable. "Who? Who is this Cunung? He's no citizen here." Alfons's eyes roll in exasperation, and his voice carries weariness. "No, he's not. He arrived with three children several days ago."

Urso turns and stomps away, "Well, I never met the man."

Alfons spits, his voice laced with a hint of anger. "Of course not. He's been busy trying to help Horst. Help us all!" Under his breath, he adds, "Something you should have been doing for months."

Urso turns back with a glare, "What did you say?"

Alfons dismisses him with a wave, "You can meet him when he returns. I shouldn't have sent him out there to investigate alone."

The bürgomeister is taken aback. He places a hand over his chest and huffs, "You did what?"

Alfons allows him to continue with his theatrical charade. "He went to see if he could find out what caused this mess."

Urso huffs a loud harumph.

There is a commotion beyond the defensible wall of the square.

Sigi calls out from beyond the gate, "Alfons! It's Kaleia and me. We brought Aileen and Baldwin." Again, Urso feigns offense at the unknown names, "And who are they?"

Urso's name is fitting. The old bear practically growls at Alfons as he asks the question. Alfons ignores him and opens the gate to allow them inside. "Quickly, into The Jolly Griff. Urso, these are two of the children that were traveling with Cunung."

The sight of the children quells Urso's fury. His face reddens slightly from his outburst. "I see. Hurry along, children. You will be safe inside." The tranquility is shattered by hooves pounding on the hard ground, growing louder from the nearby path.

Evorik offers, "Shall we close the gate? It doesn't sound like Schraega." Jud agrees, "Can't be too careful."

Evorik and the other man move to close the gate. Alfons stops them. "Wait. Horses."

Alfons points. Ilurien's company marches into view through the trees. Gregor rides with Ilurien. The company of Lumanesti strides toward the town square.

Alfons motions toward the company. "Ilurien."

Urso's anger once again grows. "And who is Ilurien? Do I even know anyone in this town anymore?" The company of Lumanesti spurs their horses on. They pass through the gate and move beyond Alfons and the others. They turn to face Alfons and gracefully dismount.

Ilurien approaches Alfons. "Where is Cunung?" Alfons replies, "He has yet to return."

Urso throws his hand up into the air in surrender. "And who are you?"

The Lumanesti meets Urso's glare with her own, "Ilurien, celestial observer, downcast, seeker of luminaries." Urso shrugs and shakes his head. "What?"

Ilurien ignores Urso, except to echo his own words back to him. "And who are you?" Urso is flustered. "I'm Urso, bürgomeister of Gryfburg. In name only, it appears, given that I am the only person who doesn't know any of these new arrivals."

Alfons tries not to laugh. He covers with an attempt at diplomacy. "I'll explain everything later, Urso. They are here to help. Gregor, this is Urso. He's the leader of the town."

Urso huffs.

Gregor steps forward and offers to shake Urso's hand, "It's nice to meet you, sir." Urso sighs and greets the boy with a handshake. "Nice to meet you, too, son. Do you know what's going on out there, Ilurien?"

Ilurien looks past Urso toward the forest and sighs. "Not with certainty. We heard Schraega's screams all night. At least ten voices were present, but we have not seen any."

CHAPTER EIGHTY-SIX

A COMING SIEGE

Horst's family is on a trail that marches from the homestead toward Gryfburg. In addition to Horst and Wigand, the two men's wives are also on the trail. Five other sons of Horst and twelve grandchildren also travel along with them. Two of Horst's sons, besides Wigand, walk with their wives.

Horst leads alongside Kl'kn. Wigand walks behind him with the reins of one of the family's horses.

There is the sound of movement in the nearby trees. Horst lifts his ax and moves toward the sound. It stops momentarily as the train of people and animals continues behind Horst. Wigand hands the reigns to one of his younger brothers and rushes over to stand beside his father with an arming sword drawn.

Horst shouts, above the commotion of the travelers in motion behind him, "Who's there?" There is no answer. The train of people continues past Horst and Wigand.

Several tense seconds pass.

A chilling scream comes from nearby.

Leaping hoofbeats resound

the tree line

terrifying form

bursts through brush

muscular creature

vague shape of a man

leaps bounds

toward Horst

long, triangular face

shaggy goatee.

wicked horns rise

crown of its head

curve back

a crude stone axe

charges for Horst

leaping – powerful, hooved legs

hooves dig deep

into the soil

kick up dirt

bounding steps

deadly vault

Horst sees it coming and pushes Wigand aside. "Run! Protect the family!" Wigand cries out as he stumbles out of the way, "Dad!"

Horst lifts the axe, focused and ready for battle. "Go, son! Now!"

Horst swings overhead

tries to defend

all that he is

from the fall

axe blade digs

creature's gut

hooves strike

Horst's chest

crushing down

into loose soil

The Schraega screams as it lands on the man. Horst's axe has disemboweled the creature. It makes a few hobbled leaps toward Wigand but drops the stone axe and collapses at his feet.

Wigand rushes back to his father. "Dad! Dad!"

Horst is pale. His breathing is labored. His lips are stained with blood. "Son. lead the family." He raises a feeble hand to point toward the train of family members, which has stopped. "Dad, no!"

Horst smiles at Wigand. "It's... okay, son."

Wigand's brothers have rushed back and stand over Wigand and Horst. Wigand looks to his brothers and says, "Let's get him to Gryfburg. Maybe Kaleia can help."

―――――――――

Cunung's voice calls over the wall. "Alfons, it's Cunung. Open up. I am back." Alfons moves to open the gate to the town. Cunung appears on the other side. He draws a cart carrying three deer. Cunung enters the town.

Alfons greets Cunung, "Did you encounter any Schraega?"

Cunung shakes his head. "No. We did catch four deer."

Alfons smirks, "That's good news. Where is the other one?"

Cunung shrugs. "Something attacked it before me. Whatever it was, it destroyed the trap and probably killed the deer. When I got there, nothing was left."

Alfons asks gravely, "Do you think it was..." Before he can finish the question, Cunung answers, "Yes." Unable to contain himself, Urso steps into the unfolding conversation. "So, you're the one who started all this? Those traps set them off, didn't they?" Cunung gives the man a stern look but doesn't answer immediately.

Alfons answers for him, "Urso! This man is a guest, and if he did something to cause them to frenzy, I'm sure it was an accident."

Urso huffs. "That kind of accident may cost us our lives. Cunung, if anyone is hurt, you'll be held accountable."

Cunung flashes a dangerous glare at Urso. "Right now, we don't have time for this. Rally the men and ensure we can hold the square."

In the distance, Horst's family approaches along the road to Gryfburg. Horst is crumpled over atop one of their horses. Wigand leaves his father to the other sons, who help to steady the man. Wigand rushes toward the town square, calling out. "Keleia! Someone bring Kaleia! Please! Hurry!" Evorik rushes inside The Jolly Gryf.

Wigand returns to help steer the horse into the town square.

Inside The Jolly Gryf, everyone awaits news about Horst. Kl'kn stands beside Cunung and whispers to his friend, "Cunung?" Cunung answers back in a low voice, "Yeah, Kl'kn?"

Kl'kn pauses a moment, almost afraid to say the words. "I know what happened." Cunung nods. "Yeah. Me too." Kl'kn winces. "Lx'trk?" Cunung looks down at the small figure with pity. "If you mean your device, then yes. Don't worry. I won't tell anyone."

Kl'kn frowns. "What happened?"

Cunung sighs and rubs his chin. "The light spooked the deer." He offers a sympathetic frown.

Kl'kn looks at the floor with tear-stained eyes. "It is my fault."

A minor assembly gathers in Gryfburg Square. The gate is closed again, and most of her citizens have moved into the public house. Horst lies in the center of the square, pale and taking labored breaths. Kaleia and his family surround him.

Kaleia kneels beside Horst, examining the damage to see if she can help. Rosalie lies crumpled beside her husband, opposite Kaleia. She holds Horst's hand. Rosalie takes turns kissing Horst's hand and pressing it against her cheeks. She lies against him in anguish.

Wigand looks to the healer, "Is he okay?"

Kaleia doesn't answer. Horst tries to speak, but his words are barely audible. He reaches for his son, Wigand.

Wigand kneels beside Kaleia and takes Horst's hand. Horst looks at his son with proud eyes and tries to smile. "Take care of Rosie..." Wigand presses his father's hand against his forehead. Tears flow down Wigand's cheeks and fall onto Horst's abdomen.

Rosalie asks through her tears, "How bad is it? Kaleia, please?"

Kaleia shakes her head. "I'm sorry, Rosalie. I'm so sorry."

Horst coughs. "...love you... Rosie."

It breaks her. Rosalie cries out. "Oh, sweet Horst. I love you, too."

Horst looks at Rosalie and smiles. Somewhere in the distance, an eagle cries. He tries to speak again, but the words choke him: "Thank you... you and the children... for my life."

Rosalie collapses onto her husband's chest. The man's breathing slows, then stops.

Rosalie cries.

Kaleia closes Horst's eyes. Tears stream down her face. "I'm so sorry, dear."

Darkness falls upon the town of Gryburg. Screams come from all directions around the town.

Norèaldur and Lumanesti move along the top of the wall with torches burning against the sky. A pair of Norèaldur guards the gate with bows drawn. Ilurien's Lumanesti archers have spread out. Each takes a cardinal direction and watches for threats. Their eyes flash blue light when they catch the moonlight.

Cunung stands with Alfons and Wigand in the center of the town square. "I'm sorry, Wigand." Wigand is crushed beneath the weight of loss and new responsibilities. It was those snares. They killed my dad."

Cunung looks to Alfons and shakes his head. "Wigand, I'm so sorry. I was trying to help." Wigand balls his hands into fists. "You did this, Cunung!" He throws his face into his hands. Long white locks of hair curl over his fingers. He begins to cry. "I'm sorry. It's not your fault. I just..."

Cunung grabs Wigand and hugs him. He tries to comfort the man. "I know. I know."

From atop the walls, the voice of the constable calls out. "Here they come! Be ready, men!"

The screams grow louder. Norèaldur men near the gate draw, aim, and loose arrows. Around the town square, more men throw arrows at the Schraega.

There is a resounding crash like thunder as the creatures kick at the town's wooden gate and stone walls.

Axe blows can be heard chopping away at the fortification.

CHAPTER EIGHTY-SEVEN

THE FIRST ATTACK

Horst is dead. His body is wrapped and sits in the middle of the town square. Rosalie stands at his head. From atop the wall comes a shout. The voice is Evorik, "They are in retreat! We must be ready for another assault; don't be complacent!"

Some of the townsmen have assembled near Horst. They lift his body and carry him to one of the watch towers' cellars. Rosalie leads the way to the tower, mourning as she walks.

The Schraega continue to scream from somewhere outside the walls. Gryfburg's defenders rush around in the background, making hasty preparations. Norèaldur and Lumanesti, stationed on the wall, watch the open fields outside the town for any sign of a more significant assault.

Occasionally, a lone Schraega steps into an open area before the walls or along a path. Any which venture too close are peppered with a hail of arrows.

Rosalie leads the men carrying Horst into the cellar.

Cunung stands with a group of men who plan Gryfburg's defense. A ring of trees surround the town in the distance. The form of a Schraega appears in the open areas spaced throughout the line of trees. Its eyes are focused on Gryfburg, burning with malice.

Defenders line the walls of Gryfburg. Norèaldur and Lumanesti forms rise above the stone walls, presenting alluring targets for the creature's rage. Most of the Norèaldur wield halberds, arming swords, or bows. Four of the Lumanesti are armed with bows. The others are armed with shashka and glaives.

Several minutes pass until Rosalie and the pallbearers march out of the cellar. Constable Curtis Weibald is waiting outside. He hands Rosalie the ax that Horst used to defend his family. "This is yours by law and tradition. I am sorry, Rosalie."

Rosalie takes Horst's ax and holds it near to her chest. "Thank you, Curt. I'm going to help the others prepare." The constable nods, then turns and hastily walks toward the steps leading up to the walls. He rejoins the defenders and watches for any sign of a renewed assault.

Rosalie rushes off toward The Jolly Gryf.

The constable looks up to see one of the Lumanesti, her gaze fixed on the woods. Moonlight catches her eyes, and they flash dazzling blue momentarily before the moon disappears behind the clouds. The constable shudders as he reaches the top of the wall. Cunung approaches him.

Constable Weibald shakes his head at Cunung as he approaches. "They still give me the creeps, Cunung. How their eyes and skin glow in the moonlight isn't right." Cunung chuckles to himself. "I understand, but they are here to help."

The constable looks defeated. "Cunung, how well do you know Ilurien? Are you sure we can trust her?"

Cunung shakes his head. "I don't know her. I know of her, and I can assure you. If this is Ilurien ev'Ythuir, we need her and her cohort."

Curtis Weibald finds no consolation in his answer. "And is she?" Cunung shrugs. "We've never met before, but she fits the description. I believe she is."

The constable sighs. "I wish I had your confidence. I have a terrible feeling. Death draws near us. I feel its presence everywhere, but I see nothing if I look around. I cannot take it in my hand, nor can I confront it. There is no reason for my fear, yet it troubles me." Cunung smiles and pats the constable on his shoulder. "Curt, we don't have much choice at the moment."

Ilurien storms up the stairs to join the two men. She nods to each of the men. "Cunung, I have spoken with each of my scouts, but there has been scarcely any motion since the last assault. Something seems wrong."

Cunung nods. "I agree. The Schraega are preparing something. If anything, they are cunning creatures."

Oriel, one of the Lumanesti scouts atop the wall, calls out. "They test the south wall!"

Four Schraega rush north toward the walls from a wood line to the southeast. Meanwhile, several other Schraega stand far beyond range and observe the assault.

The other Lumanesti scouts quickly maneuver toward the southern wall of the town and unleash concentrated volleys at the Schraega, which charge toward them.

Men of the town armed with bows rush to assist. A Schraega falls to a volley of arrows. They cover half the distance to the walls when a second stumbles and collapses to arrows that rain down upon the group.

There is a sharp, cracking sound of stone against stone as something beats against the southern wall of the town.

Rosalie cradles Horst's axe as if it were her husband. She has a look of fierce resolve. She takes the axe as a weapon and walks toward the door. Berun, Rosalie's youngest son, takes his mother by the arm. "Mom, please stay. We lost dad, we need you."

Rosalie's face falls, and she bursts into tears. She drops the axe, and it crashes to the ground with a heavy thud. Rosalie turns and embraces her son. Her body quakes as she begins to wail for her lost love. Berun cries with her. "It's okay, Mom. It's okay. I love you."

The remaining Schraega close the gap and powerfully leap toward the wall. One of these clambers up and pulls itself onto the top of the wall near Cunung. As it begins to rise, Cunung slips the blade of his katzbalger beneath the creature's neck and kicks its lifeless body off the wall. "Evorik! Where's that spear? It would be a fine day for it!"

Evorik laughs and calls back from the other side of the south wall. "Oh, you know. It's just lying around. I should finish tempering the head!"

Cunung grins but presses, "This katzbalger is only helpful if they breach the walls." Evorik shrugs and laughs. "Then let's hope it stays useless!"

Cunung laughs.

The last of the Schraega strikes the wall repeatedly with a heavy axe. The stone axe takes more damage than the wall.

The Schraega backs up to try and leap onto the wall. It proves to be a lethal mistake. The Schraega steps into the field of fire and is quickly cut down by concentrated arrows thrown from Ilurien's scouts.

The constable shouts, "Barricade any building we can in case they breach the walls."

Cunung nods. He shouts to Alfons below, "Yes! Alfons, can you see to it?"

"Yes, just make sure our efforts are unnecessary."

Alfons rushes inside The Jolly Gryf.

Sigi runs toward him. "Alfons! Is everything okay? Is there anything that we can do to help them?"

He hurries to answer and begins to organize those in the public house. "Yes! A Schraega made it to the top of the walls. Cunung killed it, but we should gather anyone not engaged in the defense into The Jolly Gryf or Urso's house."

Sigi asks, "Places they can't set aflame?"

Alfons nods. "Yes! Once everyone who isn't fighting is sheltered in one of those buildings, we can start to fortify the entrance. If the Schraega breach or climb over the walls, the defenders will pull back into The Jolly Gryf. We will make our stand here."

Sigi frowns at the thought, but she nods. "Kaleia, Rosalie, and I will get everyone into the buildings. You take anyone you need and begin gathering materials to fortify them."

Alfons motions for everyone to hurry. "Come, let us prepare. I hope we don't need it."

Baldwin, Gregor, Kl'kn, and Horst's sons follow Alfons. Everyone else joins Sigi, and they all leave The Jolly Gryf.

Chapter Eighty-Eight
Final Preparations

Alfons pounds against the stone door of Urso's manor. It is locked to prohibit the Schraega from reaching the Bürgomeister.

"Urso! Open up immediately! We need more room!" Alfons' voice echoes with urgency. "Urso! If you don't open this door, we will tear it off the hinges! Open up now!"

Several seconds pass, and Alfons starts to pound on the door again when the sound of a lock working can be heard. After another moment, the door opens. Urso stands at the door. His voice trembles with fear. "Fine. Bring them in, but be quick about it! Those beasts could get inside at any moment."

Alfons catches a whiff of smoky sourness and heat in Urso's breath. He is appalled, "Have you been drinking?"

Urso stammers as his voice cracks with emotion. "Uh, uhm. No. I may have had a tipple to settle my nerves."

Alfons shakes his head. His disappointment is palpable. "You should be ashamed. You ought to be out here, leading these people!"

Urso pleads with Alfons, "You know I'm not good in a fight. I'm more of a thinker."

Alfons' frustration turns to rage. "Why don't you **think** of a way to stop the Schraega? Or at least protect the people of this town!"

The bear huffs and tries to regain an offensive posture in the conversation, "Oh, you make it sound..."

"I don't have time. Lives are at risk. We can talk tomorrow. If any of us survive." Alfons turns and walks away, leaving Urso to *think* of a response.

Alfons stops to give instructions to Barun before he rushes away toward Evorick's workshop. "Try to fit as many women and children inside as you can. We need every one of the men who can fight out here. Send them to Cunung, Ilurien, or Curtis for arms and instructions."

Alfons turns and rushes off to the workshop. Urso steps outside with a finger raised toward Alfons to demonstrate some witty retort, but it's too late. He's gone.

Urso drunkenly wanders off to try and catch up to him.

Cunung prowls at the top of the wall as he scans for any sign that might give away the Schraega's plans. He looks very concerned about what just happened. Constable Weibald walks alongside him and looks even more nervous about their situation. "What is going on out there?"

Cunung's face is grim as he looks toward the constable. "No idea, but something felt wrong about that last attack."

Curt's hands tighten their grip on his halberd. "What do you mean?"

Cunung points into the distance, "Did you see the watchers? That was meant to expose our weaknesses. They are probing to see what works." The constable suddenly realizes, "They're looking for a way to get in?"

Cunung nods. "I think so. They're beasts, but cunning beasts are very dangerous." Curt asks, "What comes next?" Cunung stops for a second and looks at the constable. He shrugs. "I don't know."

Evorik races to his workshop with his assistants, Jud and Timmer.

Jud is the first to speak as they quickly move toward the shop, "You know we won't have time to finish Cunung's spearhead before the next assault?" Evorik laughs, "Not the point. All the old stuff we never sold? Tonight, it'll all see some use."

Timmer half-grins, "Hold, even the cast-offs?" The man looks excited—perhaps a bit too excited. Instead of calming him, Evorik directs the energy toward a purpose: "If someone can't swing it, throw it, or wear it, we will use it to barricade. Just help me carry it out!"

Timmer flashes a grin, and he nods. "Yes, sir! Hey Jud, I could get used to this Evorik."

Evorik opens the doors to his workshop as Alfons makes his way up the path with four other men to help move materials and equipment from the shop.

Inside The Jolly Gryf, the flames that once warmed the hearth have been extinguished. Their absence leaves the room in chilling darkness as much of Gryfburg's population prepares for a possible siege. Outside, metal can be heard scraping against stone as men move makeshift barricades into position to create a maze through which attackers must funnel themselves.

Women and children still enter the building and huddle together in the back. Aileen stands beside Sigi near the entrance. Rosalie and Kaleia are beside the wall on the opposite side of the doorway.

Sigi looks around the room and realizes that someone is missing, "Aileen, where are Gregor and Baldwin?" Aileen points at the door, "Baldwin wanted to help Cunung. He left to find him. Gregor was with him."

Kaleia looks upset. "What? Baldwin should be here! He has no business roaming about, especially with that injury! Oh, that boy."

Aileen grins. Sigi looks at Aileen quizzically. "What is it, Aileen?"

Aileen shrugs, "It's just not like Baldwin."

Sigi shakes her head. "Should we go chase them down?"

"I'll go. Can't be too careful." Kaleia rushes out of the entrance, looking for the two boys.

———————

Baldwin and Gregor run toward the wall when a curious, ticking sound distracts them.

Gregor looks excited. "What's that sound?" Baldwin grins at his friend. "Do you want to find out?"

Gregor answers, "Yes! Let's go!"

Instead of heading up the stairs to find Cunung, they turn and head down the street toward the noise.

They turn a corner and almost run face-first into Kl'kn, who is walking with X to find Cunung. "Whoah, whoa, whoa! Watch where you are going, young man! What are you two doing out and about? The town is under attack! Wait, I know you!"

"Hi! Uhm, Kl'kn?" Gregor offers. "Yes, and you are Gregor. Does Cunung know that you are wandering the town?"

Gregor looks for a way out: "We were going to find him, but we..."

Baldwin chimes in for his friend, "We heard your thing making noises and wanted to see what it was!"

Kl'kn seems annoyed once again at the callous treatment of his creation, "*It* is an autonomous servant. *She* is my friend. *Her* name is Xtr-Nk. Now, *who* are *you*, boy?" Baldwin nods. "I'm Baldwin. I'm a friend of Gregor."

Kl'kn fusses, "You both could learn some manners, but we have no time now. We should find Cunung. I need to see where X and I can best assist the defense. Let's go now."

The boys turn back and head around the corner with Kl'kn. The four of them rush up the stairs of the north wall and turn toward the eastern wall to find Cunung.

CHAPTER EIGHTY-NINE

DEFENSE OF GRYFBURG

The Lesser Light hangs high in the air. It is a large and ominous waning gibbous.

Tension hangs in the air.

Norèaldur defenders look nervously around atop the wall as the Lumanesti scouts stand a stoic vigil.

Suddenly, the night erupts into terrifying screams.

South of Gryfburg, forms begin to break forth from the tree line into a pouncing charge toward the south gate.

"Attackers! They come against the south wall!" The voice of Oriel, one of Ilurien's scouts, cries out from atop the wall.

The defenders rush toward the south wall to mount a defense. Almost everyone focuses on the southern assailants when a mass of fur and horns breaks from the forest to the east of Gryfburg. A second force, consisting of over a dozen Shcraega, charges the eastern wall.

Immediately, there is a shout from Pyruil, another of the Lumanesti scouts.

"More come from the east!"

Cunung curses under his breath. "Curt, hold this wall. I'm going to help with the attack from the east." Constable Weibald nods. He looks into the distance and raises an arm. Norèaldur and Lumanesti begin to lift their bows, then draw. Everyone holds their draw. "Loose at will!" The constable shouts. Archers release arrows, which rain down upon the Schraega force.

A pair of Schraega along the left flank immediately drop. Archers redraw their bows. A handful of arrows fall into the charging Schraega. A third beast tumbles beneath the charging mass. Its wild screams of pain trail off as the rest of the attackers near the wall.

The remaining creatures leap toward the south wall. Their hooves bite into gaps between the stones, and the Schraega scramble toward the top of the wall.

Constable Curtis Weibald calls the men nearby, "Engage them before they secure footing!" The constable rushes to the edge of the wall and makes a sweeping strike, cutting deep into the neck of one of the Schraega. It topples backward and falls from the wall, but the creature's weight wrenches the halberd from Curt's hands.

The constable regains his footing and draws his sidearm, but it is too late. A second Schreaga has topped the wall and gores the man in the throat with its deadly horns. It picks him up and thrashes its head back and forth, throwing the man over its back and off the wall outside of Gryfburg.

The constable's spirit is mercifully gone before his body touches the ground.

Alfons and Evorik both try to move into position to kill the beast, but it leaps off the wall and rushes into the streets of Gryfburg.

A third Schraega scrambles on the wall as a militiaman swings a halberd at the creature. The creature grabs the weapon's haft with both hands and lifts the man off the ground.

The man begins to scream before the silver blade of a glaive carves through the back of the Schraega, which causes the beast to drop the halberd and collapse upon the stone wall of Gryfburg.

One of Ilurien's sentinels looks over the Schraega's corpse, smiles, and nods at the militiaman.

Urso prowls the streets near his home in a frenzy. "Alfons! Where are you? Blast it, man!" Urso stomps north toward the makeshift maze of metal debris that impedes the way to The Jolly Gryf.

He begins to navigate the crates, metal bars, and other hazards as he seeks his opportunity to get in one last jab.

Urso shouts into the darkness. "Alfons! Constable Weibald! Cunung! Anyone?" Hoofs clap against the stone behind the Bürogmeister.

The man turns around and sees a Schraega. The creature charges at him.

Urso screams, "Noooo!"

Cunung races toward the eastern wall and sees Baldwin, Gregor, and Kl'kn running down the wall toward him. Cunung shouts a warning, "Kl'kn! Lookout, Schraega!"

Cunung points out toward the east. Kl'kn looks to his left, and his eyes grow wider. "X! Target lock. Arm ordinance. Aggression level alpha. Fire at will."

X stops moving and turns to face eastward. A hatch at the top of the spherical body opens, and a slender folding rod extends. A dart-shaped device rests atop the rod. A ticking noise begins as the rod traces the incoming group of Schraega.

The ticking noise stops.

Sparks begin to spray from the tail of the dart-shaped rocket.

The missile doesn't move.

Kl'kn leaps into action to save his mechanical friend. 'No, no, no, no!" Kl'kn rushes to Xtr-Nk with his wrench raised over his shoulder like a misshapen war hammer.

The spray of sparks halts. Kl'kn swings his wrench like a baseball bat, striking the rocket and sending it catapulting through the air toward the group of Schraega. The missile falls harmlessly to the ground and bounces twice before it halts a few span ahead of the main force of the Schraega.

Kl'kn sighs in relief and brushes the sweat from his brow, "Whew. That was close."

The rocket explodes with surprising force as the first of the Schreaga steps over it. The blast vaporizes the first Shcraega and sends two others careening backward and to the side.

Gregor's lips curl up into a smile. "Whoah. That was awesome!"

Everyone on the east wall turns to appreciate Kl'kn for a brief moment. The diminutive figure blushes. "It should have flown there! My calculations were... I'll explain later. We don't have time! X arm all systems. Engage at will."

X leaps with joy. The rods that held the rocket retract, and more slender rods extend. X is armed with an autocannon and a device that crackles with blue arcs of energy in the air. The autocannon begins to focus on the group of creatures.

Kl'kn turns to Baldwin and Gregor. "We should go back. *Now!*" Kl'kn shoos the boys back toward the stairs.

Gregor seems upset that he'll miss the excitement but agrees. "Oh, fine!" Baldwin, Gregor, and Kl'kn turn to flee back toward the stairs leading down into Gryfburg Square.

Kaleia rushes up the stairs and sees the boys and Kl'kn. She flashes a glare at them as she races toward the group. "Baldwin! Get back here! You know they could attack at any moment!"

A Schraega with bloody horns and hooves rushes toward Kaleia as she runs up the stairs. She reaches the boys, who are pointing at the creature. The Schraega tops the stairs and begins to charge.

Cunung once again shouts a warning from the far side of the town's walls. "Look out!" Kaleia turns around and realizes the danger. She interposes herself between the boys and the creature.

Kl'kn commands Xtr-Nk, "X, new target."

Ilurien begins to whisper and move her hands in an enigmatic pattern, weaving light and energy into existence. She is a calm force among the raging chaos that surrounds her.

"Enuthil r'yshva." She whispers, but the words explode into the world. A blast of wind surrounds Ilurien, who stands near Cunung at the far end of the eastern wall.

A series of fist-sized meteorites crash from the skies, each striking the charging Schraega. In total, seven strike the beast. Each fierce blow slows it until, at last, it collapses and slides to a halt, a mere span from Kaleia.

Ilurien winks at Cunung. Her eyes radiate a fierce blue aura in the dim glow of the Lesser Light.

Kaleia grabs both boys' hands, and they rush back toward the stairs with Kl'kn. "X follow!"

The tinker frantically orders the automaton, but it's of little use amidst the confused melee surrounding them.

A Schraega has clambered onto the wall between X and her fleeing companions. She targets the creature with her autocannon. The barrels whir into action, unleashing a burst of metal bolts that pepper the beast and drive it back momentarily. The bolts leave red, hexagonal welts all over the creature's chest but don't have the energy to cause lasting harm. The creature realizes it isn't dead and charges forward. It grabs X by one of the legs and lifts it off the ground.

Kl'kn realizes he can do nothing and rushes off with the boys and Kaleia. They scramble down the steps and toward the entrance to The Jolly Gryf.

The Schraega takes another of X's legs and tries to pull the automaton apart.

X brings taser to bear

strikes Schraega chest

creature lets go

she crashes down

a terrible clatter

More Schraega take the eastern wall, and a fierce melee begins. Kl'kn reaches the entrance of The Jolly Gryf and looks back to check on his friend. "X to me! Please!"

The enraged Schraega roars and stomps on X's spherical body.

a whirring sound

she ceases to move

kicked from the wall

She crashes into the street near The Jolly Gryf.

"No!" Kl'kn wails in sorrow.

Baldwin grabs Kl'kn and pulls him into the doorway.

Chapter Ninety

Gryfburg Shall Stand

Cunung charges over the eastern wall. The Schraega that destroyed X looks up and begins to bound along the wall toward Cunung. Three Lumanesti sentinels and four militiamen join Cunung in the charge.

Pyruil unleashes a final arrow toward the Schraega that still charge toward the wall. The arrow sinks into the chest of a Schraega as it leaps toward the wall. Its body smashes against a stone and tumbles back to the ground. Pyruil throws down his bow, draws a finely crafted saber, and follows the others charging into the fray.

Schraega begin to pull themselves onto its battlements along the wall's length, breaking the charge into several distinct melees. The militiaman behind Cunung stops to engage a Schraega standing between the two men.

He strikes the Schraega in the left arm. It is severely injured and enraged by the blow. The beast lowers its head and butts the militiaman. The force knocks him off balance. He drops his halberd, falling from the wall into the street below. The creature snatches the halberd from the ground and charges toward the next defender, one of Ilurien's sentinels.

The sentinel is distracted, fighting another Schraega. The blade of the glaive sweeps across his opponent's thigh, which staggers backward.

The glaive turns and gracefully carves upward across the chest and through the neck of the beast, which topples backward.

A moment later, the body of the sentinel is flung off the wall by the mass of a mighty halberd blow from the wounded Schraega. He falls from the wall and out of the city into the dark field. The vibrant blue glow of his eyes fades as he descends into darkness.

Cunung reaches the far end of the wall and strikes the Schraega that destroyed X. Ilurien desperately tries to reach Cunung but has only made it halfway down the wall.

Cunung's katzbalger pierces its belly, and the creature absorbs the blow. It grabs Cunung and continues to charge. It leaps with Cunung off the wall. Together, they crash down onto the street below.

"Cunung! No!" Ilurien leaps from the wall onto the roof of a nearby building. She runs along to see where the pair crashed from the wall. There in the street lies a mound of fur. Cunung is visible beneath the creature. The pile is motionless. Ilurien's face falls, but there's no time to mourn the man's loss.

Instead, she scans the wall for someone she can help. The Schraega, with the halberd, cuts down another of the militiamen.

She hears a groan from the street below—Cunung fights to free himself from beneath the Schraega's corpse.

"He's alive!" Hope fills Ilurien's eyes. She looks back up at the wall. The Schraega, armed with the halberd, hears Cunung as he struggles on the street below. Hope once again fades. "No, no, no." Ilurien begins to compose energy. "Inir ethilwe, ishin. Eb il eth onorim."

The beast screams and charges toward Cunung, who manages to pull himself free of the corpse and tries to stand. He struggles to get to his feet.

Ilurien continues concentrating on weaving arcane energies together, "Mirono hte li be. Nihsi, ewlihte"

Schraega leaps from the wall

Halberd raised over its head.

It crashes toward Cunung.

Ilurien's words distort time in a sphere around the Schraega. "Rini!" With a pop, the Schraega vanishes from the present. Ilurien shouts down to the dazed figure below her, "Cunung! You have five seconds!"

Cunung groans in pain. "Ugh, what?"

"Temporal reset. Three seconds. Get off the X!" Ilurien frantically tries to warn him. Cunung shakes his head to regain his senses and steps toward the wall. A Schraega screams from above.

A great form leaps over Cunung. A halberd slams down hard where Cunung stood seconds before.

With the last of his strength, Cunung thrusts his blade deep into the creature's back. It screams one last time and collapses to the ground.

Cunung falls to his knees.

Cunung and Baldwin stand talking with Wigand. Cunung looks mournfully at his friend. "I am sorry, my friend. My commitment to help remains."

Wigand shakes his head. "Thank you, Cunung. You impressed my dad. I said it was your fault, but I was just..." Wigand trails off. He can't complete his thought. Cunung places a hand on Wigand's shoulder. "I understand. It's okay, Wigand. It's okay to be angry. I would understand if you hate me."

Wigand can't speak. He shakes his head as his eyes fill with tears.

Aileen, Gregor, and Kl'kn are speaking with Alfons and Sigi. Horst's other sons and grandsons surround Rosalie.

Alfons tries to speak, but his voice breaks up. "He wasn't an evil man. He... he didn't deserve that."

Sigi hugs him from the side, comforting her beloved. "I know, I know."

Alfons scolds himself. "I shouldn't have called him crusty-butt."

Aileen puts a hand over her mouth. It's too late. She laughs, which causes the others nearby to laugh as well. When they regain their composure, Sigi intercedes for Alfons. "No, sweetheart, but let's be honest. There is a chance, however small, that he was being a crusty-butt. Urso could be like that sometimes. He knows you were friends and didn't mean anything."

"I know. I'm sorry. I don't know what to say. I didn't think anything would happen to Urso." Alfons laughs through his tears as Sigi tries to wipe them away. The group shares more rueful laughter as the grandfatherly man fights to keep it together.

Other survivors of the Battle for Gryfburg slowly make their way up the ancient road to gather near the large burial mound.

Evorik walks alongside Kaleia. "I'll miss him, you know."

Kaleia nods. "Curt was a good man. We should remember him with gratitude for serving as our constable and all his good deeds."

Evorik nods. He turns to Kaleia and smiles. "Can we have dinner sometime? Forges are just one type of flame I know how to work."

Evorik winks, and Kaleia smiles back at him. "We will see about that. I'll bring some herbs from the garden."

He pumps his fist. "Yes!"

Once the crowd has gathered, the conversations meld into an incoherent roar. Several seconds pass before Alfons calls out over everyone else: "Everyone! We are ready to begin!"

The roar continues as the man tries to take control.

Alfons cries again, "We are ready, everyone! Hey! Shhh!"

The crowd slowly begins to quiet a bit.

Cunung releases a sharp whistle, which pierces the cacophony. "Alfons is ready!" The air falls silent.

Alfons looks to Cunung and smiles. "Thank you."

Alfons clears his throat and begins. "A few days ago, we lost many friends and family members who were very dear to us."

Baldwin looks up to Cunung and smiles with pride. He's thankful to have met someone he considers a mentor and friend. Alfons continues the eulogy, "Some never left our little town. Some had only just arrived. They touched my life. I am sure their loss leaves something missing from our lives."

Alfons pauses. "I'm sorry. I didn't think it would be this difficult."

The man takes a moment to compose himself. "We should all be grateful for the precious time we were gifted to get to know them. I'm sorry, that's all I can say. Thank you for coming."

Alfons starts quietly weeping and wiping tears away. He turns back to Sigi. She holds his head, kisses his cheek, and hugs him tightly. "It was beautiful love." She again kisses his cheek.

One by one, a procession forms as people make their way to visit their loved ones inside the burial chamber. A fresh stone rests against the mound's entrance. The names of the fallen are inscribed on the stone's surface.

Heroic citizens, fallen in our defense:

Horst Ulfart, Constable Curtis Wiebald, Hort Vieger, Bürgomeister Urso Grefner, Tyren Ereben, Hevert Ereben, Launs Thormet, Traede Van Lofren, Jeren Wilsham, Meorit Vefen

Below are written the names of heroic allies fallen in our defense:

Xtr-Nk, Yriel Uvenuir, Aranuir Evaleon

Horst's family remains alone in the burial chamber.

Rosalie lights a lamp. Her children gather alongside her. Wigand hands her Horst's axe. She holds the lamp in her left hand. Horst's axe rests on her right. She walks to the tomb. Others form a line behind her.

Rosalie's sons carry bags of corn to remember their father's trapping skills, and Horst's daughters carry snowdrop flowers to mourn their father's absence.

The procession moves slowly inside to the patriarch's tomb. As it makes its way forward, Rosalie sings softly.

Why o mount,

   dost thou stand strong?

For my beloved

   has left the throng.

Why, o sea,

   must thou still rage?

With my beloved

   cast from the stage.

Rosalie pauses here, trying to recompose herself before entering the mound. Wigand places a hand on her shoulder to comfort her.

Why, o Lord,

must I still stay?

When my beloved

has gone away.

She steps into the burial mound to say goodbye.

Evorik stokes the fires of his forge. Cunung walks toward the shop. When Evorik notices, he waves and greets the man. "Cunung! It's great to see you, friend!"

Cunung looks eager for whatever business he has. "Is that spear ready yet?"

Evorik motions to the rack near the side of the workshop. "Yeah, I just finished it up yesterday. Feel free to grab it off the rack over there."

Cunung walks over to the rack. "Is this a joke?"

Evorik looks puzzled. "What do you mean?"

Cunung holds up a beautifully carved wooden stave. "It's just a staff."

Evorik stops what he's doing and walks over. "Where's the head? It's no joke, Cunung. It's a beautiful spearhead! One of my greatest works! We must find it!"

Evorik looks all over. "I'm so sorry, Cunung, it was right here! I need to figure out what's going on."

Cunung flashes a grin. "It's okay, Evorik. I have an idea. Can you make another one? I'll pay as soon as I can."

Evorik is apologetic. "Uh, yes, of course! I'm sorry, Cunung. I don't know how this happened."

Cunung laughs and claps the man on his shoulder. "Thanks Evorik."

CHAPTER NINETY-ONE
A New Adventure

S moke rises from a stone-lined pit in Evorik's backyard. A metal grate is raised on stone piles at each corner above the smoke pit, and various meats are laid out to roast.

Evorik and Kaleia laugh in the small clearing as Cunung approaches the couple. Aileen, Gregor, and Baldwin play near a line of trees at the edge of the clearing. Alfons and Sigi stand across the fire pit, talking with Evorik and Kaleia.

Evorik sees Cunung approaching and calls out. "Glad you could join us!"

Cunung offers lightheartedly, "I wouldn't have missed seeing you cook Evorik. Have you burned anything yet?"

Evorik laughs at the jab. "Nothing yet, but there's still plenty of daylight. I am surprised the forest loosed its grip on you; I never see you anymore."

Cunung sighs and nods. "I know! I am sorry, friend. We are in a much better position now. We can do this more often. There are still a few months before we must leave."

Alfons grins at Cunung. "Time together would be a nice change."

Sigi nods in agreement.

"And your room? Are you ready to abandon the common room of The Jolly Gryf yet? I know you have done well and have plenty of coins, but we have the room available for you. Please reconsider Cunung." Alfons again offers boarding to Cunung.

Sigi chimes in here. "Alfons is right Cunung. Stay with us. It would be an honor to host you for the remainder of your stay. I know the children would enjoy having you there as well."

Cunung thinks for a moment and nods. "I would be grateful for the room if you are sure it's not an imposition. I'll let Ghert know I won't need to board next week. Thank you both."

Kaleia smiles. "It will be good for Baldwin. He misses you, Cunung. See how well his wound is healing! He does nothing but talk about you. You have made quite an impression on the boy."

Cunung takes a deep breath and frowns. "I hope I haven't set unrealistic expectations of him about how life is supposed to be. I fear I have dragged them into something I wouldn't wish upon any child."

Everyone shakes their heads dismissively. Alfons motions toward Baldwin. "Children should yearn for their lives to mean something. You're inspiring them. Someday, that young man could be your most outstanding achievement."

Cunung looks at Baldwin and smiles. He then turns his attention back to Alfons with a grin. "How does it feel to be a Bürgomeister? I've been meaning to congratulate you."

Alfons sighs. "Eh. The manor is enormous. It's also lonely. I prefer the cozy life that I built with Sigi. I'll keep the title as long as Gryfburg needs me, but someone else can take over soon." Alfons grins and looks at Cunung.

Cunung waves it off with a great laugh. "Don't even think it. I can't settle down anywhere for too long."

Alfons laughs. "I tried. At least the manor gives us extra space to share. Your little friend seems to enjoy the solitude as well. He has remained in the room I lent him in the manor for days." Alfons thinks for a moment. "I do wonder what he's doing in there."

Cunung smiles.

Evorik takes a long fork and flips each large roast on the grill. "Looks like we're getting close."

The adults lounge at a table, continuing to talk as they finish their dessert. Aileen, Baldwin, and Gregor play near the edge of the woods. Baldwin looks around. Convinced no one is paying too much attention to them, he asks, "Want to explore a little? We don't have to go far."

Gregor grins, "Yeah, Aileen, are you in?"

Aileen looks excited. "Sure! Let's go!"

The three children walk off into the woods. As they make their way, Baldwin grabs a stick shaped like a sword and strikes it against trees like he is fighting monsters.

Gregor watches Baldwin with some concern. "Baldwin, be careful. You're still healing."

Baldwin sighs. "Oh, come on. I'm just having fun. Why are you so worried?"

Gregor raises an eyebrow. "You're kidding, right?"

Baldwin laughs. "I'm fine, Gregor. Kaleia took good care of me."

Gregor sighs. "Alright, alright. Let's get those Boglins!" Gregor picks up a long stick that could be used as a stave. He runs over and begins poking the trees. "Take that!"

Aileen laughs as she watches Baldwin and Gregor play. "Look out, Gregor! It's a griffin!" Gregor looks up. "Oh no! It's got me." Aileen's sing-song voice echoes through the woods.

Gregor found a griffin nest.

A griffin spurred him on his quest,

stabbed him once and made him rest,

still as a wooden doll.

Gregor looks at Baldwin. Baldwin shrugs. "Just go with it."

She continues with the next verse.

Gregor tumbled from the sky.

How I wished that he could fly

because I thought he might die

when that griffin made him fall.

Aileen laughs. "Help Gregor! It's coming for me now!"

Gregor laughs. "Oh no! Aileen! We're coming!"

Baldwin and Gregor rush over to rescue Aileen from the imaginary griffin. They begin striking the air above Aileen with their makeshift wooden weapons while running in a circle around her.

Gregor cries out, "You got it, Baldwin!"

They stop running around Aileen, and everyone settles for a moment.

Aileen pants. "That was close."

Baldwin looks around, then motions forward. "Yeah. Let's keep going."

They walk a little farther before Gregor stops them. "Hey, what are we doing?"

Baldwin rolls his eyes and laughs. "We're playing Greg."

"No, what are we looking for? Or are we trying to save someone? What's the adventure." Gregor rolls his eyes.

Baldwin lights up, "Oh!"

They stop for a moment.

Aileen has a thought. "We should go find ancient armor for Baldwin."

Gregor looks excited at the idea. "Sure! Let's go!"

Baldwin cheers, "Yes!"

The kids march further into the forest.

CHAPTER NINETY-TWO
LOOKING FOR TROUBLE

Everyone rests at a wooden table near the grill in the clearing. Evorik, Kaleia, Alfons, Sigi, and Cunung enjoy a pleasant conversation. Cunung's gaze shifts towards the tree line. His heart skips a beat as he realizes the kids are missing.

Cunung takes a moment to scan the clearing—a peaceful glade in the heart of a dense and foreboding forest. He stands and asks in a steady voice, "Has anyone seen the kids?"

Sigi scans the tree line where they had been playing. "They were playing make-believe. We can go look for them."

Cunung asks, "Evorik, do you mind staying with Kaleia in case they return?" His voice is full of concern for the children for whom he has become a steward. Evorik nods and looks concerned at Kaleia. The others rise and begin to walk toward the woods.

Aileen, Baldwin, and Gregor race through the woods to search for the cavern where the Blackguard Vondru has taken the relic.

The heavy plates of Baldwin's armor clink together as they bounce with his sprinting strides. Gregor's robes flow in the wind as he runs alongside the bold knight.

A small and vicious Boglin charges. Gregor extends a hand. "Kashakabammm!" A bolt of energy crackles with power as it flashes toward the creature. The creature wails as the bolt strikes it. The force of impact shakes the canopy throughout the forest.

The air fills with the smell of burning ozone. The sound of the impact reverberates in their ears.

The creature freezes in place, transmogrified into just another of the great trees in this forest. Another Boglin rushes from the other side, blindsiding the powerful magi. Baldwin intervenes. His mighty sword strikes the creature, turning it into a tree. "Take that!"

The children laugh as they roam through the forest.

Aileen calls for them to halt. "Wait! I see it! The Blackguard went in there!" She points toward a cave entrance.

The group stops running and walks over to the dark opening. In the darkness, there is the sound of heavy breathing. The voice has a chilling echo that sends shivers down their spines. Something beckons from within the pit. It is sinister, oppressive, and dark. Barely audible above the rustling of leaves, it whispers, "Yes. Come, children."

They take a step back and look at each other.

Aileen looks at her brother. "Did you hear that?" Gregor replies, "Yes. A voice?"

Aileen nods.

It calls again—a deadly whisper from the shadowy hollow. "Don't be afraid. Come closer. I need to see you. Touch you."

The kids take another step back. Their faces contort with fear and curiosity. They are terrified of what might emerge from the abyssal hole in the world.

———

Cunung, Sigi, and Alfons run through the woods as they seek the children. The children's voices ring nearby. They sound frightened, so the adults rush toward the sound.

The three children slowly back away from a small, dark opening on the side of the mountain. Sigi scolds. "Gregor, Baldwin, Aileen! What are you doing out here?"

The youngsters look over their shoulders and see the group. They turn and run to them. Baldwin begins, "We were just playing, I heard something!"

Cunung is visibly angry with the group. "Come on. Let's go." Aileen pleads. "Cunung, something is in there." She points to the dark opening in the mountain.

He is frustrated but looks toward the cave. "That is even more reason that you shouldn't be near it. It looks like a snake pit." Gregor looks at Aileen and shakes his head.

Aileen again tries to convince Cunung to investigate the opening. "It wasn't a snake, Cunung."

"Stay away from there!" He snaps, then softens. "I believe you, Aileen. We don't have to look for trouble in every dark crevice. This is all my fault. Life isn't supposed to be this way. It's not just chasing danger all the time, you three! Let's go." His voice is filled with concern and frustration. His mind races, thinking of his responsibility for the children and the dangers lurking in the cave. They take the children and march them back toward Evorik's house.

Cunung turns to Alfons as they walk. "I should get going anyway. There's one last stop I want to make before heading out to bait the last traps for the year."

Alfons looks impressed, "You're done?"

Cunung shrugs. "I'd like to get at least one more good day in, but we'll see how it goes. I haven't seen many signs of deer lately."

Alfons nods.

The group makes its way out of sight. In the distance behind them, a slender black figure steps in to view them. She whispers at Cunung, too low to be heard.

Her voice is silk and razor. "Aww. Sweet puppy. It is you."

***

Cunung walks up to the door and knocks. "Kl'kn? It's me, Cunung."

A key turns. The door cracks open.

Kl'kn's eyes peer out at Cunung. "Oh. Hello, Cunung. It is nice to see you. I'm busy at the moment. Maybe tomorrow?"

Cunung grins and asks, "Why don't you come out anymore? Everyone misses you."

Kl'kn doesn't budge. "You know, just... working on a project. Are you still doing your trapping thing?"

Cunung laughs. "I'd like to see you."

Kl'kn sighs. The door opens a little further. The T'nKrnl squeezes out in awkward steps. He shuts the door behind him. "Fine. I need to get back to work soon. Did you want to discuss anything specific? I've recently been researching using vapor fusion to achieve magnetic lift."

Cunung looks puzzled. "What? No, I'm not sure I could keep up. I was more interested in your research related to *necessary repairs*. *Scrounging, acquiring*? That sort of thing."

Kl'kn looks panicked briefly before his face falls. He seems ashamed. "I'm sorry, Cunung. I just..." Cunung cuts his friend off. "I want to see her!" His voice is full of longing and anticipation. His eyes are lit with a spark of hope.

Kl'kn sounds shocked, "What?"

Cunung knows Kl'kn and has accepted the strange tinker as a friend. "I don't care that you *acquired* my materials for repairs! You have the spearhead, right?"

Kl'kn gulps. He sheepishly answers. "Yeah. I'm so sorry."

Cunung continues, "No, no! It's okay! I would love to see what you've done with the spearhead. If you're fixing up X, I want to see her! *She* was my friend, too."

Kl'kn immediately perks up. "Oh! Yes! Of course! Come on in!"

Kl'kn opens the door. Beyond is a cluttered workshop full of strange contraptions. In the center of the room, a bronze orb lies on a table. Both men enter. Kl'kn picks up a detached leg—the bronze surface sparkles in the dim light. The leg ends in a dark iron spearhead. "Is this the item you were interested in?" he asks, his voice filled with pride and anticipation.

Cunung smiles, "No, Kl'kn. I'm interested in X. The spearhead is beautiful, but it is yours, or better said, it is *hers*. Consider it a gift from a friend."

Kl'kn blushes. "Thank you. After the battle, I decided she should have some way to protect herself up close."

Cunung nods. He is impressed with the tinker's ingenuity. "Great idea!"

"That's where your gift comes in..." Kl'kn twists a gear on the leg.

A wooden sheath with leather trim inside slides in an arc to cover the spear's tip and then clicks up into place. He twists the gear in the opposite direction. The sheath pops off with a snap and spins out of the way.

CHAPTER NINETY-THREE

HUNTED FOR LOVE

C unung walks by the light of his lantern through the woods near the mountain's base. He heads toward a large box trap. Absent is the hallmark "improvement" crafted by Kl'kn. It's late. Snow begins to fall.

Cunung looks into the box trap and sees that it's empty. "Smart deer got away with a free meal."

He reaches into a pouch, retrieves a bag, and pours corn into the trap. "Hope it enjoyed it. I should get back. I'm sure no one's waited up for me this late."

Cunung turns back toward Gryfburg.

Cunung makes his way back to the public house along the dark streets of Gryfburg. The silhouette of a female dressed in dark clothing follows. She opens a wooden box, and haunting music begins to play. She gently places the box on the street and joins the melody. Her girlish voice haunts the night.

At the sound of her voice, Cunung stops walking.

Sweet little puppy at my door.

Annoyed, he grumbles under his breath as she continues to sing. "I'm not your puppy."

You nipped me once, and now it's war.

Cunung's head drops.

Cute little puppy, my best friend.

The time has come to meet your end.

Cunung growls. "I'm not even a pup anymore."

She laughs. "Found you! You're it!"

Cunung looks back over his shoulder at Elizabelethereth. He sighs and turns around, shaking his head. "Not now."

She wears dark clothes similar to a harlequin or carnival clown but with no discernable color.

Her face is visible in the dim light of Gryfburg. It is the face of a porcelain doll. Her skin is smooth and unblemished. In the dim moonlight, she is stunningly beautiful, except for an odd look of madness. Behind the facade, something reeks of death and decay, like an ancient mausoleum that rots from within.

She has blue eyes that stare at Cunung. She holds a sick perversion of love—the kind of emotion that a serial killer might have for a victim. Her face is painted pale, with dark tears on her cheeks. Her lips curl into a smile, but it is empty, like the smile of a predator that has found its prey.

Snow continues to fall. It sticks to the black and grey clothing, a sharp contrast in the dim light. "You should not be here, Cunung."

Cunung stares her down through the darkness of the empty street. "Neither should you, Elli."

"My name is Elizabalethereth; get it right, sweet child." She snaps. For just a moment, her eyes betray her wickedness. Whatever remains of her glamour is cast down, exposing the monster for what she is. Cunung rolls his eyes and shakes his head dismissively. "Yeah, I'm not saying all that."

Elizabalethereth snarles at him, "Then you die, my pet. Such a shame, I've missed my little puppy soooo much."

Cunung rolls his eyes. "You were going to kill me anyway."

Elizabelethereth laughs. It echoes hauntingly through the empty streets of Gryfburg. "Maybe."

"Besides..." Cunung shrugs."... can't live forever."

Elizabalethereth laughs. "I could. It's so... good... to see you, *love*."

She winks and blows a kiss before drawing a pair of cruel, curved blades.

He reaches for his katzbalger but shakes his head. He mutters, "No, I wouldn't stand a chance with this." Cunung flees toward Evorik's workshop.

Elizabelethereth angrily bounces. Her hands clenched into fists. She stomps her feet and huffs. She sheathes her blades and turns to retrieve the music box. With the music box still playing in her hand, she follows Cunung. "You're ruining the moment, *love*! Our chance to spend some alone time together!"

Elizabelethereth doesn't rush. She half-swaggers and half-dances through the streets as she relishes the hunt. All the while, she continues to giggle.

"Why do you run, you silly boy? I'm not going to hurt you." Her eyes flash. She speaks in a sinister, low growl. "I'm just going to kill you."

Cunung continues toward Evorik's workshop. Elizabelethereth rolls her eyes. She shouts after him, "Come back, *love*! You can borrow one of my swords if you want. I am giving them both to you anyway."

Elizabelethereth laughs. It is an ominous sound in the still night air. Gryfburg is silent except for her flirtatious threats and the haunting lullaby of a music box. The falling snow muffles the sound. Aside from Cunung's lantern, the town is engulfed in the black shroud of night. Even the Lesser Light has chosen to give the pair their privacy.

Elizabelethereth picks up her pace, although she seems content to keep her prey in view. "There's no need to rush off so quickly. You're starting to hurt my feelings."

Cunung makes it to the workshop. He looks around momentarily before remembering where Evorik had promised to place the spear.

"Come back; you don't want to keep me waiting, do you?"

He rushes to the rack and retrieves the spear. The black iron of the head shines in the light of his lantern. Cunung hangs the lantern on a hook and turns to face Elizabelethereth. "Don't worry, Elli. I'm coming."

Elizabelethereth returns her music box to the street. Once it rests securely on the ground, she stands to face Cunung. She claps with glee and giggles again. "Who is this Elli, *love*? Should I be jealous?"

The music continues to play.

Cunung holds the spear in front of him defensively. He stands uphill from Elizabelethereth before Evorik's workshop.

She charges toward Cunung, and the battle begins.

Cunung aims the spearhead at Elizabelethereth.

"You're so cute." Elizabelethereth sprints uphill.

She performs a front handspring at the last possible moment.

She flies

forward over

Cunung's spearhead.

He strikes

with spear

she grabs haft

vaults higher

She flips backward once and gracefully lands atop the roof of the workshop. She draws her blades.

Cunung curses under his breath.

She playfully drops off the roof.

blades

slice down

toward Cunung

They carve a gashing pair of wounds into his back.

He stumbles forward, turns, and positions the haft of his spear defensively. He carefully backs away.

"You never..." She unleashes probing strikes. She looks for a way through Cunung's defense.

"...even sent..." More slashes force Cunung back. He tries to get a slight advantage with distance.

"...me flowers!"

Elizabelethereth steps into Cunung. She presses the spear's haft down with a blade. She cuts his left arm with her other sword. He pulls back and winces in pain. Elizabelethereth laughs and lets Cunung go. The music box continues to wind down as Cunung bleeds.

"Oh! This is *precious*!" She wiggles in excitement. A broad smile crawls across her face. "*You've* changed *so* much over the years. It's like we're meeting again for the *very* first time!"

Cunung cringes, "You have mostly stayed the same. Like a pool of stagnant water."

She sneers. "*I've* gotten better. *You* know it. *I* know it. You could have killed me once. *Long ago.* "

Cunung makes a piercing jab with his spear. Elizabelethereth steps to the side and deflects the blade away.

"You've improved. A little. Not enough." Cunung concedes. He swipes with the butt of the spear, striking her in the hip.

"Ouch! That's going to leave a mark." She backs away.

"Like my outfit? I wore it just for you. I planned this *whole* night for you." Cunung jabs at her again.

"Our first..." Elizabelethereth deflects the quick jab and steps closer again.

"...official..." She's close enough to kiss him now. Cunung frees the grip of his spear with one hand. He uses it to take her hand and stop a sword blow. Her blade still manages to dig into his outer thigh, leaving a painful cut.

"...date!" She kisses him and backs away. Cunung stumbles backward, now bleeding from the several wounds in his back, left arm, and right thigh. Reflexively, he spits and wipes his mouth. Elizabelethereth drops her jaw and recoils in shock, "How rude!"

Cunung falls back further up the hill toward The Jolly Gryf, further from the flickering light of his lantern.

Elizabelethereth mocks. "You're *cute* when you're *scared*."

"Scared? No. Disgusted? Yes." Cunung again raises his spear. "You should leave Elli. I don't want to kill you."

She laughs. "Oh, sweetheart. I believe you. I do. There's just one problem. You see? *I* want to kill you. *I* planned this *special* night for us, and you're **ruining it**!"

She charges again at Cunung.

She is in a fury.

He parries her thrusts and strikes as they disappear into a sea of shadows between his lantern and those surrounding the Jolly Gryf. Blades and the spear tip occasionally reflect the dim light or spark as they strike against each other. The melee moves into the ring of light surrounding the public house.

Cunung is exhausted. Numerous fresh wounds mark his arms, legs, and face. Elizabelethereth bleeds from her shoulder, where she has a tear in her outfit.

The music box continues to play. It slows a bit. The sound becomes more ominous as it winds down. "Do you see this snow? Do you know how cold it is in these tights? Why won't you die already?"

Cunung's heavy breaths mix with the chilling sound of her music. The noise fills the town square with desperation.

Cunung sees an opportunity and strikes at her legs to slow her pursuit. She daintily leaps onto the tip of his spear and forces it down to the ground.

She stands on the tip of his spear and smirks. She draws back both wicked blades.

With an impish grin, Cunung smashes the spear's haft toward her face.

Elizabelethereth tries to flip backward off the spear, but it's too late. The blunt end of the spear crashes into her nose, breaking it.

Her blades clatter down hard on the cobblestone.

Elizabelethereth tumbles backward over her shoulder. She returns to a stance a few span away. Cunung sighs in relief.

She puts her hands to her nose in shock. She pulls them away and stares at the blood covering them. "Cunung, *my love*! Why? How could you? I'm hurt."

She moves toward her sword; blood pours from her nose, marring her lower jaw in crimson.

Cunung's spear tip jabs at her. He forces her back and steps forward to ensure he holds his ground and guards her weapons.

She stumbles back in shock at his behavior. "*You* wouldn't hurt a harmless lady, would you?"

Cunung growls, his voice firm and deadly. "No. Of course not."

She again moves toward her swords. Again, Cunung's prodding speartip blocks her way. "You're no lady."

Elizabelethereth gasps and throws her head back, feigning grief. "Oh, Cunung, *you beast!*"

She pantomimes sincere crying, slowly turns, and slips away into the shadows. She moves back toward the workshop.

She emerges in the light of Cunung's lantern and retrieves her music box. "You ruined it. It was going to be *beautiful.* I planned all of this just for you."

Cunung is in shock. He slowly retreats toward the public house.

She slowly walks into the night singing.

Poor little puppy,

sad and alone.

I'm coming back soon,

gonna take you home.

The music box winds down and stops with her final line.

She takes three more steps, and there's a loud snap as she slams the lid shut. With that, she disappears into the night.

Cunung slowly returns to the public house. He stumbles up the stairs, heads inside, and backs into the corner. He collapses into a seat facing the door, cradles his spear, and waits for morning.

He watches all night.

The streets are covered in a soft, white blanket of snow. The door to the manor house opens. Aileen, Baldwin, and Gregor rush out to play.

Aileen and Gregor throw snowballs at each other as they race downhill toward The Jolly Gryf. Baldwin laughs at their game.

Aileen squeals as she runs past, "Don't throw any at us, Baldwin! It wouldn't be fair!" Aileen and Gregor stop near the old public house.

Aileen pelts Gregor in the back with a snowball. He cries out, "Hey!"

He stoops to pick up a snowball of his own. Baldwin runs past them, laughing. He turns to watch their fight when he notices a glint of light reflected in the snow.

He rushes over to investigate.

Aileen calls, "Not fair, Gregor! I was touching base!"

Gregor quickly scoops up and throws another snowball. "There's no base in a snowball fight!"

Aileen laughs as she unleashes her own. "Take that cheater!"

Gregor catches the snowball in his face. He spits and wipes away the ice, then charges at her, laughing. "You little brat!"

Baldwin reaches down and pulls a deadly-looking, curved blade from the snow.

He ensures no one sees him and tries to hide the weapon as best he can. "I need to go back inside for a minute. I'll be right back."

Gregor and Aileen are distracted and don't notice the sword. "Okay, see you in a second, Balds!"

Baldwin runs up the street, takes the steps, and sneaks into the manor unseen.

Chapter Ninety-Four
Hot Drink, Cold Day

A thick layer of snow covers the ground surrounding Alfons' home. Aileen, Baldwin, and Gregor rush outside in a fit of laughter. They wear heavy clothes that Cunung, Alfons, and Sigi gave them, purchased to help keep the children warm through winter.

Aileen exclaims, "It never snows in Riverview! I love the snow! Will we ever come back here after we get home?"

The question hits Gregor like a punch to the gut. He stops playing, caught up in profound thought. "I don't know, Aileen. I hadn't thought about that. I hadn't considered that we might never come back here. We might never see all the friends we made here again."

This brings the same grim expression to Aileen and Baldwin.

Baldwin sarcastically remarks, "Wow, Gregor. Way to ruin the moment."

This shatters the moment of somber reflection, and the three smile again. Gregor apologizes, "I just realized I hadn't even thought about it."

Baldwin laughs. "" I know. I was kidding. You're right. We should come back someday if we can. Alfons and Sigi are like second parents now."

Aileen and Gregor nod in agreement.

Gregor asks, "Hey! Want to explore today?"

"Sure." Baldwin thinks for a moment. "If we're exploring, I want to take something with us. You can't tell anyone, okay?"

Gregor looks curiously at Baldwin, "What? What are you talking about, Balds?" Alfons and Sigi walk up the path toward the home to visit. Before they get within earshot, Baldwin answers. "Nevermind. I'll tell you later."

Gregor grunts. "Ugh, fine."

Baldwin waves to the older couple. "Hey, Sigi! Hey Alfons!"

The pair wave to the children. Alfons calls out. "Hey, Baldwin! Hey Gregor. Hey, Aileen." Sigi adds with a wry smile. "What would be perfect for a frozen day like today?"

Aileen and Gregor look at each other knowingly.

Aileen cheers. "Steamed sweet milk?" Sigi laughs and nods. "I thought I might make some for you. Sound good?"

"Yes!" Aileen is bouncing and nodding her head vigorously in excitement.

Gregor asks, "Can we go explore after? It's been dull inside lately."

"As long as you bundle up and stay close, I don't mind. Have you asked Cunung?" Sigi replies. Gregor shakes his head. "No, not yet. I'll ask him. Thanks, Sigi."

Everyone except Sigi is gathered around a low table, sitting on pillows on the floor.

Cunung taps his fingers on the table. "Have things gotten any better with the new job?" Alfons sighs and shakes his head. "No, not really. I enjoy helping people, but the work of a leader wears on me, Cunung. Often, I'm just caught between two families who insist on bickering with each other. I see why Urso was so grumpy and never got anything accomplished."

Alfons trails off. He is lost in his thoughts for a moment before he chuckles. "Old crusty-butt got me again."

Cunung bursts into deep, rich laughter that fills the small room. "I understand that sentiment well. I'm sorry, Alfons."

Alfons grins. "Ah, it's fine. I shouldn't complain. How are you holding up now that we've trapped you away from your beloved woods?"

Cunung smirks, "It's a nice change of pace. I wouldn't want to stay cooped up too long, but I have enough to occupy my time."

Alfons' curiosity is piqued. "Oh?"

Cunung laughs. "Someone has to keep an eye on Kl'kn. He might blow up the whole town." Alfons laughs. "Truer words I've never heard. He packs quite a lot of danger into such a small frame. He is a brilliant fellow, though. I've grown quite fond of him."

Sigi enters the room carrying a tray of steaming drinks. "Well said. That little fellow brings more trouble than men four times his size. Yet he is somehow adorable." She sets the tray on the table. Three wooden mugs are filled with a warm, thick, chocolate-colored liquid. A mint leaf hangs from the side of each mug. The other three are filled with steaming tea.

Everyone grabs a mug and begins to drink.

Aileen cheers. "Mmm. Thank you, Sigi! It's great!"

Baldwin also thanks her, "Yes, thank you!"

Gregor nods in agreement and smiles with bulging cheeks at Sigi.

Sigi smiles at the children. "You're welcome. I'm glad you're enjoying it. Cunung, do you have any plans for the day?"

Like Gregor, Cunung caught off with a mouthful. He looks up from his tea and takes a moment to swallow. "I'll be visiting Kl'kn later. This morning, I'd like to split some logs for firewood. Nothing pressing. Do you need me to handle anything?"

Sigi shakes her head with a grin. "No. Thank you for asking. I was just curious. Gregor had something he wanted to ask you, though."

She winks at Gregor. The boy asks, "Can we explore today? It's boring staying in the yard all the time, Cunung. We might not get to see Gryfburg again."

Cunung sighs and thinks for a moment. "Fine. Just be careful, and be home before lunch. Don't go beyond Horst's... er, Wigand's home."

Gregor smiles.

"We won't Cunung! Thank you! Can we go now?"

Cunung smiles but gives Gregor a stern gaze. "Why don't you finish your milk first? Sigi made it, after all." Gregor apologizes, "Yes, sir. Sorry, Sigi."

Sigi smiles at the boy. "It's fine, Gregor. I want you to enjoy it. I hope it will help keep you warm."

Gregor nods and smiles.

CHAPTER NINETY-FIVE

CAVE AND COIN

The door bursts open once again, and the children run outside.

Baldwin catches Gregor and explains the plan. "Alright, Gregor. Let me get it. I'll meet you in the woods."

Gregor and Aileen walk toward the tree line while Baldwin runs around the side of the house.

Aileen's eyes sparkle with anticipation as she turns to Gregor. "What do you think Baldwin's hiding from us?"

Gregor scoffs, "He wants to show *me* something, not you." Aileen huffs at Gregor. "Fine. What do you think he wants to show *you*? I bet it's an animal."

The kids arrive at the edge of the woods. Their small figures form a silhouette against the shadows of the forest canopy. They turn back to wait for Baldwin.

Gregor looks at Aileen. "Nah. I don't think so. Why would Baldwin leave an animal outside in the cold? I bet it's a book about monsters." Aileen rolls her eyes. "Why would he need to keep a book a secret?"

Gregor shrugs. "Maybe they don't like books around here."

Aileen smiles and shakes her head. "Here he comes."

Baldwin runs around the corner of the house. He quickly checks that no adults are outside, then flashes something toward Gregor and Aileen as he runs.

Gregor's jaw drops. He's impressed. "Whoah..."

Aileen and Gregor both gasp with mouths agape.

Gregor exclaims once Baldwin is within earshot. "That's awesome!"

Baldwin rushes up to the pair. "Yeah, it is! What do you think?"

Baldwin motions into the woods and walks through the brambles, into the trees, and out of view. Everyone makes their way into the woods. Out of sight, Baldwin withdraws a wicked, curved blade.

Gregor is astonished. "Where'd you get that Balds?"

Baldwin smiles. "I found it lying in the snow!"

"No way!" Gregor asks, "Can I try swinging it?"

Baldwin suddenly looks incredulous. "No!"

Gregor is hurt. "Why not?"

"It's not yours," Baldwin answers.

Gregor replies, "It's not yours either."

"It is now." Baldwin wears a broad grin and tightens his fingers around the hilt.

Gregor shakes his head and laughs, "Fine. Let's go. You should lead since you have a sword!"

Aileen stares at the razor-sharp blade. "That's cool, Baldwin."

The children make their way through the forest, searching for the base of the mountains and the small cave they once found.

Aileen peers into the shadows that surround them. "Are you sure this is the right way, Balds?" Baldwin shrugs. "No." His answer does nothing to comfort Aileen. "Okay."

Gregor stares at Baldwin in disbelief. "Really?" Baldwin bobs from side to side. "Yeah, but I think we're close. It's hard to tell."

They step into a clearing. The canopy opens above them, revealing a vast turquoise sky spotted with a few white fluffy clouds.

They cross the clearing. A piercing, shrill cry high above cuts the silence. The sound echoes through the forest. They look up to see a Griff circling above the mountain. It's hard to tell if the creature is defending its aery domain or circling prey. The sight of the majestic creature fills them with awe.

Baldwins stares with his jaw hanging open, "Gregor?" Gregor is enthralled with the creature as well. "Yeah, Balds?"

"Are you seeing this?" Baldwin is absorbed by the beauty of the Griff's flight. Gregor seems distant as he replies, "Yeah." They all stand in silence to admire the sight.

When the creature finally disappears below the peaks, Gregor continues. "I don't believe it."

He looks at Baldwin, and they smile at each other.

"Let's go see what was in that cave!" Baldwin raises the sword's tip into the air as if leading a charge, and they continue onward.

A dark, mysterious opening sits like an abscess on the side of the mountain. The children approach. Their footsteps echo in the silence.

Baldwin cries, "This is it!"

"Yeah, this looks familiar." Aileen's voice sounds thrilled as she recognizes a familiar sight.

The trio walks into view. Baldwin approaches the cave with an air of confidence. The others join him and form a semicircle around it.

There's no voice this time. The air is still.

Gregor peers into the darkness, "Yeah, this is the right place. Is anyone in there?"

There's no reply. Baldwin grows disinterested. He turns and plays make-believe by chopping at a tree.

Gregor calls into the black void again, his voice full of anticipation. "Hello?" Aileen stands behind Gregor. Her voice trembles with fear and excitement. "Want to come out and play?"

After a particularly loud chop, Gregor gives Baldwin a stern look. Baldwin stops and shrugs as if to say, "What?"

Gregor makes an expansive, expressive shrug and motions toward the cave. Baldwin rolls his eyes but walks back over. "Hi?" Baldwin calls into the dimly lit cave. There's no reply. The trio duck low and step inside. They only make it a couple of steps when they reach the back of the cave.

Gregor sighs. "Empty? Well, that was a bust."

Baldwin echoes disappointment. "I know I heard something the other day. At least, I'm pretty sure I did."

Aileen nods. "I thought so, too."

"Do you Want to look for another Griff? Or something else interesting?" Gregor turns to leave the cave. Baldwin follows, "Sure!"

The two boys run back out into the light outside.

Gregor calls back to his sister, "Come on, Aileen!"

Aileen's eyes widen in disbelief as she spots a glimmer in the mud. She bends down and picks up a golden coin, her smile growing wider. "Look what I found!" she whispers, hiding it in her hands.

Aileen exits the cave and enters the brilliant sunlight radiating from the snow. Outside, they begin to walk away when Gregor stops, his eyes widening in surprise. "Hey, look!" Gregor points at a half-span long stone crystal lying alongside the edge of the mountain's base.

Baldwin looks down at the rock formation lying on the ground. "That's a pretty cool-looking crystal, Gregor."

Gregor clarifies, "It moved." Looking closer, Baldwin asks. "Really?"

Gregor nods.

They step closer. The stone crystal is shaped like a lizard. It suddenly sprints away with clattering steps.

Gregor exclaims, "Wow! What was it?"

Baldwin gasps with delight. "I don't know. Let's go ask!"

The kids turn back with great big smiles and head home.

CHAPTER NINETY-SIX

SPEAR AND SWORD

The children walk through the woods, full of questions about what they've seen. Aileen walks in the back. She continues to examine the golden coin. When the boys stop or look back, she hides it from them.

Leading the group, Baldwin proclaims, "I can't believe we saw a Griff!"

Gregor bounces in excitement with each step. "I know! It wasn't as big as I thought, but it was much faster!"

Baldwin is filled with wonder. "Yeah! What was that crystal lizard thing?"

"I don't know, but I can't wait to find out!" Gregor ponders.

*Whir... tick... **thud.***

*Whiiir... tick... **thud.***

Strange noises interrupt their conversation. A thudding sound accompanies each whiiir. Something is headed their way. Kl'kn walks into sight of the children. Immediately behind him is a modified X. "Whoah, what are you children doing out here? Does Cunung know where you are?"

Gregor waves, "Hey! Yeah, he knows. How are you, Kl'kn? You're fixing up X! Awesome!"

Kl'kn smiles proudly. "Oh, why yes! Of course! I couldn't just abandon her."

Baldwin tries to hide the sword, but it's too late.

Kl'kn asks, "What's that?"

Baldwin drops his shoulders. "I found it in the snow. It's a pretty cool sword, isn't it?"

Kl'kn awkwardly replies, "Yes, it is! Quite *cool*."

The kids all laugh.

Kl'kn looks confused. He asks, "What? Did I say something wrong?"

"No, you just said it funny. You're great, Kl'kn." Aileen answers, giggling. He blushes and smiles at the girl. "Do you know who owns the sword Baldwin?"

Baldwin stammers. "Uhm, no. Not really. I found it, so I was going to keep it. Please don't tell."

Kl'kn sighs because he knows he would do the same if he found something *cool*. "I don't know, Baldwin. Cunung may be very angry with me if he finds out I didn't tell him."

Baldwin looks pleadingly at the tinker. "Please, Kl'kn? What would you do if you found something like this lying around? I've never had anything like this before. I just want it to protect us. I won't hurt anyone with it!"

Kl'kn looks at the spearhead attached to X's right front leg. Overcome with guilt, he concedes. "Fine. I won't tell, but if you get caught... don't tell on me either, young man. Finder's keepers, after all."

Baldwin sighs in relief, "I promise! Thank you, Kl'kn!"

Kl'kn continues, "And be careful with that thing! Don't hurt yourself or anyone else! I don't care how *cool* it is. It is a weapon. Treat it as such." Baldwin nods.

Aileen asks, "Can we see X? What have you done to her?" Kl'kn smiles at Aileen. "Yes, come here, and I'll show you. I have only had time to attach four legs, so she's still unstable."

He points to the leg with Cunung's spearhead. "This is a subtle improvement I recently made. I realized that X needed a better way to protect herself up close. Cunung generously *donated* an armament, which I modified to provide an additional layer of defense at close quarters. I anticipate this will increase her efficiency in self-defense scenarios by 11.297%."

The kid's eyes are large. They nod but don't understand much of what the tinker said.

Aileen gasps. "Oh, yeah. That, that's, uhm, great. Excellent work, Kl'kn!" The tinker looks proudly at the girl. "Thank you, Aileen. You must be the one with manners."

She blushes and laughs. "Yes, that's me."

"Hey!" Gregor laughs, but he concedes. "Fine, that's all right. Aileen, you can be the nice one." She laughs and hugs Gregor. "It's okay, Gregor. You can be the smart one."

Baldwin flexes, and Aileen and Gregor both laugh. "That makes me the tough one."

Aileen shrugs, "I guess? If that's who you want to be."

Baldwin thinks momentarily and declares, "I want to be brave!"

Gregor interjects with a grin, "You're on your way."

Baldwin pumps his fist. "Yes!"

"Alright, tough guy. Ready to head back home?" Gregor points toward Alfon's house. Baldwin asks, "Home?" Gregor clarifies, "I mean, Alfons' home."

The three kids walk back with Kl'kn and X.

CHAPTER NINETY-SEVEN
Haunted Hearth

The kids trudge along the snow-covered path to Alfons' house. Their steps quicken with each familiar sight. They go through the front yard toward the door, seeking sanctuary from the biting cold. Aileen's teeth chatter. Her body shivers uncontrollably. She claps her arms with her hands and desperately tries to generate some warmth. "I can't wait to get inside. It's freezing out here!"

"Yeah, and that cave was a complete bust. I can't believe there wasn't anything inside." Baldwin's excitement over the day's events comes through despite his minor complaint.

Gregor's voice quivers as he ponders, "The voice from the other day... Do you think it was the crystal lizard thing?" Aileen's eyes widen in disbelief. "Nah, it didn't seem like that could talk."

Gregor nods. "Sigi could make us something warm to drink. I hope she's here!"

Baldwin grows more excited with the thought, "Yeah! I love Sigi and Kaleia. They've been good to us!" They bust through the door and rush inside the house.

Kl'kn and X lag behind. "Let me look you over, X."

He takes a moment to check on X. He rubs her spherical dome and brushes some spots on her legs. "Good girl. You stay out here and be good. I'll be back out in a second. Don't worry."

X rubs her body against Kl'kn as he hugs her affectionately.

She sits down to await her master's return.

Kl'kn turns and heads in after the children.

———

The kids huddle around the table in the center of the room. The sound of meat searing carries a fragrant aroma from the kitchen and warms the dining room. Cunung's voice calls out. "Almost done!"

"I'm famished!" Baldwin's stomach growls in agreement. He sniffs at the air. Tantalizing scents continue to waft into the room. "It smells divine!"

"It's not Sigi's cooking, but I hope you enjoy it!" Cunung enters the room. He carries a large wooden trencher adorned with a succulent roast in the center. The aroma of the perfectly cooked meat fills the air. Potatoes and carrots line the side of the roast. Juices flow out into a moat carved into the wooden board.

Baldwin smells the air with a look of wonder. "That looks amazing, Cunung!"

Cunung laughs.

Gregor agrees, "Yeah, that looks great! Thank you for cooking for us!"

Aileen adds to the growing list of compliments, "I can't believe you made that yourself!"

"Leave me alone at home for a day, and I can get creative." Cunung sets the trencher down in the center of the table and sits with the children. "Let's bless the meal quickly and then eat."

Gregor nods. "Great!"

"Father, thank you for the life of this deer. Thank you for nourishing us with it." Cunung raises his head and smiles at the children. "Let's eat!"

The kids all raise their heads and smile.

"I'm starving!" Aileen leans into the table.

They take wooden utensils that look like singular, thick chopsticks, begin to poke into slices of meat and pull them to their corner. Baldwin grabs a potato and bites. He then sinks his teeth into a slice of the roast. Everyone digs in and begins to eat.

Aileen speaks between her bites, "This is great, Cunung. Thank you!"

"Yes! It's delicious!" Gregor agrees. He feels ashamed that he didn't say so sooner.

Baldwin nods and tries to agree. His words are muffled and unintelligible because his mouth is full.

Without warning, one of the carrots flips through the air and strikes Aileen on the cheek with a force that makes her cry out in pain. "Gregor! That hurt!"

Gregor looks shocked. He holds his hands up. "I didn't do it!"

Cunung watches in awe. He looks very concerned. "Aileen, that wasn't Gregor."

He reaches his hands over the food and then moves around the room with outstretched hands, probing for something to ensure that no one unseen is sneaking around.

Gregor looks frightened. "What's wrong, Cunung?"

"I don't know. Go ahead and finish your meal. I'm going to build a fire." Cunung leaves the dining room and heads into the living room.

Baldwin whispers to Gregor, "Gregor? What's going on?"

"I don't know Balds. Are you okay, Aileen?" Gregor looks very worried for Aileen.

"Yeah. It just hurt."

Chapter Ninety-Eight

Unwanted Possession

Aileen, Baldwin, and Gregor sleep in a spacious guest room with two beds at Alfons' house.

Aileen sleeps in the bed nearest the door, Baldwin in a bed near the window beside the outside wall, and Gregor rests on a makeshift mat in the center of the room. The window is shuttered to keep out the cold. The Lesser Light streams in and casts a dim, bluish light in the room. The only source of warmth is the doorway adjacent to the living room, where a cozy fire burns. A shadow, darker than the night, occludes the light from the fireplace.

A sinister, low voice whispers from the shadow. "Aileen."

Aileen stirs for a moment but goes back to sleep.

"Aileen." The voice is louder this time. There is a long pause. The covers are ripped from Aileen and thrown onto the floor beside Gregor.

Aileen wakes up abruptly. Her heart pounds in her chest. She looks around the room, her eyes darting from one corner to another.

She notices the shadow. Its form shifts and contorts, forming a threatening silhouette against the warm light from the fireplace in the living room. She screams, "Gregor!"

The shadow disappears. Gregor leaps to his feet. "What? Aileen? Aileen, are you okay?"

Aileen looks around the room. Her eyes are full of confusion. "I think so. Maybe it was just a nightmare. I'm sorry, Gregor." She feels a pang of guilt for disturbing her brother's sleep.

"It's okay, sis. Are you sure you're okay?" Gregor is holding his chest.

Aileen thinks for a moment. "Yeah. Thanks, Greg. Goodnight."

Gregor takes a deep breath and lies back down.

"Goodnight, sis."

***

Cunung makes his way along the white streets of Gryfburg with urgency. He approaches Gryfburg Manor. The doors swing open, and Sigi steps outside. He rushes toward her. His face is flushed with urgency as he calls out. "Sigi! Can you spare a moment?"

Sigi waves at Cunung. "Of course! Good morning, Cunung. How are you and the children?" Cunung meets Sigi with a forced smile. "We're not pleasant, unfortunately."

Sigi looks gravely concerned. "Are the children okay?"

"Yes, but I need to ask. Have you ever experienced anything in your home?" Cunung asks matter-of-factly. Kaleia can be seen walking toward the manor. She sees Sigi and Cunung and approaches.

Sigi asks, "What do you mean?"

"Last night at dinner, something inexplicable happened. A carrot flew across the room and struck Aileen's cheek. It was a hard enough blow to make her cry. No one threw it, Sigi. There was nothing and no one with us." Sigi responds, her voice tinged with disbelief, "Really? What do you think it was?"

Cunund nods. "I don't know. I'm just asking. Have you ever had trouble before?"

"No, never. Are you sure it wasn't one of the boys playing a trick?"

Sigi smiles at Kaleia as she arrives. Kaleia has overheard part of the conversation and seems intrigued.

Cunung greets Kaleia and resumes, "That's precisely what I might have thought. I was reaching for a potato and saw the carrot fly myself."

Sigi pauses for a moment. Her expression shows a look of shock. "No. Nothing like that has ever happened there before, nothing at all."

Kaleia greets the two apologetically. "Good morning, Cunung and Sigi. I'm sorry. I don't mean to intrude, but I couldn't help but overhear. I might be able to help."

Cunung looks at Kaleia. "Good morning, Kaleia. It's no intrusion. I welcome any advice you have."

"Has anything changed around the home recently?"

Cunung ponders the question. "No, not that I am aware of. Why?"

"Have the children brought something in with them?" Kaleia's idea brings Cunung to an epiphany. "They were exploring yesterday morning, and this happened at dinner. I heard something moving around the house last night but could never find anything."

"We should search the house." Kaleia offers.

Sigi agrees to join them. "I'll help look. Let's go."

Cunung, Alfons, and Sigi make their way toward the home.

"I'll check around out here. You check inside." Cunung splits from the group and walks toward the backyard. Sigi and Kaleia enter the home. Kl'kn approaches with X.

Kl'kn follows Cunung to the backyard. "Hey Cunung.'

"Morning, Kl'kn. I'm sorry, but I have to find something." Cunung talks to Kl'kn but remains focused on his search.

Kl'kn tries to look surprised. "Oh? What's that?"

"I don't know." Cunung looks up briefly toward Kl'kn, then returns to searching. "The kids may have found something. If so, I need to find out what it was."

Kl'kn blushes but says nothing.

Cunung looks under the house near the guest room window.

He retrieves a wicked-looking sword. "Something like this."

Kl'kn tries to look surprised to see the weapon. "Oh, wow! Is that yours?"

Cunung shakes his head. "No. The kids must have discovered it yesterday. I need to get rid of it."

Kl'kn reaches out to take the weapon. "If you'd like, I'll dispose of it."

Cunung hands it over, glad to be rid of the reminder of Elli. "Thanks, Kl'kn, I would be grateful. Take it away from here." Kl'kn smiles and takes the blade.

He turns and runs off.

————————————

The kids are sitting around the table. Cunung stands with Sigi and Kaleia. "We found a sword hidden beneath the house. I don't care who saw it or why you took it. I want you to be safe, and taking things that don't belong to you can only cause you harm."

The kids all look embarrassed.

Sigi warns them of the dangers of the situation: "Please be careful, children."

Cunung wants to confirm the situation's seriousness without making them more uncomfortable. "Yes. It's okay, I'm not angry. I want to ensure you understand how dangerous strange items can be."

The kids nod.

————————————

The kids are asleep. Aileen dreams. Warm light from the living room streams into the guest room. A shadow occludes the warm glow of the fireplace. It stretches out like tendrils until it reaches Aileen's bed.

Tears form at the edge of her closed eyes. She whispers. "Cunung? It wasn't the sword. It wants me. Help."

Sinister, low laughter fills the room, chilling the air. The shadow fades, and peace returns to the room.

CHAPTER NINETY-NINE

SAYING GOODBYE

Snow melts, signaling the changing of seasons. The path away from Alfons' house has almost cleared. It has been their home for much of the year. A loaded horse stands in the center of the path. Cunung stands beside the horse and holds the reins. Baldwin and Gregor play nearby, each wearing a heavy backpack full of travel gear.

Aileen bursts out of Alfons' house doorway and runs toward Cunung. She is wearing a large backpack full of supplies, and her loaded pack threatens to engulf her. Her face is flushed with excitement and anticipation. "I'm coming! Don't leave me!"

Cunung laughs. "We would never leave you, Aileen. Did you get everything?"

"Yes! I'm ready to go!"

"You look like you've packed for a grand expedition. Ready to head back home?" He regains his composure, and the group sets off down the path, leaving their former home behind.

Gregor ensures he's out of reach and quips, "Hey, sis, can you fit anything else in that pack?"

She grins, "Shut it, Gregor."

They both laugh.

Baldwin looks back at Alfons' house. A mix of nostalgia and excitement fills his eyes. They have grown to think of the place as home. "I can't believe today is the day. We're going back to Riverview!"

"Hooray!" Aileen tries to jump for joy. The weight of her pack holds her stuck to the ground. Gregor smirks. "You need to let some of that weight go, Aileen."

Aileen looks at Gregor with a mischievous glare. "No!"

Kaleia is outside preparing the soil in her herb garden when the group appears on the path leading to her home. The scent of fresh earth and herbs fills the air. She greets them with a warm smile.

Evorik is beside Kaleia. He sets his shovel aside and turns to join her in welcoming them.

Together, they meet the travelers at the border of Kaleia's land. "Baldwin! Are you leaving us so soon?"

Baldwin replies, "Hey, Kaleia. Yes, we wanted to stop to tell you goodbye."

Evorik smiles and approaches. "It's a shame. We will miss you all very much. Cunung, how's that spear working out?"

Cunung looks at the spearhead and gives a sharp whistle. "It's been a lifesaver, but I haven't used it much over the winter. It's got a keen edge. You did great. I will treasure it for many years."

"I hope someday you'll find your way back here." Evorik offers. Cunung smiles and nods. "I'm certain that one day, I will."

The men shake hands and then pull each other into a hug.

"I couldn't bear to leave without saying goodbye, Kaleia. Thank you for taking care of me." Baldwin gives Kaleia a heartfelt hug. She kneels to accommodate his embrace.

Aileen watches and adds in a voice full of gratitude and affection, "Thank you for saving Baldwin. We were all so scared."

Gregor nods. "I thought I was going to lose my best friend, Kaleia. Thank you." Gregor rushes over and joins Baldwin, hugging her. Kaleia tears up just a bit. "You're welcome, sweet children. Aileen, have you had any more trouble sleeping?"

"I still have nightmares, but maybe it's a little better? It's hard to say. I feel like someone is always watching me."

Kaleia frowns at the young girl. "I'm so sorry, sweetheart. Is there anything else you can think of that could have something attached to it?"

Aileen flashes a look of anger but quickly masks it and returns to a more somber expression. She shakes her head. "No, I'm sorry. I hoped it would stop when we got rid of the sword."

Baldwin sighs heavily, his voice full of regret. "I'm sorry, Aileen. I didn't know it would bring trouble with it. I didn't realize it might be cursed." His words carry a burden of guilt, reflecting his deep sense of responsibility.

Aileen smiles at Baldwin. "It's not your fault."

"I hope not." Baldwin frowns deeply. His expression shows that he blames himself for her ordeal. Cunung notices and tries to change the subject to keep Baldwin from thinking any more about what he might have caused. "We should get moving. I'd prefer not to camp out in the wild. We've had enough unwelcome visitors these past few months."

The group heads toward the opposite side of Gryfburg. Kaleia leans into Evorik, and they wrap their arms around each other. Everyone waves goodbye.

Wigand and Rosalie are outside the manor speaking with Kl'kn when Cunung and the children arrive.

Aileen waves at everyone enthusiastically, "Kl'kn! Hey Rosalie! Hey Wigand!"

"Hello, Aileen. You truly are the polite one. Aren't you?" Kl'kn winks at Aileen, and she laughs.

Baldwin smiles at Kl'kn and asks out of curiosity, "Hey, Kl'kn. Are you leaving, too?"

"Yes. X is doing well enough that it is safe to travel now, so we shall. We have been a burden here long enough. Besides, you never know when those nasty Obviin might show up!"

Cunung shakes his head at the comment.

Gregor's interest is piqued. Over the months, he's grown fond of the tinker and his little companion. "Where are you headed, Kl'kn?"

Kl'kn shrugs. "I have yet to decide."

Rosalie looks at Cunung, then touches Wigand. Wigand reaches forward and shakes Cunung's hand. "Thank you for helping us make it through winter."

"I'm sorry for your loss. It was the least I could do. Thank you for sharing the profit with me. You have been very generous." Rosalie smiles at Cunung. "Nonsense. It was the least we could do."

Cunung smiles sadly as he reflects on the friend responsible for his success in the region. "How are you, Rosalie? How is the rest of the family?"

"It has been difficult adjusting to Horst's absence, but we will make it. Horst was a good man. He knew our maker in life. He is with him now." She fights back tears. "I'm sorry... I look forward to joining him someday, far in the future."

She wipes her eyes. "Now, I look to his grandchildren."

Cunung smiles and nods. "You have a beautiful family. There is much to enjoy. I am glad you will be together with Horst again."

"If you ever find yourself in Gryfburg, you must visit us. We would be honored to have you as a guest anytime. That goes for you and the children." Rosalie struggles to complete the thought and is grateful when the door to the manor opens.

Alfons and Sigi walk outside. Before they walk down the steps toward the street, the children turn and run up to the couple, wrapping them in hugs.

Sigi sighs at the children's adoration for her and Alfons. "Oh, I'm going to miss you, sweet children."

Baldwin chokes up as he tries to thank Sigi for caring for him. "Thank you, Sigi! You rescued us from the woods. I thought I might not make it. Thank you!"

"Hey! What about me?" Alfons speaks with a laugh, but Baldwin pulls away. He sniffles, wipes his nose on his sleeve, and embraces Alfons. "You too! I meant you both!"

Alfons laughs. Baldwin is overcome and is crying and laughing at the same time.

Even Cunung has a few tears running down his face.

"It's okay, Baldwin. Calm down, boy. There, there. It's okay." Alfons tries to calm the poor boy.

Aileen looks up at Sigi. "I'm going to miss your cooking. Your steamed milk was the best!"

Gregor turns and looks at her with a great smile, "It was incredible!"

Sigi smiles and blushes. She wipes away a tear. "Oh, sweetheart. Thank you. Maybe it was you who inspired it to be so. I'm glad you visited us. Next time, please come without injury!"

Alfons wipes his eyes on a sleeve and replies, "I second that!"

Cunung joins in. "Thank you both. We appreciate the room and your rich hospitality."

Alfons and Sigi smile proudly at the man. Alfons speaks. "It was our pleasure to host you all. I hope we see you all again someday, perhaps when the children are older."

The children smile warmly at the couple.

Gregor speaks up, "We hope to. It's a long way, but we discussed that the other day. You've become like second parents to us."

Alfons and Sigi get choked up by the comment. Sigi responds, "Oh, stop it, young man. You're making a silly old woman cry."

Alfons tries to speak but stops and shakes his head. Whatever he wants to say, he can't quite get it out.

Cunung tries to change the subject, "Have you given up on finding your replacement?" Alfons shakes his head. He wipes away a tear, holds up a finger, and tries to compose himself. Finally, he responds.

"No, I just haven't found anyone interested yet." Alfons laughs, and Cunung joins him in laughter for just a moment. "If you haven't by now, I doubt you will. You are a great leader, Alfons."

Alfons shoos away the idea. "Pssh... The indoors must be driving you crazy. I'm more of a hunter like yourself. We are more suited to something other than a desk..." Alfons looks at the robes he's involuntarily wearing. "... or fancy clothing."

Cunung and Wigand both laugh.

Wigand adds, "Those fine clothes do look rather handsome."

Cunung nods with a great smile.

Alfons rolls his eyes. "Then you come and wear them! You know, you've always been a troublemaker, Wigand."

Again, Wigand laughs.

Cunung stirs the group toward home. "We should be going. We will miss you all dearly."

The kids hug Alfons and Sigi again for a long time. They walk down the steps and rejoin Cunung. The group turns north along the road toward the gate heading toward the Mourning Mountains. Kl'kn walks alongside them.

Baldwin asks, "Are you coming with us, Kl'kn?"

"Don't be so presumptuous, child. *Tough one* is still to be proven, but you certainly are the *stubborn-headed one*." Kl'kn's sly grin tells that he is joking. He has become quite enamored with the children over the months. Aileen and Gregor both laugh. Cunung smiles and enjoys the show.

Baldwin asks, "So, you're coming with us then?"

"We may accompany you for a time, but I must stop soon to work on X. She still needs some minor tuning." Gregor raises his eyebrows at Kl'kn's answer. "X and I are not babysitters for indolent children. That job belongs to him." Kl'kn points a sharp, bony finger at Cunung. The Nachtulfen drops his jaw and raises his eyebrows. Cunung flashes a shocked smile at Kl'kn. "Did you just call me a babysitter?"

The children burst into genuine laughter.

Chapter One Hundred
Parting Ways

K l'kn halts and steps off the path with Xtr-Nk.

Cunung looks at Kl'kn and tries to convince him to join them one last time. "Are you sure you won't go any further with us?"

"No. This is where our paths diverge. It has been most pleasant traveling together, but I need to adjust X. Her stabilizers seem to be acting up." Cunung nods. His eyes reflect their shared experiences. "I have no idea what that means, but it sounds important. It has been an honor to meet you, Kl'kn."

"The privilege has been mine. Children, be kind to each other. Listen to Cunung and take care of what you *acquire*." Kl'kn waves to the group.

The children wave goodbye to the tinker before the group resumes travel. Kl'kn turns and tinkers with the internal mechanisms of his beloved X. The group makes their way north along the road out of Gryfburg toward the summit of the Mourning Mountains. This treacherous yet majestic range separates Ostenplatz and Ulfreich from the rest of the world.

The road is well-worn but twists and turns as it winds through the forest. Gregor ponders all the things they've seen as they explore. His eyes sparkle with curiosity. "Cunung, do you know where we're going next?"

"We have to cross the Mourning Mountains. It is a place with a history of great sorrow and mystery. We'll have to take The Broken Pass, a treacherous route known for unpredictable weather." Cunung flashes a mischievous grin at Gregor, hinting at the adventure that awaits them.

Gregor rolls his eyes, "No, I mean, what city? You said your home is Ulfreich. Do you know if there are any things to see along the way?"

"I've passed through, but I must admit that I'm not familiar with Ostenplatz." Cunung motions toward the mountains they are traveling toward. "On the other side of the Mourning Mountains is Centervale. We won't make it to the city, but we will stay for a night on the outskirts. We'll see if we can find something entertaining to do along the way."

The children all wear broad smiles.

Baldwin asks, "So, we will only visit briefly?"

"We might stay somewhere for a day or two if you see something interesting, but we must take advantage of the pleasant spring weather to get you home." Cunung tries to focus on the roads. He feels someone has been watching them since they left. His mind returns to his encounter with Elli, and her voice rings, "*Coming back soon to take you home.*"

Aileen's is full of excitement and anticipation. She pulls him out of his memories. "I can't wait to get home!" Her eyes shine with hope, but Cunung winces as the word home echoes again in his mind.

"We only stayed in Gryfburg so long because we'd have been killed if we had tried to travel very far during the winter," Cunung explains, his voice burdened with regret.

Gregor looks astonished. "Really?"

"Animals and monsters seem exciting. Mundane, silly mistakes cause the most significant harm, Gregor."

Baldwin hangs on every word. "The Goblins, Mehr, the Gnoghl that attacked me. Those aren't dangerous?" he asks, his voice filled with curiosity.

"That's not what I said, Baldwin. Those things are deadly, but we rarely encounter them. We always travel with ourselves. Our carelessness is always there with us, threatening to cause trouble." Cunung thinks for a moment, his face grim. "Allow me to phrase it another way. That creature that attacked you, the Gnoghl. Why was it chasing Aileen and Gregor? Had it been stalking us, and we didn't notice it?"

Gregor suddenly realizes, "It stalked us before it attacked?"

Cunung nods and frowns. He seems bothered by the situation. He feels guilt and shame. "Yes, I am certain of it. It was a mistake for us to split up. It was my fault. I'm sorry." Cunung sighs and pauses for a long time.

He finally continues his train of thought. "I've thought about it. I have felt terrible about the situation. What if my mistake caused your injury, Baldwin? I will always carry that guilt."

Baldwin shakes his head with large eyes. His voice is full of conviction. "No! You saved us, Cunung! Don't say that."

"Survival is not just about escaping danger. It's about avoiding trouble in the first place." Cunung's words hang in the air. They carry with them decades of wisdom.

Baldwin nods his head as he absorbs the knowledge. "The creatures may be dangerous, but our actions put us in danger."

Cunung shakes his head, winks, and points toward Baldwin. "You got it. Exactly."

Aileen rubs the golden coin in her hand. She pays no heed to the conversation.

CHAPTER ONE HUNDRED ONE
FIRESIDE CONVERSATIONS

Warm breath forms white vapor in the crisp mountain air. The four travelers trudge along the winding road that leads them higher into the mist-shrouded peaks. A small group of merchants pass alongside the group traveling toward Gryfburg. The temperatures dissuade them from acknowledging each other.

Aileen clings to her golden coin. Her eyes dart suspiciously at every passerby. Her heart throbs with fear and anticipation.

"Hey, Aileen, you okay?" Gregor calls back to Aileen from in front.

"I'm fine, Gregor." Aileen's voice is a growl. Gregor doesn't notice her harsh tone. "Still having those nightmares?"

"Yeah. Just leave me alone. She's fine." Aileen starts the sentence in a low voice. The last two words again come out in a guttural snarl.

Gregor looks back at Aileen. "What?"

"I'm fine, Gregor. Just leave me alone."

Gregor looks toward Cunung. The two meet eyes. Cunung shakes his head as if he knows something.

The road turns and cuts back on itself. Someone follows up the pass, but it's impossible to tell who it might be. Baldwin looks down at the traveler. "Hey Cunung, someone's down there where we were."

"Yeah, I saw it. Are you going to let them catch up with us? It would be a shame to get passed by a merchant caravan." Cunung laughs, but he's haunted by a song he can't quite get out of his head.

I'm coming back soon,

  gonna take you home.

It has been stuck repeating in his mind for days now.

"Think they're following us?" Baldwin asks. Cunung snaps out of the dark memory.

"It's a busy road, Balds." Cunung thinks for a moment. "Are you trying to make me paranoid?"

"Sorry." Baldwin and Gregor both laugh. Another train of travelers passes them. They continue further up the mountain path. When these travelers pass, Cunung decides to confide. "It's okay, Balds. I'd like to tell you about something that happened in Gryfburg. Can you remind me later?"

Baldwin is shocked at first. He smiles and nods at Cunung with pride. "Yes, of course!"

"Great. I look forward to sharing the story with you."

The group returns to silence as they continue up the trail.

A campfire blazes. Its heat drives away the cold, night air.

Aileen is in her tent for the evening. She tries to sleep, but it is fitful. She tosses and turns. Her dream is full of incomprehensible whispers.

Cunung patrols the camp's perimeter as he watches for something or someone.

Aileen's voice calls out from her sleep. "No. No. Please, no."

"Another nightmare. I wish I could do something." Gregor sits with Baldwin.

Baldwin spreads his hands near the campfire and adds, "I do, too. What do you think's wrong? Aileen never had nightmares back home, did she?"

Gregor shakes his head. "I don't think so. She never mentioned them to me."

Cunung walks back into the camp. "Are you two okay?"

Gregor sighs. "Aileen is having nightmares again."

Cunung shakes his head. "I worry about this. It's been constant since that day at Alfons'. Something is wrong."

Gregor nods.

Baldwin asks, "Cunung, I'm worried for her. Is there anything we can do?"

Cunung sighs and shakes his head. "Only if we find out what's going on."

Gregor and Baldwin both frown.

"Help! Gregor! Help!" Gregor rushes into the tent and rouses Aileen. She awakes with a gasp. "Gregor, what's wrong? Why did you wake me?"

Gregor's expression is bleak. "You were screaming, Aileen."

Aileen is perplexed. Her nightmare is lost in memory. "What? I'm fine, Gregor. I just need rest."

Gregor leaves the tent, defeated. "Goodnight, Aileen. I hope you sleep well."

Gregor sits back down with Baldwin and Cunung.

Baldwins changes the subject. "Hey Cunung?"

"Yeah, Balds?"

"You mentioned a story earlier. Can you tell us now?" Baldwin asks.

Cunung thinks for a moment. He sighs but resigns himself to share with the boys. "I had an unwelcome visitor back in Gryfburg. On my way home from checking the traps, it was late one night."

The boys are intrigued. Baldwin inquires further. "Who was it? What happened?" Cunung sighs. "I call her Elli. She tried to kill me. Did you ever see who was following us up the trail?"

Baldwin and Gregor both look shocked. Gregor turns his head away from the fire to look at Cunung. "When? How? Did she get away?"

Cunung shakes his head. "Gregor, I got away."

Baldwin's eyes widen, "What?"

Cunung looks to the side, ashamed to meet Baldwin's gaze. "She's dangerous, Baldwin. Did you see who was following us?"

"No. I'm sorry." Baldwin admits.

"Gregor?"

"No. Are we okay?" Gregor sounds nervous.

Cunung's voice trembles with regret and self-doubt. 'I've thought a lot since we met. I feel like I've led you all into great danger. I'm sorry. I intended to bring your sister back safely and return you all home. I fear I've failed.'

Baldwin laughs. "We'll be okay. We're on our way."

Gregor smiles at Baldwin's confidence. He treasures his friend for this moment of encouragement. "You can't blame yourself for all that happened. You've kept us safe through all the bad stuff. I still don't know what we'd have done without you."

Baldwin adds, "I don't know what I'd have done without you. I didn't want to go on this trip, but now... I wouldn't change anything. Thanks for letting us come with you."

Cunung continues to avert his gaze. He shakes his head. "I regret that decision."

"Why?" Baldwin sounds angry now.

"I..." Cunung tries to cut in, but Baldwin cuts him off. "Cunung, I have wanted to be brave my whole life, and you're the only one who has ever shown me how!"

Cunung thinks for a moment. Finally, he replies, "I get it. I wish there had been some other way."

Baldwin stands up and walks toward the edge of the campfire's light. He stands alone, his back turned to the campfire. Baldwin looks down into a valley far below the mountain.

Pins of light burn in the windows of homes and buildings of some small town.

The beauty of their light carries hope to Baldwin.

He takes a deep breath.

"I think there was a plan for this. I'm ashamed to admit it, but what if this was the only way I could ever overcome my fears, Cunung?"

CHAPTER ONE HUNDRED TWO

GRIFF'S NEST

The path carves its way through the peaks of the Mourning Mountains. On one side, a cliff face rises; on the other, an abrupt descent falls ten span to an outcropping hidden by vegetation. The group cautiously traverses the pass, known for its treacherous nature. Each step is a potential hazard.

Gregor points out into the distance. "Look! We've crossed over to the other side!"'

A lush green horizon is broken by snow-capped peaks, the only thing obscured by vibrant blue skies. It's a beautiful day.

Cunung scans the horizon and nods. "Excellent observation, Gregor. We made it!"

Gregor smiles.

Aileen shivers in the cold air as if she has a fever. "It's so cold up here. I miss Sigi's warm drinks."

Cunung tries to encourage her. "It won't be long, Aileen. When we get a little lower, it'll warm up."

Aileen looks unhappy. "What about the warm drinks?"

"We can find someone who can make something for you. Are you okay, Aileen? You haven't seemed happy in a long while." Cunung inquires, worried about the girl's health.

Aileen frowns. "Yeah. I'm sorry. It's just... nothing. I don't want to talk about it."

Cunung looks concerned. "Are you sure? Everyone here cares about you, Aileen. You can tell us anything that is bothering you."

Aileen sighs. "Maybe later."

Baldwin walks closer to the edge of the pass. He looks down into the valley and whistles. "Long way down. I wouldn't want to slip and fall in there."

Gregor nods. "Yeah. That drop is terrifying."

Both boys step a little further from the ledge.

A scratching noise captures Gregor's attention.

Gregor walks over to the side of the pass to get a better look. It's a steep slope down to an outcropping some twenty span below.

"Careful Gregor."

He stops and looks back toward Baldwin. "Alright, Balds, I won't go any farther." Gregor turns around to face his friend and smiles. "This would make a great painting, wouldn't it?"

Baldwin starts to nod when the talus along the edge of the slope slides away under Gregor. The snow on which Gregor stands tumbles down. He falls down some twenty span and crashes into the brush below.

"Whoah!"

Baldwin's voice cracks as his friend disappears over the edge. "Gregor!"

His cry echoes through the mountains, a desperate plea for his friend's safety.

———

Gregor skids to a halt at the edge of a Mountain Griff's nest—the mother nests with her young hatchlings.

Up close, she's not at all what he expected. A Mountain Griff differs from the larger Prairie Griffins he has seen in Beaumont. This creature is a depiction of agility. She's a nimble aerial darter and ferocious fighter. Her body is muscular, but she is much smaller than a Griffin. Her chest is shaped like that of a shepherd dog. Her forelimbs end in large paws instead of the sharp talons of a Prairie Griffin. A fluffy tail complete with razor-sharp quills marks her end. A dark, sticky oil coats the soft tail.

Gregor has only a moment to process all this information. It feels like an eternity.

She rises.

Gregor stands and tries to back away. He wants to get distance from the nest.

There's nowhere to go except toward the edge.

A cliff that drops further off the mountain.

Nowhere to go.

———————

A commotion rises from where Gregor has fallen, but for a moment no one can see what's unfolding below.

Gregor steps out of the vegetation and appears at the edge of the outcropping. He cautiously backs away from the nest.

The mother rises and growls at Gregor as he backs away.

His heart pounds in his chest.

Gregor steps closer to the edge. His fear is palpable. "It's okay, girl. It's okay."

She prowls slowly closer.

His voice trembles as he tries to calm her. It's too late. She turns and swipes her tail at Gregor. It strikes him above the chest.

A venomous barb pierces his flesh.

"Aeigh!" Gregor cries out in pain. The dart penetrates his shoulder.

The shoulder hurts momentarily before Gregor feels pins and needles, and his arm goes numb. In shock, he grasps the arm and massages it, but he cannot wake the limb that has fallen asleep.

Cunung murmurs, "Oh no."

Something captures the Griff's attention. She turns away from Gregor to attack it and disappears behind the thick vegetation. The beak strikes something metallic. A sound rings through the air like the sound of a church bell.

Cunung shouts. "Gregor, we'll find a way down to you! Just get out of there!"

Gregor takes another step away from her. He grows weaker. He stumbles at the edge of the cliff and rolls down the mountain.

"Gregor!" Aileen's voice is filled with terror. Her eyes are fixed in shock, and she fears for her brother's safety.

Cunung quickly covers the eyes of both Baldwin and Aileen. He tries to shield them from seeing something terrible happen to the young boy. His limp body rolls and slides down the slope of the mountain until he slips out of view beyond the trees. Cunung pulls the children close to comfort them. He continues to hold their eyes covered.

"It's okay. Gregor will be okay. We have to find a way down to him." Cunung lets go of the children's eyes and hugs them both.

Baldwin asks, "What can we do to help him now?"

"He's on the other side of the mountain. We can only cross over and find a way down. I'm sorry." Cunung looks devastated.

Aileen looks at Cunung with a deep frown and furrowed brows. "How will we get to him?"

Cunung shakes his head. "I don't know. I see a road near where Gregor landed. Maybe someone along the route will spot him. Let's go!"

The three rush along the trail, their steps quick and determined, as they desperately search for a way down the mountain to reach Gregor.

Acknowledgements

Thank you, Jesus, for being the author of my life's story. I pray that it brings you joy.

Thank you, Julie, for never giving up. Thank you, Chase, Drake, Christian, Kristofer, and Grace, for teaching me how to love. Thank you Savannah and Katie for walking home with my sons.

Thank you, Nanny, Day Daddy, and Mom, for the beautiful stories you shared. May ghosts dance in the dim light of a train, and fae dance in rings of broken glass beneath the trees until we meet again.